TH

Edward Joh [barcode: MW00810452] s born
in 1878 to a e Irish
peerage, dating to 1439. Growing up, he split time between London and
the family properties in Shoreham, Kent and Dunsany Castle in County
Meath and was educated at Cheam, Eton, and the Royal Military College,
Sandhurst, which he entered in 1896.

Dunsany was an extremely prolific writer, producing a body of work
comprising some eighty volumes in various forms, including short
stories, plays, poems, novels, nonfiction, and autobiography. His earliest
published works were poems contributed to periodicals in the 1890s, and
by 1905 his first volume of short stories, *The Gods of Pegana*, appeared. In
this volume and in several more collections of stories and plays published
over the next few years, Dunsany wrote within the fantasy genre, many of
his tales focusing on an invented pantheon of deities who dwell in Pegana.
These early stories have been cited as influences on J.R.R. Tolkien, H. P.
Lovecraft, Ursula Le Guin, and others.

Dunsany's first novel, *Don Rodriguez: Chronicles of Shadow Valley*, appeared in 1922 and was followed by two more well-regarded fantasy
novels, both considered classics of the genre, *The King of Elfland's Daughter* (1924) and *The Charwoman's Shadow* (1926). Among his later books,
notable highlights include *The Curse of the Wise Woman* (1933), a semi-
autobiographical mixture of realism and fantasy set in late-nineteenth-
century Ireland, *My Talks with Dean Spanley* (1936), adapted for a critically
acclaimed 2008 film, and the *Jorkens* books, collections of short stories in
which Joseph Jorkens, a middle-aged raconteur, would recount fantastic
stories to anyone who bought him a whiskey and soda.

Dunsany's wide-ranging interests included hunting, shooting, chess,
and cricket, and, despite his love of hunting, he was an advocate for animal rights. He was also involved in Irish literary circles and numbered
Lady Gregory, George William "Æ" Russell, Oliver St. John Gogarty, and
W. B. Yeats among his friends. His other contributions to Irish literary
life included major donations to the Abbey Theatre and championing the
work of the poet Francis Ledwidge.

Later in life, Dunsany transferred Dunsany Castle to his son and heir
and settled with his wife, Beatrice, in Shoreham, Kent, where he continued to write and publish until his death in 1957 from an acute attack of
appendicitis.

Both popular and critically well regarded during his lifetime, Dunsany's stature has continued to grow after his death, with most of his
works still in print and his importance to the fantasy genre increasingly
recognized, with Neil Gaiman, Guillermo del Toro, Jorge Luis Borges,
Michael Moorcock, and many others, citing him as an influence.

By Lord Dunsany

The Gods of Pegana (1905)
Time and the Gods (1906)
The Sword of Welleran and Other Stories (1908)
A Dreamer's Tales (1910)
The Book of Wonder (1912)
Five Plays (1914)
Fifty-One Tales (1915)
Tales of Wonder (1916)
Plays of Gods and Men (1917)
Tales of War (1918)
Unhappy Far-Off Things (1919)
If (1921)
Don Rodriguez: Chronicles of Shadow Valley (1922)
Plays of Near and Far (1922)
The King of Elfland's Daughter (1924)
The Charwoman's Shadow (1926)
The Blessing of Pan (1927)
The Travel Tales of Mr. Joseph Jorkens (1931)
The Curse of the Wise Woman (1933)
Mr. Jorkens Remembers Africa (1934)
Up in the Hills (1935)
Rory and Bran (1936)
My Talks with Dean Spanley (1936)
My Ireland (1937)
Plays for Earth and Air (1937)
Patches of Sunlight (1938)
The Story of Mona Sheehy (1939)
Guerrilla (1944)
While the Sirens Slept (1944) (autobiography)
The Sirens Wake (1945) (autobiography)
The Year (1946)
The Man Who Ate the Phoenix (1949)
The Strange Journeys of Colonel Polders (1950)
The Last Revolution (1951)
His Fellow Men (1952)
The Little Tales of Smethers (1952)
Jorkens Borrows Another Whiskey (1954)

THE CURSE OF THE WISE WOMAN

LORD DUNSANY

With a new introduction by
MARK VALENTINE

VALANCOURT BOOKS

The Curse of the Wise Woman by Lord Dunsany
First published New York: Longmans and London: Heinemann, Oct. 1933
First Valancourt Books edition 2014

Copyright © 1933 by Lord Dunsany
Introduction © 2014 by Mark Valentine

Published by Valancourt Books, Richmond, Virginia
http://www.valancourtbooks.com

ISBN 978-1-941147-39-9 (*trade paperback*)
Also available as an electronic book.

Set in Dante MT 10.5/12.7

Cover: Adapted from the original jacket art from the 1933 Heinemann first edition by Heather "Herry" Perry (1893-1962)

INTRODUCTION

Lord Dunsany is mostly read now for his ornate and fantastical tales of gods and the unfortunate mortals who encounter them. They are written in some of the richest, most sonorous language ever used in English, driven by the stately rhythms of the King James Bible. These tales achieve a remarkable combination of strange fancy and worldly irony: exotic worlds, described in an archaic vocabulary enhanced by resonant invented names and words, prove still to be full of perennial human follies. Starting with *The Gods of Pegana* (1905), Dunsany published about ten volumes of these bizarre and exquisite pieces, together with plays in a similar vein.

But it must have become obvious to him that there was a limit to how often he could revisit these dream realms, journeying across the border from the "fields we know" to the outer marches of faery. It has also been speculated that the First World War, in which he served as a Captain in the Royal Inniskilling Fusiliers, caused him to put an end to these fey visions. Whatever the reason, he soon began writing instead longer works; novels and romances.

At first, as in *The King of Elfland's Daughter* (1924), these were set in a similar milieu to his earlier tales, and it is true that Dunsany never left the haunts of faery altogether in any of his work. But gradually he began to write more of "the fields we know" than of the fields beyond: and, in particular, he turned to his own country, Ireland, for inspiration. *The Curse of the Wise Woman* (1933), written in his early fifties, is the finest work he produced from this new (and old) source: and arguably it is Dunsany's most haunting and thoughtful book.

Edward John Moreton Drax Plunkett (1878-1957) succeeded to the title as the 18th Lord Dunsany at the young age of 20 in 1899, and also to the family home of Dunsany Castle. This is situated not far from one of Ireland's most celebrated monuments, the Hill of Tara, citadel of the ancient High Kings of Ireland: he grew up on the very threshold of legend and romance. Dunsany was a man of prodigious energy and many interests. Some of these were fairly conventional for his class and era: soldiering, hunting, cricket, socialising. But others were much less so. He was a keen chess player, and (despite his hunting) an advocate of protection for animals. And, most of all, he was a dedicated writer: his work in the end embraced stories, poetry, plays, autobiography, travel essays, lectures and much else besides.

This literary work brought him into contact with artistic and bohemian circles and in particular to an acquaintance with many of the leading figures of the Irish Renaissance, including W. B. Yeats, the poet and mystic 'Æ' (George William Russell), Oliver St. John Gogarty, Lady Gregory and Padraic Colum. His plays were performed at the Abbey Theatre, Dublin, the centre of this circle. But he also valued the acquaintance of lesser-known figures. He championed the impoverished poet Francis Ledwidge, a grocer's boy whose verses he discovered, and he found a particular affinity with the ex-miner and English artist Sidney Sime, who illustrated his early books: they worked so well together that for one of the volumes Sime made the pictures first, and Dunsany wrote the stories to go with them. Sime visited Dunsany Castle several times, where his original cast of mind was appreciated. Asked for the time once, he replied "Later than it ever was".

Although Dunsany mingled with the leading Irish literati of his day, he seems not to have been considered fully a part of their circle. He recalled in his autobiographical volume *The Sirens Wake* (1945) that the immediate stimulus for writing *The Curse of the Wise Woman* may have been—though he is not sure—a reproach from Yeats that he never wrote about Ireland. There was in a literal way some justice in the comment, for Dunsany's earlier dream-world work barely had its soles on any part of the earth, still less a particular locality. On the other hand, in its celebration of gods and heroes, quests and journeys, it certainly did have some kindred with early Irish

wonder stories and sagas, and Yeats might have been expected
to see that better. In any event, Yeats welcomed *The Curse of
the Wise Woman* and acknowledged that Dunsany could now
be regarded as a more fully Irish writer.

Beatrice, Dunsany's wife, recorded in her diary in 1933 that
her husband "wrote his Irish novel in three and a half breathless months: bits of it have been in his mind for years and I
never let it be forgotten for too long and then it came suddenly" (Mark Amory, *Lord Dunsany: A Biography*, 1972). The
long thinking that went into the novel is evident in its depth.
There is nothing tentative about Dunsany's evocation of Ireland in the book. It is imbued with every significant element of
the country: its politics, its religion, its gentry and peasantry,
its hills and its bogs, its skies and its streams, its shrewdness
and its whimsy, all the bleak realities of its visible world, and
the hovering presence of its otherworld. All this was drawn
from Dunsany's direct experience: as Mark Amory notes, "The
story—of a boy spending his holidays from Eton in Ireland
shooting snipe and grouse on the bogs with the keeper, his
mother dead, his father soon to disappear, is the most autobiographical of his books."

We may also sense that there was a careful and deliberate
choice about Dunsany's method of narration. For the book
is written as the memoir of an Irishman in exile, far away in
another country that might seem marginal as well as liminal.
He has been made a diplomatic minister of the Irish Free State,
a servant of the newly independent nation. This is perhaps a
Dunsany that might-have-been, and he must have meant to
imply that he could be as loyal to the new Ireland as any more
flamboyant Celt. But his narrator is also lonely and still possessed by his past, and here Dunsany was acknowledging
something of his own stature, as an Irishman of letters never
quite accepted because of his background: his class, his Anglo-
Irish origins and assumed allegiances: and perhaps also, more
personally, because of his idiosyncracies and his elaborate,
exotic fantasy world.

The first study of the Irish peer, *Lord Dunsany: King of Dreams*

(1959) by the American hostess and traveller Hazel Littlefield suffers from a somewhat breathless style and a rather particular focus, chiefly related to the occasions of the author's own social associations with Dunsany. However, it has some sound observations, including this passage very relevant to the writing of *The Curse of the Wise Woman*: "the Irish heart of him loved the wildness of the bog and the moors, the long glimmering evenings with a soft wind in the grasses, and storm clouds, like ghosts of gods, passing over the mountains. He knew how it was with those who have a true love for any piece of earth where their roots have gone deep into the soil." That country is a powerful presence in the book.

In the two young friends whose journeys we witness, and even more so in the mother of one of them, the wise woman of the title, we see this understanding of the call of the land lyrically conveyed. But Dunsany had another knowledge too, an insight into the nature of spiritual exile, and that is just as keenly evoked in the book. It is this that gives the story its delicate melancholy, its sense of quiet tragedy, an intangible impression lying like a pale watermark within all its pages. The book is in one aspect an elegy for, as the narrator says at the outset, "an Ireland that they tell me is quite gone".

We can date the beginning of the exile's recollections of his youth by a reference to a particular event: the fall of Khartoum and the death of General Gordon, in 1885, when the narrator says he was sixteen. This tragedy made a dramatic impression on the British public, and indeed Dunsany's fellow writer of supernatural fiction, Arthur Machen, whose work he admired and introduced, recalled that he was so moved by it that he announced the news to his clergyman father in ancient Greek, as it seemed the only fitting tongue. Many felt that Gordon had been betrayed, and that a strange soul had gone from the world (a sense that not even Lytton Strachey's satirical essay on him in *Eminent Victorians* quite dispelled). A mourning for lost noblesse is therefore hovering in the book from the start, even around a passing point in chronology, and it is soon augmented by what we learn of the boy's background.

The young Charles James Peridore, who we know is later to become the lonely exile, is a delicately changed version of Dunsany himself. He is not the heir to a castle and an ancient title, but to a diminished estate and a Jacobite dukedom (and indeed Jacobite forenames), romantic but honoured only clandestinely. The Old Cause and the Old Faith are still observed in the house, and this makes him some degrees closer to the people of the land. One of the great appeals of the book is the subtly depicted friendship between this son of a lost cause and Tommy Marlin, the peasant 'bog-watcher' who is also the son of the local seer, the prophetess Mother Marlin. Whatever tense politics may be stalking the land—and they are keenly depicted in the thrilling opening passages—and whatever peculiar magic may be living in the marshes, the book sticks close to the alliance between these two different young men. Dunsany understands the simplicity and stolidity of such comradeship, found and fostered in long walks over the marshes and the stalking of the wildfowl in the watery waste.

The strength of *The Curse of the Wise Woman* over Dunsany's earlier fantasies and fables is this concern with human qualities. Edward H. Bierstadt, studying Dunsany's plays, wrote in 1919: "His place is that of pure thought, devoid of emotion, so neither in his gods, nor in the world they rule do we find a trace of passion either human or divine." He praised the musical language of his dramas, but noted, "not once do we know the poignancy of the familiar. He realises but does not experience: he perceives but does not feel." Others thought the same of his tales: they were sonorous but heartless. There are in fact very fierce motivations in the gods, heroes and desparadoes of his stories: love, longing, lust for glory, jealousy, greed. However, mostly the mortals in that earlier work are ethereal dreamers, roaming among ruined cities or fabulous palaces; or schemers who think, unwisely, that they can steal something from the gods. They may, though, seem formal and stylised, as in the old sagas, and not fully fashioned from the weft of human fabric.

By contrast, all the individuals in the novel have complex

dimensions to them. The boy of the marsh cannot read letters, but he can read the skies and the mosses. The taciturn steward knows more than he ever tells. The dark-haired assassin looks to the well-being of the man whose father he would have murdered. Those whose mission it is to kill cannot defy a holy relic. With gentle irony, Dunsany celebrates the ambivalences and contradictions and paradoxes in any mortal worth their salt.

These may also be felt in the main themes of the novel. A contemporary critic doubted if it would do well because the male readers who would like the shooting and hunting scenes would not like the mystical passages, and those who liked these would be deterred by the blood sports. In fact, as Dunsany knew, that might not only be true of men: Laura, the young woman that Charles James Peridore woos in the book, is a keen Artemis of the chase, and the nearest she gets to the mystical is the hope that heaven will prove to be "Galloping down wind for ever".

But it is certainly true that by today's standards the devotion to wildfowling and foxhunting that is central to the book may dismay many readers, for all that they appreciate the closeness to the land, the keen observation of birds and animals, that accompanies them. Dunsany had addressed head on the question of why he, so devoted to campaigns against cruelty to animals (he particularly fought against the practice of docking dogs' tails), should also take pleasure in chasing and slaying them. "Of course I am inconsistent," he admitted, "and when you consider the power of the pulls of heredity and environment upon all of us, like the sun and the moon pulling different ways at the tides, we must all be as inconsistent as the sea." His biographer Mark Amory thought that "he was aware of the paradox that those who really love the country are frequently those most dedicated to killing the creatures that live in it" and that this always "nagged at him". It was such human inconsistencies that he put into his book, and they are a strong part of its compelling authenticity.

But if Dunsany had shown he could write convincingly in a naturalistic way, far from his mannered fantasies, he had certainly not deserted the unearthly entirely. The hovel of Marlin's mother, though it is of ragged thatch and reeks of peat smoke, is as much on the edge of the world as the uncanny cottages in his tales of dream visions. It is the last place before the bog begins. The bog itself, so broodingly evoked, is itself a marginal land, where we understand that the rules are not the same as in the settled lands. And at the end of it, so her son, the bog-watcher Tommy Marlin says, there is the sea, and beyond the sea is Tir-nan-Og, the pagan Irish otherworld to which, in peril of his soul, he has devoted himself.

This paradisal, but dangerous, realm sometimes advances further towards the human domain, and can be seen in aspects of mortal country: in the blossom on an apple bough, for instance, or in the lying of snow or the glinting of dark light in the pools of the marshes. Dunsany had told Hazel Little-field, she recalled: "In the blood of man there is a tide, an old sea-current rather, that is somehow akin to the twilight which brings rumours of beauty from however far away, as drift-wood is found at sea from islands not yet discovered." These rumours of beauty—and mystery—are rarely more beauti-fully expressed than in the glimpses of Tir-nan-Og that haunt the book, shadowing the natural world throughout with the suggestion of a world beyond.

Nor is this the only supernatural element in the book, for in Marlin's mother he memorably depicts a witch who listens to the North Wind and has visions of the future, visions where the renewed Ireland will be "free again" and where the emis-saries of far-flung empires and republics, and also seafarers and merchants, poets and dreamers will flock to its shores. It is as if, through her, Dunsany sees his original worlds of marvel meshing with an idealised version of the country of his birth. Before that can come into being, though, there are struggles to be won against those with narrower souls: and in the final part of the book, Dunsany achieves a most subtle and ambiguous splicing of the natural and the supernatural.

It was probably this dimension that most appealed to John Masefield, himself the author of books where magic is abroad in the land, when he chose the book as the winner of the annual Harmsworth Award for "the best work of imaginative prose by an Irish author", and indeed the book was generally well received. Dunsany went on to write over twenty more books, including novels where he explored again the Ireland he knew, its land, its people, and its legends. But it is fair to say that he never quite achieved again the fine mingling that gives *The Curse of the Wise Woman* its particular allure.

Like the boy in his book, Dunsany could never keep away from the red bog for long, and he was out unsuccessfully seeking snipe just a few days before his death in the Autumn of 1957. He left his gold watch and chain to his gamekeeper of thirty years, and a poem for the birds he had so long pursued, telling how they would rejoice at his passing. In his going, as in his life, he was no less a glorious paradox.

Mark Valentine
September 17, 2014

CHAPTER I

I am in a foreign town now, with little to do, and with nothing at all that is so interesting and soothing as letting my memory roam. My memory is not what it was. If Monsieur Alphonse, as I call him, for I can never quite get his queer Balkan surname, were to suddenly ask me what day it was, I might not be able to tell him, and yet the scenes of my youth are as clear as ever they were, and many men and things you may see in the course of a day that you will not remember as vividly that same evening as I remember the things of fifty years ago. Monsieur Alphonse is almost the only man I ever see to talk to: he comes in nearly every day to have a glass of absinthe with me; and when he goes I sit and think of the past. And only the other day, while the sparrows were all chirruping outside my window in sunlight, and my memories were even more vivid than usual, it struck me that it might be as well to write them down, for they are memories of an Ireland that they tell me is quite gone. And it seems to me that if the scenes of those days be allowed to be quite lost, the world will miss a memory of a beautiful and happy country, and be the worse for that. Or was it a sad and oppressed country, as some say? I don't know. It didn't seem so to me.

Well then, my name: Charles James Peridore. The date: I do not remember. But I remember hearing the names of Gordon and Gladstone, and one day the loss of Khartoum flashed from the news; and I must have been about sixteen. Well, somewhere about that time; for it is not the date that is vivid and bright in my mind as the leaves of the lime-tree just outside my window, but the things I saw as a boy; somewhere about that time I was sitting before the fire with my father late one winter's evening in our house called High Gaut. Of the date of the house I can tell you nothing accurate. It was built by a forbear of ours who was a historical character, but it is just about that

time that the history of Ireland begins to be fabulous, so that it
is truer to tell you merely that the house was very old. Of the
period of its furniture and its fixtures I can tell you at once: it
was no period at all. As chairs and such things wore out they
were replaced in different generations, and the only thing that
they all had in common was that they were all bought by the
same family. There is a right and a wrong place for antiquity:
it is right in walls, wrong in carpets; wrong too in curtains and
wall-paper and hearth-rugs. We had antiquity everywhere. My
father kept only one housemaid to do the work of the large
house, and though she did what she could, it was clear in every
room that the spider was gaining. And another memory I have
of that day, that is almost as clear to my mind as the memory
of my father and myself before the fire in the library; and that
is the picture of a long man in a frayed black coat that came
below his knees, galloping down the street of a village in which
all the houses were thatched, and all had low white walls shining in sunlight. I should not call it a memory, because I never
saw it, but I pictured the scene so clearly when I was young,
when the man came up to High Gaut, and said: "I galloped all
the way from Lisronagh to tell you that the geese are in on the
bog," that the picture is still here among my memories. And a
keen joy stamped the picture clear on my mind, for shooting
was the greatest adventure I then had known, and a pheas-
ant the largest bird I had ever shot; and that grey traveller the
goose, with his wariness, his rarity and romance, was a greater
prize to me then than any that the world could offer me now.
And my father would not let me go to Lisronagh, because I
had not done my holiday task. It was a book of Dickens, and
everyone else in my division at Eton would do it in the train
going down from Paddington. I see now that fifty minutes in a
crowded railway carriage may not be enough in which to read
one of Dickens' novels; but the feeling that my father did not
understand is deeper and older and stronger. Yes, it is with me
yet.

So in the evening we were sitting before the fire in the
library, and it was late, and he had sent for the glass of milk

that he always drank with whiskey before going to bed. There were only us: my mother had died years ago. We were alone in the large house but for the cook and the kitchenmaid and the one housemaid: the butler lived half a mile away, and had long gone to bed. And there was a boy, living over the stables, who did odd work in the house by day. We were not talking much. Perhaps I was sore about not having been allowed to go to Lisronagh; I don't remember now. Of course I had had ample warning about the holiday task; my father had often told me to do it and I had not started it yet: partly laziness; chiefly, I suppose; and partly that feeling that my father did not understand the attitude of the world to a holiday task: my world, I mean. I obeyed my father as much as most boys do; but there was one curious thing over which he seemed to exert all his personal force, all that was left to him as he grew old, and even more, as though he called up hidden reserves of power; and that was that one day in that room he might say to me "Look at the picture," and if ever he did I was to go immediately to a little Dutch picture at the end of the room and watch it; I forget for how long, but I was to watch it minutely. And, if ever he said those words, I was never to think that he did not mean them, or that it was a joke, or that there was time to spare. He told me this often. Why? He never told me why.

Well, there we were sitting, and the house was all shut up; my father always went round every shutter himself to see they were properly fastened, and I used to think it rather unnecessary, for we knew everybody all round us; but once when I said something of this to my father he had replied: "You never know who might come over the bog." And certainly on the other side of the bog there were hills of which we knew nothing. Yet the idea that, even over there, could be anyone with enmity for my father, seemed, I remember, absurd to me: for one thing he did not seem active enough to have his share of such enmities; but that was a boy's idea, forgetting he had been younger.

We were talking when at all about Lisronagh, for I wanted quietly to find out what day I might go; when the housemaid brought in the milk, a tumbler of plain milk which he used to

mix with the whiskey himself, after tasting the milk to see that
it was not sour. The housemaid left the room, and he put his
hand to the tumbler that stood on a table beside him. I can see
him now more clearly than I can picture faces seen yesterday;
tall and thin, with fine profile, with the firelight in his greying
beard. And I was talking of Lisronagh. I thought he would
have let me go next day, till he said definitely: "Not this week."
I remember the words because they fell on my ears with such
a sense of disaster, yearning as I was to get to Lisronagh before
the geese had gone, and because they were the last words but
four that I ever heard him say. He lifted the glass of milk to
his lips and then put it down again, and turned to me and said:
"Look at the picture." And he said it with none of the authority
I had expected, if ever I really expected he would say those
words at all, with less authority by far than that with which
he forbade me to go to Lisronagh; but as though he were very
tired.

I did as I had been taught. I went without thinking he did
not mean it, or that there was time to spare: I went to the
little Dutch picture and gazed at the tiny figures, skating past
churches and windmills over grey ice. The picture was near
the door, the only door in the room, which was shut, until it
was opened from outside, and four tall men came in. Then I
looked round, and my father was gone.

I saw at once that the men were from the other side of the
bog; they were dark and strange and like none of our men.
They peered round the room, then one of them looked at me
fixedly and said: "There is no one we have a greater respect
for than your father, but it is a pity he mixed himself up with
politics the way he did; and it's the way it is we want to speak
to him, and no one could be sorrier than myself that I have to
say it."

Then I knew they had come to shoot my father.

So I said: "He is up in his room, but I'll go and fetch him."

"You will not, sir," said the same man. "But we will come
with you."

So they looked amongst all the curtains in the library, and

behind a sofa that there was, and found nothing, and then I walked slowly up the stairs, and they came with me. So slowly I went that one of them shouted: "Come *on*, now." And at that I started forward and ran up a few steps, and fell at the top of a flight. I got up slowly, and then limped a little. All this gained time.

When we came to the door of my father's room I knocked, but they shoved in past me. The room was in darkness and I got a match for them and lit a candle: they looked round the room carefully, and we gained time there.

I said: "He must be in his study." And then I added: "Perhaps he is in another bedroom. Shall we go there first?"

But the man who had spoken before said: "You will go to the study." So I did as he told me and we all went downstairs. All the time I was calculating how far my father could have got. How he had got out of the library I had no idea; there was only one door and all the shutters were shut; but gone he had. And even if he went by some narrow passage, and difficult steps in the dark, I calculated that with our various trifling delays, that all add up, he had gone by now as far as we had, and that that should have just taken him clear of the house. He would make of course for the stables: that was a hundred yards. And then he would have to get in, and saddle his horse and get out again, and past the gate by the house, before one could think him safe.

When we entered the study I think they saw at a glance that my father was not there, and never had been. It was not only that the fire was unlighted, but the look and feel of the room told you at once that it never was used by anyone. And indeed, except for meals, we never used any room at all but the library. And they all looked at me in a rather nasty way.

"If you don't show us where he is, we'll burn the house," said one of them that had not spoken before.

"You will not," I said, looking straight at him.

And his face fell at that, and I saw the eyes of all of them turn downwards. For they knew, whoever they were or wherever they came from, that we kept a piece of the true

Cross at High Gaut, and had done for ages, ever since it had
been granted to us for the help my family gave in a war of one
of the popes. I saw they were thinking of it, and did not have
to remind them that if a man burned that, the flames might
not be so easily quenched. They would flicker about his soul
all through eternity.

But you do not always know, when you invoke powers like
that, whom in the end they will benefit. The leader turned
to me and told me to get the cross. It was a crystal cross and
part of the crystal was hollow, and in the hollow the piece of
the true Cross was. I knew what they wanted it for: they were
going to swear me on it. And I grew suddenly afraid of the
cross, and afraid of the men.

I had to get it: it was in that very room; in a little golden box
on a marble table. It was never locked up; there was no need
for that. I went across the room to get it, and they all drew
their pistols as I went. They took them out of their pockets,
in which I knew they had them, but they had not shown them
before. Now they were getting annoyed because they had not
found my father, and I saw that they were not going to let me
escape from swearing to them on the Cross. They were long,
single-barrelled pistols, old even then; nothing like the auto-
matics they use nowadays.

When I came back with the relic I saw that they had me
covered. I came up to them and lifted it in my hand, and they
all dropped on their knees. "Do you swear," said the leader,
kneeling before me, but still covering me with the long black
pistol, "to the best of your knowledge and your belief that
your father is still in this house?"

And while he spoke I heard the clip clop, clip clop, of my
father's horse coming out of the stables. But it was only coming
at a walk. That was of course so as to make less noise, and then
there was a gate that he would have to open, but somehow I
had thought he would gallop. Almost at once he got on to the
grass, and they had not heard him, but he had to come right
past the house. I could still hear every step of the horse, but I
suppose it is easier to hear what you are listening for, if you

are listening as I was; while they were all watching me and the cross that I held and waiting for me to speak, and they never heard the horse coming by on the grass. But they would have if I hadn't spoken just when I did. He wasn't safe till he'd opened the gate another fifty yards on. "I swear," I said, "to the best of my knowledge and my belief," speaking slowly, spinning it out as long as I could, to drown the noise of the hooves, "that my father is in this house."

I suppose one puts one's soul in danger oftener than one thinks, and in less good causes. The risk frightened me when I took it. If it wasn't the true Cross, and (God help me) I've sometimes doubted it, then no harm was done. If it was, could it be on the side of these four men and against my father? But I was not easy about what I'd done, for a single moment, till I went to Father McGillicud and told him all. "And would you murder your father," he said, "and with the true Cross in your hand?" Then I knew that I'd done right.

When I had sworn I put the relic down, and they all rose from their knees, and as they rose I heard the hoof-beats stop. My father was opening the gate.

That is the scene that remains with me today, so far away from Ireland, as clear as any picture that one could hang on the wall; the old room in my home, and the four men kneeling before me with their pistols. It takes a wealth of experience in many peaceful years to make a man forget having looked from the wrong end along fire-arms; and the first time he probably never forgets; but it is their earnest, devout faces that I see in my memory as vividly as their weapons.

When I put the relic down they began to search the house. My father must still have been fumbling with the gate, for I did not hear as yet the sound I was waiting for. It was one of those gates that you had to dismount to open. I went with them from room to room; and suddenly, in the first room that we came to, I heard my father's horse. It was trotting now. I began talking hurriedly, and still they seemed not to hear the horse. There was the lodge still ahead of him, and the lodge gates, but I felt he was almost safe now. I never knew how these men

had come, whether on horse or driving or on foot, and did
not know what means of pursuit they might have; but I felt
he was nearly safe, though I wished he would gallop. We went
from room to room, and they searched thoroughly, paying no
attention to my suggestions that I made to drown the sound
of the trotting hooves, growing fainter and fainter; but, in
the hugeness and the stillness of the night, they were clearly
audible all the way to the lodge. Sometimes the four tall men
stopped suddenly still and listened, to hear if my father was
moving about the house before them, but they never heard the
hooves. Large deserted rooms that we never used we passed
through, with a feeling of emptiness and damp about them,
and so little suggesting the presence of either my father or any
living man that one of them said to me: "Was there ever a ghost
here?" And partly because of the look and feel of the room,
with only one candle burning, and partly because of the habit I
had picked up from the people all round me of rather avoiding
a straight answer, I said: "I wouldn't trust it." I think that
hurried them on, which is what I should most have avoided;
but, as they came to the last room, I heard all of a sudden ring
out in the heart of the night the sound of a horse galloping.
It was my father, clear of the lodge, on the high road. It must
have been half a mile away, but the sound of a horse at night
galloping is a sound that they could not have missed. They all
stood still at once. "It's himself," said one. They looked at me,
but gave up any notion of my complicity; then they turned to
their own plans and began to hurry towards the hall door. I
started making conversation with them about shooting. One
of them listened to me, and soon I was telling him of the geese
on Lisronagh bog. It was a safer topic than some that they
might have started, if left to themselves. To look at him you
would have said that he was the worst of the four, and yet he
told me little things about shooting that are pure gold to a boy;
and, when he saw how keen I was on the geese, he said to me
just as they all went out through the door: "And a goose takes
a long time to get his pace up. Don't aim so much in front of a
goose as you do at other birds."

And then when they'd all gone he opened the door again and put his head inside, and said, word for word as I write it: "And if it ever comes to it, and God knows the world's full of trouble, aim a foot in front of a man walking, at a hundred yards."

CHAPTER II

It was pretty late when the four men were gone. I went back to the library, the room we used every day, and began to look round it with new eyes. There was only one door, as I told you, and I had been standing near it while it was shut, and in half a minute while I was not watching him my father had left the room. There was a large mirror with heavy wooden frame at the far end of the room from the Dutch picture, and two dark cupboards of carved wood. I suspected the frame of the mirror, but how you moved it I could not see. So I left this mystery and tried to find out the other, what warning my father had had; for the men had not reached the stairs, and there was no sound of steps when he vanished. And the second mystery I discovered. I think that now that my father was safe, and the men had gone, the strongest emotion in me was curiosity. I sat in the chair in which my father had been sitting; I looked so as to see everything that he could have seen, sitting there; I tried to remember all that he could have heard, as the housemaid came in with the milk. But it was not sight or hearing that warned him. I sat as he had sat, holding the glass of milk; I even raised the glass to my lips as he had done. And then I got it, even after so long; for there was still hanging over the milk the scent of the queer black tobacco they used to smoke in those parts.

The men had come by the back door and through the kitchen. How much had Mary, the housemaid, seen of them? What did she know of their purpose? These things I never knew. But the smell of their black tobacco had lingered upon

the milk. With no men of our own in the house the meaning
of that pungent smell on the milk must have been clear enough
to my father. And he may have been expecting those men for
years. When you've anything like that on your mind you can't
afford to miss warnings, if ever they come.

Then I put out the lamps and went to bed, without saying
a word to Mary. Why did I go without telling her that her
master, to whom she was much attached, had left the house
that she had tended for years and loved? It's hard to explain.
"Vox populi, vox Dei," is a saying that gives some hint of it.
She cared devotedly for our family, and yet I think that in her
very blood was a feeling that the people couldn't be wrong. I
believe she would have fought a burglar single-handed if one
had entered our house; but this vengeance that came from
the hills over the bog was something that I thought she might
have strange feelings about, stronger than all her kinder sympathies, something I can only compare with the feeling that
the Englishman has for the law. And it's no use pretending to
you that I do not sympathise with the Irish point of view: an
Englishman honours the law, and a very convenient thing it
is for everyone that he does so; but it's a dull thing when all's
said. Now an Irishman will honour a song, if it's worth hon-
ouring, though his doing so is of no convenience to anybody;
but he'll never honour the law, however much it might suit the
community, because a law is not sufficiently beautiful in itself
to work up any enthusiasm over. It's a point I sometimes try
to explain to Monsieur Alphonse, who is fond of songs, but he
will not understand.

But to return to my story, I told Mary nothing, and in the
morning I saw by the tears running down her face when she
called me, that she had found out for herself. "Mr. Peridore is
gone," she said. "The poor duke is gone."

I should explain that a forbear of ours who had followed
James II to exile had been given a dukedom by him. One day
on the shore of France, looking across to the cliffs of England,
he had made him Duke of Dover, and my family had used the
title for so long as they remained in exile, but we do not use

it now. Oddly enough the peasantry all round about us still remember it; they are the only people that do.

Well, Mary in tears told me what I knew well enough, that my father was gone, and saved me the trouble of telling her, but one thing she told me that I had never thought of, "We'll never see him back again," she wailed. Had I undervalued the four strange men's persistence or the power of those that sent them? And then, in spite of everything, there suddenly dawned on my mind, the gloom of which had just been deepened by Mary, a thought like sunrise breaking on misty lands; I could go now to Lisronagh.

So I dressed and hurried down. Did I tell you the date? No. Well, I never kept a diary, and I scarcely remember any dates; it is not they that shine in one's memory after all these years. But this one date I do remember: it was December 26th. I remember it because the night that the four men came was Christmas. I don't think it was chance that brought them then. I think that they were afraid of what others had told them to do, and that they found some sort of shelter in the sanctity of the day. But there's no knowing.

Well, I went down to breakfast; and the old butler was all silent. I suppose he saw in my face, he must have seen, some reflection of the joy with which my whole heart was turning now to Lisronagh; probably all my attitudes showed it too. It is not that I did not sympathise with my father, and the sympathies of youth are strong; but my longing for the quest in the wild lands was stronger, where heather and mosses and rushes and soft black earth, and a million pools, stretched away out of my sight and beyond my knowledge. So the old butler thought his thoughts to himself, and would not share them with me. I saw that the view that he took was a very grave one. But I did not want to discuss it; discussion could do no good, and the less I understood of my father's going the better. Once more I looked round the library, trying to find the door to a secret passage; but soon I gave it up, deciding that if I kept out of politics I should never have any need of it. Soon I was off to the stables, whose grey buildings of large stone could have held over twenty horses and the men to take care of them, but there was only one man there, and, now that my father had gone away on his hunter, only one horse, the carriage-horse: sometimes a boy might be seen working there, and sometimes not; otherwise the man was alone. I went to get the carriage-horse so as to drive to Lisronagh bog. Ryan was the coachman's name, and in conversation with him I began that morning the habit I increasingly held to, to talk about my father little and vaguely. Well, he put the horse into a light trap for me while I went round to the gun-room. God forgive me, I have sometimes hoped that there may be a gun-room in Heaven. Instead of taking one's happiness there on trust, as one should, I used to be foolishly wondering if it could be complete without that deep contentment one knew as a boy in a gun-room in the morning, with the various implements of sport awaiting one, all the more mysterious for a rather dim light; outside, the north wind blowing, and the sky full of portents. It was like that now; but I needed no portents in a stormy sky, for Marlin had told me that the geese had actually come. We had a gamekeeper, who had taught me all I knew about shooting, so that it seems like ingratitude, looking back over the years, that anything Marlin told me I treated as some rare and wonderful knowledge, while old Murphy's sayings, sound and wise as they were, seemed to lack magic. But then one had mostly to tell of orderly woods inside what we called "the demesne," and the other of things that began where man's cultivation ended, and sometimes even of things at the boundaries of man's experience. And it's queer that what is luring my memory back to those days is not our house nor the woods nor clear landmarks, that would be such good guides for one's fancy travelling into the past, but things that he used to tell me of those that haunted the bog. He was bog-watcher for my father, which means, well, very little, except that he lived in a white thatched cottage by the side of the bog of which part was owned by my father, and Marlin's mother lived with him. Where my father's boundary ran I have no idea; the bog went on and on, over the horizon and out of my knowledge.

Sometimes along the sides of it, or perhaps a quarter mile in, one saw small cottages of men who had rights in the bog, and sometimes the crumbling walls of those that the ancient desolation of that untilled space had defeated; but once one had gone ten minutes over the heather, all the things of man were behind one. Of all the enemies of man I think that the red bog, as we call in Ireland that wide wilderness of heather, seems the most friendly. It cannot be called a friend; it threatens him with death too often for that, and is against him and all his ways, and is untamed by him and unsubdued; only by utterly destroying it does man gain any victory over the bog, and eke from it a difficult living. But it lulls him and soothes him all his days, it gives him myriads of pieces of sky to look at about his feet, and mosses more brilliant than anything short of jewellery, and the great glow of the heather; and if ever it seize him, luring his step with its mosses, it so tends him and cherishes him, that those that chance upon him and dig him up find one whose face and skin are as of their own contemporaries, yet not the oldest in the district know him, for he may have been dead for ages. Well, I've said enough to show you that, though I was only driving four miles, I was going to as strange a land as you might find in a long journey, a land as different from the fields we inhabit as the Sahara or Indian jungles.

I got my gun and cartridges and started off with Ryan, and we hadn't gone down the road a hundred yards from the lodge when we met Marlin coming towards us. How news travels! I saw by his face, and by a certain carefulness about his silence, that he had heard already about my father. When he spoke it was to say: "I thought you might be coming to the bog, Master Char-les." So he had walked a good three miles. We talked for a while about the geese: they were not in the bog now, but would be in by nightfall, his mother said. Ryan gazed down the road with all his mental powers obviously concentrated upon not overhearing our conversation. This duty he assumed partly out of politeness, but it taught me that there is between shooting and hunting that slight division that there is in religion between sects that seem almost identical: the educated faithful do not notice it, but the simpler folk that have only the faith, they see the rift and cherish it. And other rifts still wider there may have been, of which I knew nothing.

Of my father's departure Marlin did not speak. Politics are talked in certain times and places, but neither Marlin in the hearing of Ryan, nor Ryan in the hearing of Marlin, would say anything to me of anyone that had been touched by politics to the extent that my father had been. Then I got Marlin up into the dog-cart, and we drove on to Lisronagh. From then on, as we neared the bog, the land changed rapidly: no actual details that I could give, and my memory is full of them, would convey the sense of that change. Little white cottages, much smaller than those behind us, with scarred deep thatches, poplars with queer arms clawing, strange willows, those little lanes that we call bohereens, rambling busily on and fading away into moss; none of these actual things convey the sense of it. I can only say that if you neared World's End, and fairyland were close to you, some such appearance might be seen in the earth and the light, and the people you passed on the way.

A great north wind was blowing, driving the geese out of the Arctic lands, as I hoped, or, if all were gone already, sending them in from sea. There are two kinds of geese that come to these bogs, which are too far inland for the Barnacles; the great grey lag and the smaller white-fronted goose. And, as though it made any surer of the geese, I asked Marlin again about them and which kind he expected. And he answered: "My mother says that the grey lags are coming."

CHAPTER III

We passed through the tiny village of Clonrue and then the bog was before us; rushy lands at first, such as we call the Black Bog; and, at the end of those marshy fields, rising twelve feet above them, and frowning at the top with withered heather, lowered the red bog. It seemed to me as I saw it then, all dark by the bright fields, to be threatening man and his cultivation; his hedges, his paths and his houses; with the might and the mystery of the ancient wildness that was before he came.

Bright and white in the fields stood the Marlins' cottage; but, as the trap stopped in the bohereen, a field away from their door, having come as far as anything thus sophisticated could come down a path so doubtfully won from the waste and the wild, I saw Marlin's mother come out of the cottage. And her tall, but bent, dark shape seemed to me as I saw it then, and always since, to be something not on the side of those that won those fields so arduously from the heather, but to be somehow akin to those forces that ruled, or blew over, the bog, and that cared nothing for man. She walked a little way and filled a bucket with water from a stream that ran by from the bog, and brought it back with her, flashing beside her darkness, and went in and shut the door. When she was back in her cottage it looked once more what actually it was, an outpost of man on the edge of the fields he had won, a fortress against the waste; but for a moment, as I saw her coming out with her pail, it almost seemed to my fancy as though the enemy held it, as though something in league with the waste dwelt in that cottage.

I told Ryan to come back for me at seven, and set off with Marlin for the bog. It was not yet ten, and I had never had so long on the bog before as I planned to have to-day. My father used to make me come in for meals. I think hope lifted my steps more than cartridges weighed them down, but I certainly had too many; I could not deal with the game that hope pictured for me with less. Marlin carried my bag of snipe-shot, but my pockets were full of others.

"Have you the B's?" said Marlin.

"I have," said I.

"Then don't be ladening yourself, sir," said he, "for you'll not want them till nightfall."

And he carried the goose-shot to the cottage and left them there with my spare stockings and boots as we passed it. I still kept threes for duck, and a few fives. I found it pleasant to talk

to Marlin of what shot I had brought, such trivial technicalities
being still fresh to me and continually bringing the possibilities
of sport closer to my imagination. But not till we reached the
bog, and could be overheard by no one any longer from any
hedge, did he speak to me of my father.

"The duke is gone," he said.

"He is," I answered.

Marlin sighed and shook his head. "He mixed himself up in
politics," he said.

"What did he do?" I asked.

"You remember Maguire?" said Marlin.

I did not; but that did not matter.

"He was a policeman in Clonrue," he said. "And there used
to be a band of men in the hills. I won't say if they're still there,
and I won't say what they did, and then you'll never know, and
Begob that's better. But Maguire knew, and he reported it. And
the Duke got to hear they were going to kill Maguire. It's not
for me to say how he got to hear it, and it's God's blessed truth
that I don't know. But the Duke walked down the street of
Clonrue that day, and threw a note in through an open crack
of the window where Maguire's wife sat knitting. And Maguire
was gone that night, and his wife after him, and they got clean
away out of Ireland. That was three years ago, but the Duke
was never safe after that, and he knew it."

"Has my father got safe away?" I asked, for I felt Marlin
would know.

"He has that," said Marlin, "and I'll tell you for why. A man
that's prepared like that, and can get away at the start, he's not
going to be caught."

"I hope not," I said.

"Not he," said Marlin.

"There were four of them came," I told him.

And I saw Marlin pondering a moment, almost as though
he were considering which four they would have been; but of
that I could not be sure.

"Did you help him to get away?" he asked.

"I did not," I replied.

"That's right," he said. "They'll have nothing against you then." And he added, so as to soothe me: "Ah, but they wouldn't have hurt you."

But I knew they would from the way they had lowered their aim to my stomach as I was taking the oath, so as not to hit the true Cross in case they should fire.

We were speaking low, but the snipe heard us, and were beginning to get up. It seems a pity, but I'm afraid that the human voice is about the most dreaded sound in all nature. Soon I was shooting at the snipe, and missing them. But Marlin had not yet brought me to the point from which he wished to start our walk over the bog, with the north wind behind us; and he consoled me with the remark: "Sure there's no man living could hit a snipe when he's walking up wind." This is not true, but was very comforting. And sure enough it's a very difficult thing, especially on a red bog, to hit a snipe except when you are walking down wind. The bird gets up at forty or even fifty yards, and has done twenty more before you fire, straight away from you, and dark against the still darker earth and the twigs of the heather. But when you walk down wind on them it is as Marlin first explained to me; they fly across you so as to get into the wind to travel against it, and they show white as they turn, and you aim yards in front. I asked Marlin why the snipe fly against the wind. "Sure it's the contrariety of the bird," he said. "And, begob, there's men like that."

We came after some while to a place at which the bog went down, with a soft black precipice twice the height of a man, to flat reaches of marsh and rushes, and the heather ended. And there we turned and got the north wind behind us, and walked away over the heather and moss to my heart's content. I remember the low hills bounding two sides of the bog, and the horizon where it seemed boundless, and beyond the horizon; yes, I remember that as clearly; beyond the horizon where my imagination, fed by Marlin's tales, saw the heather, the pools, and the mosses reaching endlessly on, till they came at last to lands that it was my joy to have heard of. Better, I think, to have heard of those lands beyond the horizon, and to have treasured some picture of them all these years, however wide that picture be from geography, than never to have cared or wondered what it was like over there. I remember too a brilliance that shone in the pale blue of the sky, as though the north wind had enchanted it. Before me in the South the sun was hidden, but behind me and to the East the dome of the sky seemed all washed clear and shining, so that often I find myself thinking that it may really be true that the days were brighter in Ireland when I was young. Under that luminous sky we walked straight for hours, with the flash of the snipe now and then, white as they flew across me, against the dark of that earth; walking, as I had already learned to walk, with both eyes watching for snipe, and yet with somehow or other a glance to spare, to see that one put one's foot safe on the heather and never once on one of the glimmering mosses that make the bog so beautiful, and that let you through to deeps of which Marlin said there's no sounding. Safe foothold and dangerous waters over unknown deeps of slime seem, from, what I remember, to have been just about equal. And all the way, as every bird got up, came Marlin's tactful consolation, or rare praise, in his quiet voice, after my shot. How slowly I came to believe what Marlin told me about aiming in front of snipe, for it seemed absurd to fire so far from where there was any bird; but at last I began to kill one for every three that I missed, which is not bad for a boy. Once a woodcock got up, looking uncouthly slow, with his heavy body and large lazy wings, after the lightning flash of the snipe; but when I fired I was yards behind him, with both barrels, and began to learn then what it took some years to be sure of, that those large wings of the woodcock do at their ease what the little snipe has to hurry so much to equal. And a hare in his couch of heather heard us coming, and leaped away over the bog, with a shower of water behind him all the way, like a half of a silver wheel.

"There goes a hare!" I exclaimed.

"Aye. Likely," said Marlin.

"But it *is* a hare," I protested.

"Aye. Likely it is," he repeated. "But you never know what shape may be took by a leprechaun."

It's curious how far, as it seems to me now, when I walked the bog with Marlin, I had entered that country of which Tennyson seems to speak:

> "Not wholly in the busy world nor quite
> Beyond it lies the garden that I love."

And of course all poets have been there, one time or another; one foot on earth and the other just touching elfland. Marlin, who knew so well all about shooting, and the habits of all the birds, and how to walk the bog, seemed also to have travelled a little further than heather grew or any road ran, and to have brought back for me, as a fairing, lore that is not of our fields.

More snipe got up, and still we went on, with the north wind hard behind us.

Once I met a man who said to me wonderingly: "But what do you *do* in the country?" Well, there is space there, for one thing; and what the use is of that I cannot say, unless to tell you that it is like drink, to one of those men who must have it and who die if you keep it away from them, as (likely as not) I am dying now, in this foreign town slowly, through not having the past to get back to nor the Irish bog. But I must not argue here with a man I met years later than that day of which I set out to tell you, and anyway argument is no good. I was arguing again yesterday with Monsieur Alphonse. But here I am only remembering. Remembering Ireland. Well, the snipe got up and we went down wind all the morning, and I had shot, I think, twelve; probably nearly as many as I had shot in all my life before. And there were still the geese before me, if that strange remark were true, that had haunted my mind all the morning: "My mother says that the grey lags are coming."

I suggested lunch. And Marlin said: "Ah, I'll not trouble with anything to eat. But I'd like a little sup of whiskey."

So we found a comfortable bit of heather and I ate bread and cheese that I had brought, and handed my flask to Marlin.

For a while we sat in silence under that brilliant sky. Then I looked up and saw Marlin's eyes full of things that seemed far away and of which I knew nothing; and I chose that moment to ask him of the thing I had wondered at ever since hearing him say it. "How does your mother know," I asked, "that the grey lags are coming?"

And though he turned his face towards me, he never called home that look. "Ah, she knows," he said, and would say no more.

CHAPTER IV

I only shot two more snipe in the afternoon: we were coming back and were not right with the wind, and I was hurrying to get to the place at which I was to wait for the geese. Probably I was hurrying unduly. If they went by our watches I might not have let my impatience run away with me; but coming, as they do, with a certain phase of the light, which we cannot predict so accurately as they can, it seemed better to allow half an hour, so as to be on the safe side, and I stretched the allowance till it was over fifty minutes. There swept by me a dozen golden plover, busy with some great journey, too high for a shot; I remember their arrow-like flight as I saw it then, and the formation in which they flew, like the point of a broad-barbed arrow, and the sound of their golden voices; one note only; were it more they would have outshone the fame of the nightingale. I remember too, that day, the cry of the curlew, as one rose suddenly some way off, from the bog. And ever since that day it is by this voice that I most remember my home. The lion, heard at night, is not more the voice of Africa, nor the nightingale the voice of romance, than the cry of the curlew seems to me to be the voice of Ireland. It utters a message so far and free from the shallowness of all phrases, that I like to think of it living, as surely it will, and nesting still in the heather, after all the follies of man. And the message? I do not know. But the messages that can never be put into words seem to me to be always the deepest, and those that words can at once express are seldom of any help; so that we seem to be sadly without guidance.

I wondered what Marlin would say of it. So I said to him: "That's a strange cry."

"Aye," he said. "My mother says that sometimes it means nothing."

"And at other times?" I said.

"At other times it's a warning."

I looked at him, rather than question him further, to see if any warning was troubling him then, but he was walking on towards the dry land in the distance, not heeding the curlew. And I was glad of this, for it was not only that the bog grew ominous towards evening, but there was something increasingly oppressing me when Marlin spoke of his mother that made me have vague forebodings as her cottage came into sight without ever knowing what I feared. Far off we saw the brown thatch, sagging in the middle, and black where it sagged; and its column of smoke going up into the air, whenever the north wind let it, from its low square chimney of wood.

Looking back on that journey all those years ago, as I approached the Marlins' cottage coming out of the bog, I seem to remember more things learned that day than I ever learned in a month from the wisest books; and, strangely, I seemed to be learning things in pairs, now something this side of the horizon, now something barely within the borders of Earth. I learned what is more important than how to shoot snipe; how to mark them. For if you cannot pick them up it is far worse than useless to shoot them. I had brought no dog, for I had been too much away at school for our retrievers to work for me as they worked for Murphy, so I was dependant for my fourteen snipe on the keen eye of Marlin, and on what I learned from him of the art of marking birds. And this art depends in the first place on never blinking after one has dropped one's bird, and never for a moment shifting one's gaze, until one comes to the spot where the bird is down. One instant's change of

one's gaze from the tuft of rush one is watching and twenty
tufts that are like it greet one's returning eye, which fast grow
to a hundred. The snipe may fall easily eighty yards away, and
one must find one's way to the spot in safety over the bog: that
is the art. If one can do that one can put one's handkerchief
down within five yards of the snipe. And then there is the cross-
line. If two men, some yards apart, both mark a snipe, where
they meet as they walk towards it should be within one yard of
the bird. And a mark should be thrown down at once as soon
as one reaches the spot, for any landmark one takes is soon
imitated by the bog again and again over an area wider and
wider. If a man alone on a bog gets a right and left at snipe it is
almost impossible to pick up both. His only chance is to throw
a handkerchief down on the spot where he fired his shots, and
then to pick up the second, relying on memory for the line of
the first when he goes back to the handkerchief. When there
are two men, as we were that day, the one that is not shooting
must mark the first bird of the two, as the man with the gun
has to take his eye off it, probably before it hits the ground, and
he has to pick up the second bird. But it was a year or two yet
before I was able to get right-and-lefts at snipe.

Never shall I forget how as we neared the cottage for the
second time that day, the brightness now all gone out of the
sky and the threat of night lowering, Marlin came nearer to
me, and nearer still, clearly full of an intention to speak, and
for some while not speaking; but when we were close to the
cottage he reached out a sudden hand and touched my elbow
to stop me, and said to me words that will never convey to the
reader what they conveyed to me. For most of what he said was
in his earnest warning voice and in his look, and I also knew the
meaning of the strange words that he used. "It's the way it is,"
he said, "that my mother's a Wise Woman."

The accent was equally on the word Wise and on the first
syllable of Woman. It was not that he said that the woman was
clever. It was nothing less than a warning that his mother was
a practising witch.

CHAPTER V

As we entered the cottage she was standing at her hearth, prodding the fire with an ash sapling under a large iron pot that hung on a chain from the darkness. When the son saw what she was at, he said: "Will you give Master Char-les some fresh tea, Mother?"

"I will that," she said. "But there's dreams in this one," pointing to the pot.

And at that there reached me a straying whiff from the pot, disturbed by the wind that had followed us through the door, and I knew she was stewing tea.

"What is there in the dreams?" I asked. For a guest cannot ignore his hostess's topics.

"All the truth that is not in the world," she said.

And then she turned all her thought to hospitality, no less observed at the edge of an Irish bog than in the salons of Paris. She spread a table-cloth and brought out cups and plates that had the air of being rarely used, and made a pot of fresh tea. Had I drunk that other tea, that had probably been stewing there all day, and had I spent a few weeks in a cottage like that at the edge of the bog, watching the ground mist rising as twilight was coming on, and hearing the curlews calling, there is no saying that I might not have seen such things as Marlin saw, or even known something of the lore of his mother: a few more days might have done it. It's hard to say, and I cannot work it out; I knew the bog, and roughly where it went to— that is to say, I believed in the maps; but Marlin and his mother had some other belief and some other knowledge, and their geography seemed to run so close to mine that I have often feared that almost at any moment theirs might float this way and mine drift out of sight, as easily as mist and clear air may change their places; and if that occurred I knew that one's chance of salvation was over. And if I did not entirely know this then, I already suspected it, and knew it only a little later that day, when Marlin told me upon what land his hopes were fastened.

As I drank the tea she was watching me from the darker end of the room, beyond the glow of the candles that she had put for me on the table. And I think she was prophesying, but she said nothing.

Had she spoken then, and had I written it down, I might have had more to tell you of my life than this tale sets forth. Would it have been the same story? I cannot tell. But probably, like my memories, there would have been gaps and vivid intensities, crowded hours and empty years, like butterflies flashing on empty levels of air. And as for truth, which lies in the meaning of all our acts, can I see that clearer looking back than she seemed to see it looking forward? I do not know, but there was an intensity in her look more vivid than any that ever comes to me nowadays, and I would trust her to have seen the truth.

As the room grew dimmer beyond the light of the candles, a new uneasiness was overtaking me and ousting the apprehensions that seemed a part of the room, an uneasiness that I might arrive too late at the spot at which I was to wait for the geese, and that they might be there before me. But dark though it was in the room, it was light enough outside, except that the brilliance had gone out of the sky, and small birds were filling the hedgerows with their voices. And then I feared that the geese might not come at all. And at this thought I turned to that strange woman who seemed to know more than Marlin knew, though he knew so much of the ways of the bog and all that dwelt in the heather, and I asked her if the geese would come that night.

"Aye, they'll come," she said.

And in my eagerness to be sure of it I asked her how she knew. And at that she broke out strangely.

"Haven't I seen the north wind?" she said. "Aye, face to face. And few the secrets he hides from me. He that whispers to the smoke of my chimney now, an hour ago was shouting to the geese. Aye, they'll come."

Marlin quietly nodded to me.

"Aye, that's the will of the north wind," she added.

And I asked her some question as to how I should get a goose, but no more would she tell me, saying: "The secrets of the north wind are not for that, nor the thoughts that the hills are brooding."

And I saw that I had tried to evoke her wisdom for too trivial a thing, and I changed my boots and stockings then and got my heavier shot, and set out with Marlin.

We had not far to go: a stream ran through the bog and past the Marlins' cottage, and about its banks there ran for some way into the heather a level space of rushes and moss and grass on which the geese used to alight, to eat the roots of a marshy relative of the buttercup, that Marlin called briskauns, that grew there. When we got there I could see by old marks that this was where they came when they came at all. I chose, with the help of Marlin's advice, a tuft of rushes in which I lay down, and he gathered a few more rushes and threw them over me and then concealed himself in another tuft near by. I shall always remember that evening; partly because of the twilight fading over the bog and night coming slowly on with stillness and voices, and partly because of the things that Marlin told me; for he talked till the hour came that he felt might bring the geese, and we waited for them then in a hush while the earliest stars appeared. Shall I tell of what Marlin said, or of what I saw myself as the western sky glowed with layers of gold and vermilion, and faded away till all the bog was dark, and wandering pinions began to whisper and sing? Rather, I think, what Marlin said to me; for I saw but the beauty of one evening hallowing the moss and the heather, but evening after evening with all their enchantments, shining in those wild waters, gleaming on moss and on heather, had been sinking year after year into Marlin's spirit, until whatever was strange in that land, whatever was lovely, dwelt in him as a very essence, of which this one evening was but a particle.

The bog-rail croaked his shrill croak a hundred times, small singing birds passed over on their way home; the rooks went by; a dead hush followed the sound of the last of their wings, and then Marlin spoke.

"They'll not come yet," he said.

And I saw that he wanted to talk to me; and, knowing that all he cared for was in that waste of peat, that the bog was his country and his patriotism limited to it, I spoke to him of the bog. I was also eager for knowledge of that strange land, over which the edge of night was already hovering. "Do will-o'-the-wisps come here?" I said.

"They do that," said he.

"What are they?" I asked.

"Jack-o'-lanterns," he answered.

I asked him: "What are jack-o'-lanterns?" And I saw I had somehow troubled him. For he was silent a long time, and said: "God help them, they are men like me."

"Men like you!" I exclaimed.

"Aye," he said, "spirits of men."

"But what kind of spirits?" I persisted.

"The damned," he said.

"Oh, Marlin," I exclaimed. "You are not damned."

"Keep your head down," he said, "in case the geese come. I'm surely damned."

"But why?" I asked him, not heeding what he had said about letting the geese see me.

"A sin that I sinned," said Marlin.

"But you can confess it," I insisted.

"It is a reserved sin," said he.

And the meaning of that (for such as have not the true faith) is that he had done something for which no parish priest could give absolution.

"You can go to the bishop," I said.

"I'd have to go to Rome itself," he answered, "and how can I get there?"

"What was it?" I asked.

"I fell to dreaming about the bog," he said, "and to wondering where it went, and to looking at the sun on it a long way off where it goes silver and golden; and, begob, what chance had I with that upbringing; and, God help me, I turned my thoughts to Tir-nan-Og."

"Tir-nan-Og!" I said. For the place, if it be a place, or the fancy that made it, and all who dwell there, if they dwell there indeed, and the very songs about it, are all purely heathen. "But can't you forget it?"

"Forget Tir-nan-Og?" he exclaimed. "Forget Tir-nan-Og! With the young men walking with the gold low light on their limbs, and the young girls with radiance in their faces, and the young blossom bursting along the apple-boughs, and all that is young there glorying in the morning, and it morning for ever over all the land of youth. Forget Tir-nan-Og! Not the angels in Heaven could forget it, nor all the blessed saints. And I saw them once in a dream, that was sent, maybe, to warn me, but it came too late. I saw the angels in a dream, all talking among themselves, more than you ever saw of ducks over any water, a multitude of them looking north and south and east, but with all their backs to the west or turning their heads away from it. And I prayed to them, and it was the last time I prayed, but they must have seen in my face that I had looked towards Tir-nan-Og, for they rejected my prayer, and I knew that my soul was lost."

"But, Marlin," I said, "how could you know that?"

"I was praying to them," he answered. "And they went on talking among themselves."

For a while I was too horrified by the finality of that vision to find any words to say; and something in his voice or his face had convinced me that it was in reality one of those experiences of the spirit that can sometimes come to men.

And then I said lamely: "But you had done no sin."

"God help me," he said, "I had preferred Tir-nan-Og to Heaven."

And I looked in his eyes in the twilight and I could see that it was as he had said. For him there would never be anything but that most heathen land. And I tried, still lamely enough, to point out some flaw in the certainty that he had of the loss of his soul.

"But if the will-o'-the-wisps are here," I said, "what have they to do with Tir-nan-Og?"

"They come over the sea on the west wind from Tir-nan-Og to the bog, and back again before cock-crow to Tir-nan-Og, but to Heaven never," he said.

"I'd pray," I said, "till I forgot Tir-nan-Og."

"Hist," he said. For there was a soft note in the air now, growing louder and fading, and then growing louder again. The duck were flighting. So I rolled back among my rushes, for once the duck came there was no telling when those wayfarers that I watched for might not arrive. And I lay still thinking of poor Marlin's soul. Was there such a place as Tir-nan-Og? If not, could Heaven be jealous? And if there were, logic said that Marlin had made his choice, and should be content with it. But logic is little use to us. There are many things that men deliberately choose instead of Heaven, and yet are ill content. And just as I was reasoning out these things, as I never clearly reasoned them again, I heard a voice far off utter two syllables.

In the silence that followed I did not of course forget about Marlin's soul, just to think about geese. But what is the use of writing my memories down if I depart from them to write things that, however laudable as expressions, are entirely un-true? I forgot Marlin and all his perils utterly. I thought of nothing in the world but those two notes, wondering if really they came from the geese, wondering if I would hear them again. And they came again, a sudden burst of voices. An ac-clamation, partly like hounds hunting, and partly like a distant people cheering. It was the grey lags.

CHAPTER VI

The bog had gone very dark when I heard the grey lags, but the sky was like enamel, no longer giving light but full of it; and against the sky I saw them. They were coming straight for me. Soon they were a black mass, very black, with enormous waving wings, and the whole night rang with their outcry.

And how I wish, vain although wishing be, yet how I wish there were anything that could stir me now as the coming of those geese stirred me. What is there now for which I would wait in the damp an hour, lying in a tuft of rushes? Nothing ever happens here to interest me but the arrival of Monsieur Alphonse to discuss certain relations between his country and the Irish Free State, and I wait for him sitting in a comfortable chair, and nothing ever comes of our discussions. But then! Then the incredible seemed on the verge of fulfilment, for I had never believed that the geese would really come within shot of me. The night seemed too big for that. One might as well hope to touch a star. And here they were.

Marlin never said a word. I remembered the advice of the man that came to shoot my father. Do not aim too far in front of a goose, he had said. But that was at the beginning of its flight; yet these geese seemed to be slowing before alighting, so I aimed as he had advised. I saw two together in one black mass quite close, and I fired at them. One dropped. With an immense commotion they all came over me then, and with a great outcry of voices, and I missed with my left barrel, and they went away as though dancing upon the air.

"Well done, Master Char-les," said Marlin. "B' the Tarrawar, but that's great."

I never heard anyone else swear by the Tarrawar, and I do not know what it is. Marlin lying flat with even his face hidden had not seen the bird drop, but he had heard the thump of it in the still night.

I waited, wondering if more would come. But Marlin said to me: "Pick it up, Master Char-les, before it gets too dark."

It is curious how I had failed to foresee the blackness with which night would soon cover everything. It seemed so easy to pick up a goose twenty yards away. But I waited a little longer, and in that short while the last of the light went suddenly out of the rushes, and I was searching soon amongst scores of black lumps, one of which must be the goose. When Marlin found the goose and gave it me, and I held it in my hand by the neck, it was one of those moments of achievement that I suppose all men hope for, and that sometimes come, bringing with them very often disillusion, when they come at all. And I suppose that if you examine all the achievements of man, one by one under the microscope of philosophy, you will find what Solomon found; you will find in every one the same taint of disillusion. Therefore let no man grudge me my goose or scorn it; it was one of those things I have known, which like some rare metal purified perhaps by the flames of a meteorite, was without any trace of disillusion.

"It's late to get out of the bog, Master Char-les," said Marlin, "but sure we'll do it."

And I realised then that the day's work was not over, and that the short and easy journey we had made to get to the place at which I had watched for the geese was now something to be undertaken in the spirit of pioneers travelling in unknown lands.

Marlin went in front, relying on some kind of instinct he must have had, for we could not see. And I followed him step by step, and he turned round once in every ten yards or so to see how I was getting on. The night was very still and menacing. It was not till I was clear of that uncertain land, led all the way by Marlin, that I gave another thought to poor Marlin's soul. And then I wondered once more how it was that merely living all his life by the side of the bog could have so utterly turned him from Heaven, and whether it was really too late. "Marlin," I said, "how could just looking at the bog make you think so much of Tir-nan-Og."

"Begob," said Marlin, "you should see it in spring." Which is of course just the time I never went there, as it was only shooting that took me. "And when the heather is first blooming," went on Marlin, "and at dawn, and when the sun's setting over it, and in storm. And the further it goes, the grander it gets. And over there where it goes out of sight men have tried to hem it in with roads and railways, but they could not spoil the glory of it, and it goes on, in spite of them all, till it comes to the sea, and a little way over the sea is the land of the young. And isn't the bog lovelier than the sky?"

And somehow I knew that he was going to argue from that that his heathen land was lovelier than Heaven. And it was to prevent him saying such a thing that I repeated something I had been told about Heaven which teaches us that it is fairer than any land that there is, or any that could be imagined.

"God help me," said Marlin, "I have chosen Tir-nan-Og."

CHAPTER VII

We walked on in silence then, I saddened a little as I hope and do believe I was, by the knowledge, now, that Marlin's soul must be lost, and yet with elations in me that no boy could have kept under, that came from the very feel of the goose in my hand; and so we came to the cottage. And in the bright candle-light I looked at the rows of feathers, wide and deep on the goose's breast. I had never seen one before. And Marlin's mother looked at the bird, whose coming she had prophesied to me, and all she said was: "Aye, they had written his name to die to-day. And had they written your father's name, he too. It's all in the writing."

Who They were she did not say. And, when I asked her how they wrote it, she only said: "With the north wind on ice."

With a boy's persistence I asked where it was written. And she flung up a warning hand, saying: "Never read that!" And I asked her no more.

I was glad of the tea that she gave me again, dark and strong now, for it was the same tea that she had made for me nearly two hours ago, kept warm by her great fire. Again, at that table, bright amongst cavernous shadows, I felt that but the lifting of a curtain, but a glance through a door ajar, but a flicker of mist, might have shown me the bog as Marlin's mother saw it, and the path of water and moss across the horizon as it was known to Marlin. I seemed for a while to be hovering between two worlds, that both claimed the same area of Ireland. I see, now, that I was wrong, I see now that Tir-nan-Og is contrary to everything we have been taught, and I know that there are no spirits haunting the bog for any other purpose than to mislead us. But in that cottage then, there was something in Mrs. Marlin's eyes alone, and in Marlin's thoughtful face, that showed me there were beliefs of the land all round us, held as strongly as any creed, though they were heathen. And the influence of those beliefs, arising from glances, dim lights, and the mere wonder of night, and confirmed, as they seemed to be, by every whisper the north wind said to the thatch, so gripped me in that cottage by the bog that the influence abides in my memory to this day, not strong enough, I trust, to imperil my soul. And yet when I look at the bog shining there in my memories I find it hard to remember the map and to say exactly where its boundaries go; rather I seem to see it crossing the sky-line and narrowing where roads and railways confine it, but a strip of it running on, till it comes to the very sand and shells of the ocean, and across that a little way westward, God help me, Tir-nan-Og.

I am afraid as I read what I have written that I have not shown any reason why my heart should have leaned even for a moment towards that heathen land; but it will be known, I trust, in Heaven what power there was in the shadows that stalked from the firelight, and the clear words of the wind, clear though in no known language, and in that strong tea, and in the mystery all round us, made by the night and the bog, a mystery hushed with the silence of one about to whisper, and in old Irish legends that gathered these things together, and in the attitude of the only two that were with me, which clearly accepted more than all I have hinted. They will estimate all these influences and know their weight, and will know that in the end I have turned my back to the West.

The wind was rising, but, above the voice of it, I heard the sound of the horse and trap that Ryan was to bring for me down the bohereen. So I said good-bye to the dark woman, and, as I shook her by the hand she peered into my face, and then said: "You will come again." She did not say it as though asking a question, or uttering a polite phrase, but as though

stating something that she had just seen. And I said something
polite that sounded foolish against the deeper certainty of her
words; and she added: "Aye, and the day will come when we
three shall be here again, two of us looking as we seem, and
one of us drifting over the bog in the night."

I did not understand her, but I remembered her words.
Glancing at Marlin I saw no surprise in his face at either of her
remarks: he merely accepted both as though she had said that
tea would be ready at five. As I left he said to me: "Then you'll
come again, Master Char-les."

He too said it as though it were something that had now
been ascertained. Which left me little to say.

The lights of the trap at the end of the bohereen glared
suddenly, as something out of a different land, as the lights of
a ship from some great city might gleam by uncharted coasts.

The things that most stand out in my memory after that
are showing my treasure to the different people I met, to
Ryan, to the lodge-keeper by the light of one of the lamps, to
our cook, and next morning to Murphy. And one other thing
stands out very clear from that day; there came a telegram
from my father. It had been handed in at Euston just before
eight o'clock, and said: "Forward all letters to the club." From
that I knew he was safe. As for the letters, my father belonged
to no club, having taken his name off the list of members even
at the Kildare Street Club, for the sake of economy years ago:
in London he had never belonged to a club. But it told me all
that was intended, and if the postmistress talked about the
telegram till others were sent to look for my father around
the London clubs, no harm was done by that. I saw that he
must have ridden a long way that night, and come to some
other line than our familiar one and caught some early train
of which I knew nothing, and so boarded the Irish mail only
ten hours after leaving High Gaut. He may have even taken
a special, so as to catch that boat. I never enquired who were
after him, well advised by Marlin; but whoever they were, my
father must have relied on them not to waste a night in sleep. I
showed the telegram to the butler without a word, and he said

nothing to me; nor did either of us talk to the other at any time about forwarding letters. It was better not.

The north wind that had blown all day had been increasing in power all the while that I was driving home; it had flapped the wings of the dead goose as I brought it into the house with me, and it had slammed the door behind me. And now it was rising still. All night it boomed and wailed, trying shut doors in anger, and mourning in aged walls. For a while after going to bed my imagination kept pace with the wind's anger, wondering what men were breaking into the house, or tiptoeing along corridors, and then in the midst of its furious tumult I slept. I woke in as deep a calm as I have ever known, the hush of an utter silence, and in the silence the snow. It lay bright over everything. The north wind had brought it and fallen.

What a change snow brings to any land that it visits: rather enchantment than change. It is as though the mountains came down to speak to the fields, almost as though overnight another planet had called for us and taken us over from Earth. Even the inside of the house was changed, a bright light dwelt in the pictures, making the work of men long dead more vivid and merrier; and on the north side of the house all the rooms seemed as though they were still curtained, and all their blinds drawn down, for the snow was clinging to the window-panes where the wind had so violently hurled it; and yet even in those dim rooms, through the grey snow, there seemed to shine gleams from the light of a strangely triumphant morning. And the first thing I thought as I saw all that snow was that my snipe would be gone; they would have risen from beside their countless pools, from their feeding-grounds of marsh and their shelters of heather, and would have gone by those bright levels along the horizon where the bog went wide through the hills, and would have taken the way of Marlin's dreams until they came to the sea. From the rushy lands they would be gone too. And even the geese, with snow on their grazing grounds, would feed tonight upon beaches beyond my knowledge. But perhaps the most essential quality of a sportsman is an aptitude to adapt his pursuits to the weather: he is not the enemy of the elements, having far more friendship for the north wind and the snowstorm than he has for the railway and pavement. It is the weather that brings him everything; and, if sometimes he try to outwit it, keeping himself warm or dry with the alliance of some stout willow, when the air is full of hail, it is a contest no more unfriendly than that between two teams of athletes. He has no more enmity for the weather than a business man has for his banks. Indeed, I think we sportsmen are somewhat nearer to the tides and the growth of trees and the night and the morning, and to whatever we call the plan that orders the planets, than many a man that does more useful things. And so I immediately thought of what the weather would bring me in place of the geese and the snipe. It would put the woodcock in. The woods should be full of them.

So after breakfast I went to find Murphy, to ask him what chance there would be of getting beaters. I found him standing outside the door of his house at the edge of one of the woods, looking out over the snow with the air of one estimating the qualities of some new neighbour. At my question of beaters a thoughtful expression came over his weather-beaten face. He said little or nothing, and I knew that the thought in his face was not concerned with how to get the beaters, but the sub- tler problem of how to speak to me without offending or even disappointing me; and I realised that the difficulty about the beaters was that I had no authority to take the men from such work as they might be doing. He would gladly have done it for me, and would have found it easier to go round collecting the beaters, working only his legs, than to work his brains to find for me appeasing temporising answers. But he could not get the men without asking the steward, and the steward ran the place for my father. Things were like that till my father's letter arrived. And this was not for another two days, two days that I spent in walking about with my gun by streams and wherever water was not frozen, to find snipe that the weather had driven out of their marshes. Two or three I found, and a teal, and the larder profited by my lonely walks.

And then one morning my father's letter arrived. It had

been posted in Paris, posted on the day on which I had woken to see the snow, arriving two days later. It showed me that my father had not stopped even three or four hours in London, but had gone straight on. I wondered at this haste, thinking he would have been safe enough there, but I was young and knew nothing of the extent of the ramifications of politics. This was the letter.

My dear Charles,

Run the place as well as you can till I return. I've told the bank to let Brophy have funds to pay the men. There are things that I want to tell you about the Dutch picture, and about other things in the library, for pictures and books are roads that may lead you far. Best of all, keep out of politics. I will write to you at greater length, but first I must be sure that my letters are not being tampered with. I have put a number 8 shot in this letter, the kind you use for shooting snipe. Write and tell me if one fell out when you opened the envelope. I know you will open it at breakfast and will easily find the shot on the tablecloth if it rolled out, but if none was there my letters are being opened.

Your affectionate father,

James Charles Peridore.

I should explain perhaps that our family have always been called James Charles, or Charles James, father and eldest son alternately, ever since our disastrous loyalty to James II. But, poor Stuarts, our loyalty to them was no more disastrous to us than our loyalty to-day. When we are called James Charles, the first name is after James II, and the second after the prince that they called the Young Pretender; when we are called Charles James, the first name is after Charles I and the next after James II. They gave us a medal and that nebulous dukedom, and that is all we got for it.

To return to the letter, the shot was there all right and I wrote at once to say so, but from that day the correspondence ceased. I got no more letters from my father.

CHAPTER VIII

The thing that at first most concerned me about my father's letter was his permission to run the place. This meant that I could have beaters. I interfered in no other way with the routine, that Brophy ran as well as he could, but I went at once to him and asked him to let Murphy have the men. Seven or eight were all he could let me have, in fact it was pretty well all that there were. So young Finn was sent for, and soon he was going round the place calling the men loudly by name. It occurred to me then, as it never had done before, that young Finn was oddly described. He was tall and greatly wrinkled, and his long beard that once I remembered to have had faint tints of yellow about the edges was now pure white. When my father called him young Finn, as he always did, I never thought of questioning the designation, which was no doubt given him to distinguish him from some Finn that I never knew; but now for the first time I questioned the appropriateness of it, though I still called him young Finn.

Young Finn, then, went shouting round the place and soon had seven men, and the morning was not too far on its way when Murphy had them all lined up at the beginning of a long narrow wood that hid the wall that shut us off from the road, a wall built too high for any man to climb, but time had given a hold between rows of stone, first to moss, then to men's feet, and fingers had done the rest, so that tracks led into the wood here and there from the wall; no one knew whose; probably the men that came to look for my father had come in by one of these ways. There were brambles here, roving a little further every year about the feet of old beech trees; and here were box bushes and patches of privet. The men went through the wood shouting: "Hi, cock; hi, cock," as they went. But the snow had so beaten down the usual homes of the woodcock that in this wood we got none at all.

"They'll all be in the fir woods," said Murphy.

So we all set off towards them, wilder woods at the far end of the demesne, with the tidy land lying park-like in front of them, and the wild hill behind. Wide rides had been cut for shooting, and I took my place at the junction of two of them. It was while standing there waiting for a woodcock, that I began to think of my father's letter. I had fully understood his reference to books and pictures in the library. Obviously he intended to tell me, as soon as he was sure that his letters came safely, about that exit from the library that was somewhere behind my back while I watched the Dutch picture. At the time it had been far better for me not to know, but who knew what the future would bring forth? And he wanted to tell me now of that secret path to safety that might one day be needed again. But one thing I had not understood when first I read the letter, and that was why he had explained to me that number 8 shot was the kind one used to shoot snipe. At the time it had rather annoyed me; now it puzzled me. It was rather I that used to tell him what shot one used for different birds, for shooting was the chief glory of the Christmas holidays, and I could not help talking of all its details; it was so new to me then; so was life. But why had my father wasted ink on telling me what shot I used for snipe? And from thinking of this I came to other things in the letter. Why was he so sure that I would open the letter over the dining-room tablecloth? As a matter of fact, I hadn't. Not that it mattered, for the two sides of the folded sheet of paper had been turned over for a quarter of an inch, the open end being towards me, so that it could not easily have fallen out at all. What then of the people that he seemed to suppose might open the letter and lose the shot? Why should they lose it? Did he suppose that they would open the letter hurriedly where there was no level surface to receive the shot if it fell out, whereas I would have the tablecloth to receive it? Perhaps. But in any case the envelope showed no sign of having been tampered with, and with a boy's arrogance I was a little contemptuous of these elder fancies, that I regarded as too complicated for reality. Another thought I had about that pellet of shot, which came again later, but just now a woodcock gliding by me put it out of my mind. I had not seen the woodcock soon enough, but there is always some excuse for missing a woodcock, if not seeing the bird in time can be regarded as any excuse: rather it is an aggravation. Anyhow, I missed it. And more came by and I missed them too, till it began to look like a morning wasted. And yet every woodcock I missed was teaching me something, and any skill in defeating this difficult bird, that I later came to share with most Irish gentlemen, I was learning then. The snow helped me. I began to see by marks of my shot on the snow how far I had shot behind a bird. And then the knack came to me: it came merely by aiming far in front of the apparently slow flight, and I began to hit them then, except when they were flying straight away from me, when an unforeseeable twist would take them out of my aim, usually just as I fired, or when they were flying straight towards me; that was the most difficult of all.

The beaters' voices came close; and now the woodcock, that glide as silently as a dream flits through the night, were flying noisily, for they were getting up close, and the woodcock gains that quiet mastery of speed that he has with a rapid flutter of wings as he rises, that is audible for quite fifty yards. One came straight towards me, giving that difficult shot that I mentioned, and I missed with both barrels. I missed with the right barrel because I aimed straight at him, and, if he had really been coming straight at me, bird and shot would have met, but the woodcock never is coming quite straight at one; to begin with he was higher from the ground than my eye, and, as he was not sinking, he cannot have been flying straight towards it; consequently I was a bit behind the bird with my right. Then he saw me, and up he went like a very irregular rocket and whirled away over the trees, while I scarcely got an aim at him at all with my left barrel. I had two or three down, and Murphy eagerly showed me where to find the pin-feathers, which then were great prizes to me. How much money or toil it takes to come by something we value, later on in life! And all the while we are losing things by the way. Would a diamond bring me now the pleasure that the pin-feather of a woodcock could give me then? I doubt it. And all the while there are people teaching youth to look forward to the solider things wrapped up in the mists of the future, and to scorn as trivial the wealth that lies all around them. What was that fable of the dog with a bone in his mouth, that saw the reflection of a better bone in the water? And can it apply here? Perhaps not.

No such thoughts as this, that trouble my mind now, came near me then, and I went on to take my stand at the end of the next beat, full of keen expectations encouraged by Murphy. There was a part of the wood there that had been swept by an old storm, and it had been replanted with spruce. This spruce was now just the right age to shelter woodcock, and its layers of greenery held up the snow like the many roofs of a pagoda. Again, as I stood there, I thought of my father's letter. Why had he turned the edges in so carefully if he had wanted the shot to fall out when the letter was opened? And there came the other thought that a woodcock had previously interrupted: what would anyone tampering with the letter do if he lost the pellet of shot and then read that it ought to be there? I turned over these thoughts, but with far less alertness than that keen fervour with which I waited for the woodcock that Murphy promised under the spruce. And, sure enough, they were there. At first none came at all; and then one came fluttering between two trees, both heavily heaped with snow, and I missed it. But it had shown me the way, for, as often happens with all kinds of birds, others flew the same line as the first: in that dense growth of young spruce there was a kind of white valley down which they came and, one after another, slipped out into the open between the same two trees. I got one, and then another. It was the one place to which they all seemed to have come for the shelter below the dense stiff branches of the spruce that the snow could not beat down. I did not get a right and left, but by the time that the beaters had come up, chanting "Hi, cock," as they came, I had ten woodcock down. It was some years before I did better than that, and to this hour

I can remember the pleasure with which I answered Murphy when he said: "Did you get one, Master Char-les?"

We picked them all up without much difficulty, which we should not have done but for the snow; for you can stand within a yard of a woodcock, dead or alive, and not see him among brown leaves or bracken. The brown on a woodcock is like the brown of the bracken, and the black bars on him are like the darkness in the spaces between dead leaves; they are more than like; they are identical. Man has to invent the cloak of invisibility in his fairy tales, but all animals that are hunted, or hunt, are born with it.

Then we went on to an older part of the wood, over that dazzling page on which Nature writes the doings of all her children. Nothing had stirred in the night, since the snow had ended, without leaving clear record of its leaps and travellings, of its escapes or pursuits. In the old wood I got two or three rabbits; then we all had lunch in Murphy's house, on that excellent dish that Ireland has given to a world that does not always understand it, for I have known cooks beyond our shores to cut all the fat off the cutlets, in order to make them tidy, before putting their sad remnants of lean and bone in the pot. Had I gone to the house for lunch, though it was barely twenty minutes away, I should have lost on the two walks and on the slowness of a more ceremonious meal, little less than an hour of the short winter's day. We went on, warmed, over the snow, and by the time the sun set huge and round through the wood I had only got one more woodcock. But the bag was good enough, and it was long before I got so many again.

That evening I went to Brophy's house to tell him of the day's sport. I remember him as a tall bent man with a very long brown beard. He had, compared with the rest of the men on the place, some sort of education, and he was a man whom I believed I could trust not to pass on my conversation with him as gossip. So I told him of my father's letter, and even about the pellet of shot. "That was a good scheme, sir," he said.

And yet I wondered about it, and still was a little puzzled.

CHAPTER IX

Days passed while the crows and the jackdaws came close to the windows for help from their human neighbour, now that all food was hidden by this sudden change in the world; so I used to share my breakfast with them and to watch the crows walking up, usually sideways, with their deep-blue heads and the purple sheen on their bodies, and their wings a little open to balance their walk, and the grey-headed jackdaws sailing suddenly down from some turret above me. Days passed, and the day came round when my father should have written again. And no letter came; nor the next day. In my growing uneasiness I looked for someone who could tell me all about it; and there was no one. It was then that the temptation came to me one evening to look for help from a source whence aid is rightly forbidden us, and to consult Marlin's mother. From which temptation I turned in time, but I still drove over to Lisronagh next morning, though not to seek help from her; for it occurred to me that among all his heathen fancies there was a streak of shrewdness in Marlin that would be as well able to see through this mystery as the wits of any I knew. We came to the old bohereen and drove only a short way down it, for we were stopped soon by a snowdrift that had found a gap in a hedge and had slanted across our way, its delicate sides smoothed out by the very wings of the wind, barring the road to the bog as though the things of the wild had suddenly come by that mood in which they sometimes weary of man and his wheels. So I got out and walked on to the house of the Marlins, telling Ryan to put up the horse and trap in Clonrue and to wait for me there.

The land lay still under that great enchantment that a whim of winter had worked with the north wind for a wand; and the bog that had held so many shades and colours was now a glistening plain with shadowy lumps, that went shining away to the sky-line, while grave white hills seemed to watch it on either side. And there was Marlin, motionless, as those slopes, gazing out over it to its furthest point, where it went unbounded by hills to a golden flood of far sunlight. It is right enough that a bog-watcher should watch the bog; and yet I thought from his rapt stillness, and from the look of his face as I came nearer, that it was not of any such work that he was thinking, but of the way over the bog to that flood of sunlight, and thence, keeping still to the bog where it curved to the distant sea, and so to that heathen land a little way over the water, whither none turn even their thoughts who hope for Heaven.

He was a few yards away from the cottage, and his back was towards me as he watched where the bog beneath its mantle of snow went over the sky-line through the wide gap in the hills. When I was quite close to him and he saw me, he seemed to bring back his gaze from further than the horizon; and so strange for a moment that gaze appeared, coming back to the fields of men, so ill-content to be here, that I wondered if Marlin was ill. And suddenly he was his old self again, my teacher in the only learning I sought. "There'll be no geese to-night, Master Char-les," he said. "The bog is frozen and they can't get at the briskauns."

"I didn't come for the geese," I said, though I had my gun.

"There'll be no snipe there neither, Master Char-les," he said, "for the river's frozen too."

For the river, though a running stream after it fell from the bog, was a sluggish line of wide pools among bright mosses before it left the heather.

"We'll go the other way," I said, pointing down the stream.

"Begob, there might be a teal on it," said Marlin.

"What shot should one use for a teal?" I asked; and no young scholar ever studied the aorist, or the tricks of any foreign verb, as I investigated such things as this. But I forget now what shot Marlin recommended.

"Will you not come into the house and have a sup of something?" said Marlin.

But I was in search of advice and I feared this house, lest

I should be tempted to seek it there; and such things are forbidden. And I answered Marlin out of such store of politeness or evasions (call them what you will) as one is bound to keep for the purpose of refusing drinks.

We had not gone far when I took from my pocket my father's letter and showed it to Marlin. "Begob," said Marlin, "wouldn't you read it to me yourself? Sure no one would read it better."

This tribute to some special skill in reading for which Marlin was giving me credit failed to conceal from me that he was unable to read himself, and probably all the better able for that to do his own thinking. So I read him the letter and showed him the actual shot and the turning of the two sides of the paper that prevented it falling out sideways. Marlin looked at these things for a moment and thought over the letter. And then he said: "Sure that would be no scheme at all."

"Why not?" I asked.

"In the first place," said Marlin, "if the shot fell out in Dublin, wouldn't they pick it up again as soon as they read it had a right to be there?"

"But if it rolled away and was lost, before they read about it?" I said.

"Sure, wouldn't they put in another?" replied Marlin.

Yes, that was obvious enough.

"And isn't the Duke a shrewd man?" said Marlin.

"I don't know," said I.

"Don't I know damned well he is?" answered Marlin. "Sure he wouldn't be alive this day if he wasn't."

"That's true," I admitted.

"True enough," said Marlin. "For they were clever men that were after him."

I made no answer, and Marlin went on. "Then wouldn't he make a better scheme than that?"

And all the questions I had asked in my mind about that letter came all together at once to a single point, kindling a light on the problem that Marlin saw in my face.

"Begob he did," said Marlin.

CHAPTER X

As we went by a willow I suddenly saw a teal on the far bank of the stream, barely twenty yards away, a male teal standing on a patch of grass that had been sheltered from snow by an aged trunk of an osier. I had never seen a teal so close: I could see the band round his eyes going along his face to the neck, a dark green patch upon his chestnut head; and I had the idea that having got so close I was certain of that teal. All this was in one instant. He seemed so large, standing against the snow that I thought he would rise as duck do, slowly and heavily. But suddenly he was off; and without any flutter, such as the woodcock makes, without any gradual increase of speed like the duck, he seemed to be instantly in the fullness of flight, like a snipe, or like an arrow. I fired at this bird, that but a moment ago seemed taken unawares as we came round the willow, and missed with my right barrel. Then he soared upwards. How far to aim above a teal soaring from the first shot, and how far in front, I think I learned during the next twenty years, but it took me all that time or a little longer; the shot that I fired with my left barrel then went nowhere near him.

"Missed," I said to Marlin, which as words go was unnecessary; but I think I must have expressed a great deal more in my voice, for he was at once at hand with his consolation.

"Sure no man could hit a teal," he said, "when they get up like that."

And I asked him how men did hit teal.

"Sure I'll drive them for you one day," he said, "and you'll get them coming over."

And he began to tell me of pools in the bog where they came, and of rushes in which I could hide while he went round to put forty or fifty of them over me; till the future seemed to be full of compensation for my present disappointment.

And just as Marlin was telling me of these things there

occurred an event; common and unimportant enough (if one has any idea of what is important or not), that dwells with me to this day, a tiny light illuminating the past for me, even in towns: a blue patch brighter than the summer sky, a speck that might have fallen undimmed from some Indian heaven, moved down the centre of the water, curving all the way with every curve of the banks, till that streak of earthly blue exactly divided the stream: it was the kingfisher.

I was silent with wonder.

"He's the one bird that goes from here to there backwards and forwards," said Marlin.

And I knew that he was talking again of Tir-nan-Og.

"He must look lovely over there," I said.

"Indeed he does not," said Marlin. "Over that water, and under that sky, and fluttering about the heads of queens that are young forever, dressed in silks outshining all the silk of the East, and with eyes outshining that, he looks very ordinary."

"Does he?" I muttered.

"He does indeed," said Marlin.

And then he told me that the swallows too go to Tir-nan-Og. But only once a year: the kingfisher alone goes backwards and forwards, and perhaps the owl.

We walked some way along that wandering stream that carried the soft bog-water I knew not where. I got no teal, and all the snipe were gone, probably by that very path along which I had seen Marlin gazing, over the bog to the sunlight, and thence to the sea; a path, I mean, for birds and for the thoughts of men like Marlin, a path through the air and over dreams, for no path led over the bog, but a series of dangerous steps, dead heather and brilliant mosses all the way, the first safe and the second deadly. Again, as we walked back to the cottage, now dream-like in the invisibility that the snow almost gave it, I saw Marlin lift his eyes to that far part of the bog where, unbounded by hills and touching only the sky, it had so clearly the air of going everlastingly on. He lifted his eyes to it as a caged eagle might to the mountains, as though his home were afar. Again that look troubled me. "Are you well, Marlin?" I said.

"Ah, well enough," replied Marlin, and once more his eyes were smiling on these fields and hedges of ours.

We entered the cottage under the thatch whose hollows were hugely filled with snow, and Marlin's mother looked at me in silence. As a student might look at a book, perhaps a little strange to him, she seemed in those moments of silence to be regarding my life; not the few years that were then past, but those that were coming. And, though I can give no proof that this was so, I seemed to read it as easily in her face as she was probably reading those years in mine.

"We walked down the river, Mother," said Marlin.

"Aye, the river," said she, "and one of the great rivers of the world, though it's small here. For it widens out on its way, and there's cities on it high and ancient and stately, with wide courts shining by the river's banks, and steps of marble going down to the ships, and folk walking there by the thousand, all proud of their mighty river, but forgetting the wild bog-water."

"What cities are they?" I asked, for I felt myself believing in them.

"Unknown, unknown to the world," she said. "But when Ireland's free and their ships go sailing out, they'll be known the world over."

I asked her when that would be.

"Aye, when?" she said. "And all the cities of the world, waiting to greet their sisters, are asking when. But there'll be a day when Ireland's ships, putting out from all our rivers, will crowd every sea. And they'll see no grander ships in all their journeys. And they'll come to all the cities that have ports on any sea, bringing their merchandise, at which the people of all markets will wonder. And the ambassadors from foreign lands, coming to greet us, will pass up our rivers and anchor under the walls of the Irish cities, and see their ships go dark from the shade of our towers and humble from the glow of our cities' pride. And when they ask of our wealth and the trade that we do with the other great nations of the world, our singers will tell them, coming down to the harbour's edge with trumpets and gonfalons and telling the men of strange lands of Ireland's glory. And the ambassadors will go back wistful into their own lands, telling what they have seen in the West, and all the nations will send costly gifts to welcome us, and to win from us treaties with far Indian kings. Aye, kings with crowns of pearl and jade will seek us, travelling from the boundaries of Earth in ships of scented timber." And suddenly she burst out wildly laughing and threw her arms up high, and dropped them again as though exhausted by that tumult of laughter, and sat down weeping bitterly.

I stood silent, and all was silent but for her sobs. Then Marlin turned to me quietly: "She's been looking at the future," he said.

CHAPTER XI

I stayed for some while watching the old witch weeping, and found nothing to say or do. And then I thought that if I waited awhile, her weeping might soon stop. But Marlin seemed to read what I was thinking, and slowly shook his head. And at that look from Marlin I said good-bye to him quietly, shook hands and went out of the cottage, and so walked back to Clonrue, haunted all the way by the memory of that wild laughter, which often troubles me yet. In Clonrue the horse was waiting in the stables behind the public-house, and the young men gathered in the doorway, or leaning against its wall, with their faces hopeful and sunlit, began at last to free my mind from the echoes of that terrible derision with which Mrs. Marlin had looked at the future. As for tears, there were none in Clonrue; and, as nothing else seemed to be afoot, several of the young men strolled round to the stables, and by the time the horse was led out there were seven or eight of them there, watching the horse being harnessed and estimating his quali-ties, for the Irish people are born judges of horses. Nor is there any sport at which they are not connoisseurs, even when they have failed to find any opportunity to follow it; so I was soon telling them that I had shot nothing that day on the bog, and they were giving me reasons why this must be, partly out of politeness and kindness, and partly because they knew the bog and its ways and were giving me sound advice. "The snow's sent all the snipe to the sea, Master Char-les," said one. "You should go to the red bog in the full of the moon," said another. And they all repeated that. Marlin had already told me this, but these men were all emphatic about it. And they were right. It is one of the few things that are known about other lives than ours, that snipe go to the peat and the heather whenever the moon is full. For each bit of knowledge like this, that we have of the wild folk's ways, there must be a hundred equally strange and romantic of which we have caught no hint.

And why were these men, of whose names I only knew two, all urging me to go shooting over there at the best time? It excited no surprise in me. Gratitude, I hope, yet no surprise. But the reader, if he dwell in towns, may feel surprised. No men in London guide him to the best shops, or advise him what to buy. Yet this was the way of Clonrue.

Then I asked of the geese, and they shook their heads and spoke more weightily. To tell the habits of snipe was one thing; it was another to bring news of the geese, to whom a hundred miles was a light journey. And then the horse was harnessed and I said good-bye to them, and they all said good-bye and urged me to come back as soon as the snow was gone, when the snipe would be hungry and back on their feeding grounds. And why? It was the Irish way.

I drove home and went straight to Brophy, and found him among the farm buildings. Of what I began to speak I do not remember, but he saw at once that it was not the topic about which I wished to speak to him, so he moved further away from the men that were working there, and when we were out of ear-shot, I said: "I am afraid we shall have no more letters from Mr. Peridore."

"Do you say that?" he replied.

"I do," I said.

"And why wouldn't the Duke write?" he asked.

"Because he never put a pellet of shot in the letter at all," I said.

"But didn't you find it?" said Brophy.

"Yes," I told him. "But I think those that opened the letter put it in when they read that it should be there. I think he meant them to do it. It was the surer way of the two."

"That would be very complicated," said Brophy.

Some time in that afternoon the wind swung round from the North, and came back to that point whence it blows so much upon Ireland, back to the south-west, whence come the clouds that wrap us warm in the winter and protect us from summer's heat, clouds bringing us dreams with their shapes and abundant crops with their moisture. Turn your back to an iron balustrade on the side that has gone rusty, or turn away from the mossy side of a tree, and you will have that wind in your face, moist and warm and gentle. It is the wind that has given us our green fields and flowing rivers, when other fields in our latitude are white and other rivers frozen. It blew once more, and a drip splashed from the eaves of farm buildings, and snow slipped softly down suddenly-slanting branches. All night the south-west wind blew, and in the morning patches of snow remained, and patches of green appeared, and patches of flood.

"It's the weather for snipe," said Murphy, when I saw him that morning. And I went to the stables to tell Ryan that I should want the trap, to drive to one of the black bogs not far away, and that I should walk home. And Ryan astonished me by saying: "The Duke's horse is home, Master Char-les."

"But when did he come?" I said; for there had been no word of it yesterday.

"Last night," said Ryan.

"Who brought him?" I asked.

"Sure, I don't know that," said Ryan.

"Didn't you see him come in?" I asked.

"Sure, it was long after I'd gone to bed."

"But don't you lock the stables up?" said I.

"Sure, I do," Ryan replied.

"Then how did he get in?" I asked.

"Begob, I don't know that," said he, with all the air of think-ing of something new. And when I saw that look I realised that I should get no more out of Ryan.

So I turned to more practical things.

"Is he fit?" I asked.

"He is," said Ryan.

"Could he carry me in a hunt?" I said

"He could that," replied Ryan.

And a new prospect was opened for the holidays.

Somehow I seemed to know, though I can't say how; it must have been merely by their expressions; that Murphy, young Finn, and all the men on the place, knew that the horse was home. But nobody ever spoke of it.

Old willows, lurking like witches by the borders of sere fields; patches of rushes, stray pools, in a world of browns and ochres; make the scene of the next few days that my memory still revisits. There I used to go with Murphy to look for snipe, which in the dark of the moon were all on the black bogs, and I suppose that Murphy told me as much of the ways of snipe as Marlin did, but I missed the things that Marlin knew, which were, or so it seemed, beyond Murphy's world, and I wanted to go out with Marlin again on Lisronagh and thought of it more and more. I was troubled too about that strange peril which he was so sure threatened his soul; and had some vague idea, which I see was useless, that somehow or other I might be able to help him. How I thought I could help him I do not know, but, trivial though it may seem, I kept away from Lisronagh because it was not the right time for snipe on the bogs of peat, and I had some shy reluctance to going there without much reason again, as I had done once when the bog was all under snow. As soon as the geese returned Marlin had promised to tell me. There was no saying to what distances they might have gone from the snow; they might by now be in Spain. So I shot snipe with Murphy; and then one day the hounds met three miles away. It was the first meet anywhere near, since the horse came back; they usually met far off on the other side of the hills.

For some days before this meet Ryan had been talking to me, whenever I saw him, about the super-equine powers of the horse that had carried my father; till I knew just how he took a double, how he changed feet on a narrow-bank, and his scorn for the walls of loose stones with which men fenced their fields down by the bog-lands.

"He'd change feet on a man's hat," said Ryan.

And, not noticing quite the surprise that his exaggeration demanded, he added: "Aye, and the man would never feel it."

"Has he wings?" I asked.

"He has not, for he doesn't need them," replied Ryan. "But he's the kind of horse that would grow them if he got into any difficulty."

"He'd grow them on top of a double," I suggested, "if he couldn't get down without."

"Begob he would," said Ryan with great conviction.

And I learned a great deal about the country from Ryan, for I only knew it this side of the hills, and the country I knew was mostly the bogs and marshes, and the woods of our own demesne. As for riding, I had been blooded in my pram from the pad of a fox just killed in one of our woods; and though I had never owned a hunter as yet and had only ridden ponies, there was probably horsemanship enough in my ancestry to be called up by the sanctifying touch of that wet pad in the hand of the old huntsman fourteen years earlier. Or are all symbols vain?

On the morning of the meet I went to the stables early to see Ryan about the bit. "Give me a curb," I said, for I was uneasy about not being able to hold him when I got near the hounds.

"You'll hold him better with a snaffle, sir," said Ryan. "The only use of a curb is for putting a horse into a ditch just as he's jumping it."

And I'm not sure that Ryan wasn't right. Many a beginner clutches at the rein just as a horse is jumping, especially as the horse lands on the bank of what we call a double, with another ditch in front of him; such clutches are apt to wreck him, and if made sufficiently hard, with the curb, at the wrong moment, are certain to. An expert horseman knows more about riding than horses do, but short of that the horse knows most, especially in a difficult country, and the less one interferes with him the better.

I had rather a fine pair of spurs; but I saw Ryan quietly looking at them so often, that, when he offered me a pair of my father's that were only an inch long, I had the sense to take them.

The meet was at eleven, and I started much too soon, urged by unreasonable fears of missing the hounds. They met at a little village straight out towards the hills, whose grey slopes grew clearer all the way as I rode, till one picked out every window in cottages lower down, and the gates and gaps in stone walls that wandered away to low clouds. Four cross-roads met in the village of Gurraghoo; and every one of the four drew, to a depth of at least twelve miles, from the countryside, all that were able to take their part in the quest and pursuit of a fox. Sometimes I had glimpses of them coming by one of the other three roads, a red coat or the flash of a button. But, from the gorse on the hill above Gurraghoo, the fox that dwelt there must have seen the commotion on every one of the roads to a great distance. He may not have known where they were going, but when he heard more voices than usual in Gurraghoo, and noise that gradually increased instead of passing on over the countryside to be dissipated in fields, he must have felt some uneasiness. And uneasiness with a wild animal is not a thing to ponder about or investigate, but a warning on which to act instantly. He probably knew every voice in Gurraghoo, certainly the normal volume of the talk of the village from which he took one chicken every night, as the hunt knew well by reading the village's claims on the poultry fund and dividing by three. So now the old warning came to him that things amongst men were different, and that the change meant danger. At any rate the fox that had dined outside Gurraghoo the night before, was gone when we drew the gorse covert.

So we jogged back through the village. And as we went, and as horses gradually changed their places in the long column, I met all the people I knew in the county, for they were all out. And I found that the news of my father's going, and the cause of it, had got abroad. I was riding beside a neighbour who was a magistrate, as we went through the little crowd in Gurraghoo, a certain Major Wainwright, whom we all regarded as "rather English," either because of his slightly uncompromising character or because he was a Cromwellian.

"We'll get those men one day," said he, "and have them all committed for trial. Of course you'll have to identify them."

"Of course," I said.

And as he was speaking to me we passed a tall dark man in a long black coat, to whom the magistrate's words must have been clearly audible. He was looking at me, and I stared back at him.

"Did you ever see me before, sir?" he shouted.

"I did not," I answered.

"Because I thought you were looking at me as though you did," said the tall man.

"No, I have never seen you before," I said.

What else could I have said? Had I said to the magistrate: "That is like one of the four men that came for my father," he would, if convicted, have been sentenced to a term of penal servitude: in a few weeks he would have been let out, and long before that I should have been dead; and my father no better off for anything that had happened.

I reined back my horse till the men in pink coats were all past me, and I was among roughly-dressed men on beautiful horses, but ill-kempt, long-haired and wild; and soon I was level with the tall man in the black coat, who was walking slowly the way that we were going.

"I got that goose," I said.

"By God," said he, "Master Char-les, that was great!"

CHAPTER XII

As a thread of the warp in the weaving of cloth runs through all the threads of the woof, helping to bind them together, so runs the fox in Ireland through all our lives; so that any man who is utterly unconcerned with the fox lives a little apart from the rest of us. Who such a man could be I do not know; for, to begin with, no one owning poultry or turkeys can be quite immune from the fear of the footfall of that red visitor, inaudible on the stillest nights, however closely you listen for it. And that is, I suppose, the original sin on account of which we hunt him, and it must have been to deal with those prowlings, too subtle for his own wits, that man first sought the help of his friend the dog in this matter. And, having sought it, this organisation in defence of his poultry spread ramifications round the very heart of man. There are towns to be found in which the name of a fox stirs no more quickening of pulses than does the mention of guinea-pigs; but not in Ireland. For in the little Irish towns no man is so far into the dry waste of streets that the sounds of the hunt, from say in the South, cannot reach him, but that some other pack on the northern side, passing the town's edge, will bring him running out to see the red coats go by, and to feed his memory with the things that the pavement can never give. And so we give you the toast from our Irish shores: The Fox (death to him!), may he live for ever. And nearly two hundred of us concerned in this matter were jogging now in the direction of Clonrue, with the hills at first on our left as we rode along at the feet of them, and then almost behind us when we had turned to our right. And who was not concerned in it? First of all we had the whole of "the gentry" for twelve miles round, and as many of their daughters as a horse could be found for; then we had from a rather smaller area as many of the farmers as had a horse that could carry them; soldiers, squireens, a few strangers, grooms,

second horsemen, and men with young horses of which they
had hopes that they had not named to anyone; but who, as a
young girl sometimes looks to Heaven, far and yet not unat-
tainable, looked to the Grand National.

There were no priests at the meet, because they are forbidden to hunt, though not forbidden to ride; and of course
if they meet with hounds while they are riding, it is no sin to
go the same way with them. All the priests in that part of the
county were out riding that morning along the road under the
hills from Gurraghoo to Clonrue.

It was a long jog to Clonrue, over five miles: that is the
beauty of Irish coverts, there are usually so few that when a
fox leaves one he has a very long way to go to the next one: and
there was a wood of wild osiers beyond Clonrue near the bog,
an almost certain draw. All the way as we went that fervour
leaped up among all who saw us pass, a fervour for the quest
not limited to those that were taking part in it; men, women,
children and dogs were all awakened from other pursuits to
let their thoughts soar up from their own fields and then to
sail with us over the grey-green plain, now shining in sunlight
far away from those hills. And if any say that our quest was
not worthy of this awakening, I can only say in argument that
perhaps whatever awakens us to any vivid intensities needs no
other test of its worth; but in evidence I can say this on oath,
that I have seen the emptiness of many things, like a white
damp wall of mist closing roads to the spirit utterly, but never
yet have I noticed it in a fox-hunt. Certainly on that day the
hope of seeing a fox killed in the open, even the less presump-
tuous hope of being there before the tumultuous gathering
at that furious feast was over, was as bright a splendour to me
as could be the hope of any statesman to see the ruin of his
enemy's land, with all its fortresses fallen. And so we moved
to Clonrue till the hills were grey behind us, and the voices
of dogs warning Gurraghoo that something strange was afoot
were faint cries adding a weirdness to the solitude of those
fields. And the dogs that guarded the houses of Clonrue took
up the cry. And, among those that waited to watch our coming

by, the first that I saw was Marlin. He was standing dark against one of the white walls, with a look in his eyes such as inspiration might have, as he gazed at the young girls riding there, and at young well-mounted men, and the young horses. And I saw then, once for all, that quiet age and calm and repentance, and at last Heaven, were none of these things for Marlin, but that, turning away from all of them, he would only look for such glories as youth can give, and would always yearn for that land whose history was the dreams of the young and that knew nought of salvation. For a moment I would have spoken one last word to save him, and was silent knowing there was nothing that I could say; and at that moment I saw a priest ride by, and I turned to him, for he could have done it, but still no words came to me; and the priest rode on, and from the look in his eyes as he went by I saw that Marlin was lost.

And further down the street we saw Mrs. Marlin, leaning upon a stick that was, rather, a crooked pole, with wisps of her dark hair hanging about the sides of her face; her eyes watched us intensely, and more than the watchful dogs she seemed to be guarding Clonrue. Or perhaps Clonrue was but her outpost, and she watched for the sake of the bog, or for the sake of that land that lay under the frown of the bog, where her cottage stood and through which the river ran, where the gnarled willows leaned, a stretch of earth that always seemed to me strangely enchanted. What desecration she feared for this land I do not know, but she eyed us intently and showed no sign of enmity.

"Shall we find in the sallies, Mrs. Marlin?" I shouted as I passed her.

"He's waiting for you," she said.

"Will he give us a good run?" I asked.

"To Clonnabrann," said she.

I have often thought of those words, and looking back on them after all these years, and with the experience that years must bring, it seems to me now that, as every cottager thereabouts knew, a strong dog-fox lived in those sallies; a southwest wind was blowing and, running down wind as they do,

Clonnabrann would be right ahead of him if he could get so
far. To say, therefore, that he would get as far as Clonnabrann
was no more than an estimate of his strength by one of those
on whose chickens he nightly dined.

There was a silence as the hounds went into the wood, a
silence that hung heavily for what seemed a long time; then
one hound whimpered; silence again, and then the whole
pack gave tongue. We were all lined up on the bog side of
the willows, to prevent the fox breaking on that side, for if
he went over the bog none but the hounds could follow him.
And there we waited for a sign from the Master that we could
let our impatient horses out. A mild man, as I have seen him
in a drawing-room, the Master; almost shy at a tea-table; but
on a horse the owner of a fiery tongue that held his field in
awe, as his whip-lash held his hounds. Only for a few seconds
he held us back; I remember the waving line of horses' heads;
I remember a patch of gorse at the edge of the wood, whose
buds had already burst into two small blossoms; then we were
off. We used to have big fields out in those days, and for a hundred yards or so it was like a race; and then each rider began
to settle down to deal with his own difficulties, to cross each
fence in accordance with the capacity of his horse, and to take
a line in accordance with his estimate of many things, con-
stantly varying, or to follow different men for different reasons, of which these are three; because he is a masterly rider,
because he is close to his own home, or because he is going in
the opposite direction to what appears the right one. Before
following the third kind one should know something of the
man, but, if he is reasonably intelligent, he must have some
strong motive for turning away from the rest. I remember the
first few fences to this day; the first of all a narrow-bank five
feet high, built of earth as thin and steep as earth will stand,
and green with sods: it seemed impossible that it would not
trip up a horse galloping at it, as it would have tripped up me
if I had tried to clear it on foot. But I was forgetting the four
hooves. Other horses cleared it, mine was hard to hold, and I
let him go at it. He rose at it, touched the top, or near it, for

a moment paused, and was on again. So my first obstacle was left behind me. The next was a narrow stream, with sides steep as those of a ditch, clear water that had cut its way through the soft black earth. As I rode at it a man that I did not know called out: "Not there, Master Charles." And I followed him, trotting along the bank. "Boggy landing," he said.

Soon we came to a place at which the far bank sloped, and there he plunged in. It was deep water, and the bank on the far side seemed nearly liquid, but the horse struggled up, and I followed. We came next to a double, a great bank thrown up from two ditches, and twelve feet high, with small trees growing along the top of it. It looked an impossible obstacle, but others had been before me through the stream and were now crossing the double in several places, cantering slowly at it and jumping as high as the horse could reach and doing the rest with a scramble, then pausing a moment and disappearing from sight. So I checked my horse and jumped where another had jumped before me, and he easily found a foothold in the soft turf for his hind-legs, while his fore-legs reached the top. With a heave we were there. Looked down on, the far ditch seemed wider than the near, wider indeed than could be jumped from a standstill, but you can't go back from the top of a double, so I left it all to my horse. He approached it as cats approach a garden from the top of the garden wall; he went down and down the steep bank till I thought he would slip to the bottom, and just as this seemed certain he sprang, and we easily reached the field on the far side. For a moment from the top I had seen the hounds, going over a field together, and somehow reminding me of the shadows of clouds drifting over the flashing grass on a windy day. The next fence we came to was an easy one, and the last we saw of its kind, for we were leaving the country of white loose stones from which they built it, a stone wall. We went fast at it and my horse hit it hard, but it made no difference, for the stones flew with a rattle, and we were in the same field with the hounds.

From patches of bracken and gorse, and pale grey stones sometimes as large as sheep, we looked to a wide plain stretch-

ing for miles in the sunlight, with large green fields and having
a tended air. It was as though that loose stone wall that I had
crossed were a boundary between the last of the things of the
wild, lying behind us, and Earth subdued by man, lying before.
Bog and the rough lands were behind us now, and the turf
good for going: the pace increased. Shall I breathe air again
that is like that air that I breathed as I galloped down to the
bright vale gathering sunlight? What vintage in what golden
and jewelled cup will ever equal it? It came in gusts as we galloped, so that we breathed it like giants quaffing wine, and
whenever one lifted one's eyes from the fields and the fences,
the rim of the plain far off shone gold as a god-like cup. Shall
I ever breathe it again? And the priest in this foreign town tells
me not to think of these things any longer; the time being
come for thinking more of my soul. But he is not an Irishman,
and has only ridden a mule.

CHAPTER XIII

The time came for holding back my horse a bit. Hitherto I had
left the pace, and most things, to him, as knowing more about
the business than I did; but as I saw that wide valley opening
to the horizon, and not a wood in sight, and hounds pouring
away down the valley, it came to me that we were in for a long
hunt. The horse was pulling still, but I held him back now,
and there was the place for doing it; for, riding down a long
slope with that wonderful vista before one, there was such a
clear view of hounds, or at any rate of the hunt, that by riding
straight where they turned a little one easily made up the
ground that one lost while resting one's horse. And I did then
too what I have done ever since; if there was a gap or an open
gate I rode for it, rather than tire my horse by the display of
jumping a fence. There were plenty of fences ahead of us, and,
if I could get over all the fences I had to jump, I should have
jumping enough. I think I had learned already, from noticing

the effect on my horse's festive spirits, that jumping one fence tires a horse more than galloping across two fields.

It is strange that during this hunt I thought of the Marlins, but the green and tidy country to which we were coming was so unlike the wild willows about their cottage, and then the bog and those watery levels shining on its horizon, and beyond that the wonderful country whither wandered the dreams of Marlin, that the very contrast made me think of them. The thought came to me that they would look fantastic among these tidier fields, and then it occurred to me that I was leaving the country I knew and riding among landmarks that I had never seen before. And still the fox ran straight with the south-west wind behind him. Sometimes we had news of him. A countryman shouted: "A fine big dog fox."

"How long is he gone?" called out the Master, galloping by.

"A fine great dog fox, glory be to God," replied the countryman.

"How long is he gone?" shouted the Master again.

But an excited man cannot easily hear what is shouted among galloping horses.

"Big as a lion," shouted the countryman.

And the hunt swept on.

And then we came to wilder country again, where brown lands, marshy and rushy, intruded amongst the green. For a while we saw no houses or roads, or even hedges, and our only obstacles were wide bog-drains. A small neat cottage appeared, thatched and white-walled, with a tiny garden beside it. We went by within a few yards of it, and a man and a woman came out and an astonished dog. Perhaps they would have seen three or four men or women pass that way in a week, and suddenly there were two hundred galloping by. For a while that lonely spot was populous, then it would be silent again. What did they make of us? Only the thoughts of their dog could one be sure of. And his sole thought was defence, his duty to that white cottage.

Then the green fields again, of the grazing country; hedges and trees once more. I had no idea where I was. We saw a

river shining, large enough to have a name that one must have
known. But what it was I knew not. I was now a long way
from home. My horse was going well, but dropping back towards the tail of the hunt, for I would not push him. Sweat
was white on the horses wherever straps touched them. And
then came our first check. It was very welcome to me. I came
up to the field in which hounds were nosing thoughtfully, and
dismounted at once. Almost immediately we were on again,
but my horse was probably fresher for those moments of quiet
breathing, and I had all that distance in hand from the head to
the tail of the hunt, towards which I could drop back slowly, as
my horse tired. For I realised now, if I had not done so before,
that only by taking the utmost care of my horse should I see
the end of this hunt that had come so far already and that gave
rise to wonderful hopes that it might be one of those events
that, though seldom told of in books, are topics of conversation in counties for years, and rare gold in old memories.

There were no longer clusters in gateways, with steam
welling up from the horses into one column; we went through
singly now. One met with riders turning away from the hunt
on horses that could do no more, horses with no more foam
on their necks, but looking as if they had just been bathed all
over in mud and water, which several of them had. One had
to be careful whom one followed now, for fear he was turning
home. These must have been riders heavier than I was, which
is likely enough at my age; it can hardly have been that they
had not recognised as soon as I had, with all my inexperience,
that this was going to be a long hunt, unless the words that
I had with the witch could really have taught me anything.
The short evening was beginning to wear away. There was
no more rest for my horse in the gaps in high hedges, where
one had earlier to take one's turn among twenty or thirty: one
crossed alone now, or followed one other. But one was closer
to hounds without these delays, and able to go easier. And still
my horse pounded on, treading good turf in which the hoof-
marks of those in front of me were cut clear and dry. The late
light hovering at the close of day seemed to over-arch a calm

through which we galloped, as dreams might glide through the still of a summer's night; and I remembered a heathen religion of Northern lands that told of endlessly riding through everlasting twilight. From this thought I turned away, but it came back more than once.

What the time was I did not know, but it must have been after four, and that meant we must have been galloping over two hours. The meet had been at eleven, but we had not moved off till after the half-hour; then we had spent some time going up to the gorse-covert and drawing it blank, and it was nearly a quarter to one by the time we returned to the village. From Gurraghoo to the covert beyond Clonrue had taken us over an hour, and the fox had left about two o'clock. The fences at first had seemed things to watch and pick carefully, when horses were fit and fresh; yet now, when the time must be coming near when one's horse would fall at one of them and lie still, breathing heavily, now they seemed no more than those strange old furrows lying wide and green, the relic of ancient ploughing, that one sometimes meets in a field. And as every fence was past that same joy rose like a flame, the same exultation at an obstacle passed and the chance of being up at the end of the hunt brought nearer. Still the hounds ran with the south-west wind behind them. A little more and the fading light would add so much to our difficulties that any fence would beat us. And suddenly above the bare green fields, and clear of hedges and trees, I saw a small town shining on a hill, in light that was flung up there from the last of the sunset. A row of houses below, then two streets running up the sides of the hill; all the town white; and, set among those two streets and the houses below, like an emerald the hill's summit. I did not know that, except in old pictures of Italy, towns were built like this upon hills. Certainly I never thought of seeing one, but believed that they belonged to poetry or romance, or to times long past or countries far away. Hounds were going straight for the hill; if I went round it, in the fading light I should lose them, but a hill at the end of that eighteen or twenty miles was more than my horse could do. Heaven and earth seemed against us,

light fading and the land sloping. It was time to pull out and
turn home; and I should not see the end of that wonderful
hunt. And suddenly in my dejection a strange thought struck
me, so that I reined back to a slow canter and soon lost sight
of hounds, but I watched instead the white walls of the houses
that were gleaming along the hill. I took two more fences,
open ditches, and just got across. And suddenly as I gazed at
the little town I saw the fox himself going up the slope to the
houses. Then the hounds. He seemed making straight for the
streets: what shelter he looked for there I could not imagine.
And then the hounds got him.

The Master and two whips were there when I came up, and
eight or nine others. The dead fox had already been taken from
the hounds by the Master, and his head and brush removed,
but I was in time to see the rest of him thrown back to them,
and to hear their voices change to that deep roar to the tune
of which a fox is torn in pieces and eaten. Then one by one a
hound with a bit of a leg or a rib walked away from the rest
to eat his morsel alone; and the whips with their ruddy faces
looked on with a deep contentment, faces that nearly matched
the skirts of their coats, which the sweat of horses and the
water of ditches were gradually turning to the colour of
fuchsias. Now window after window up on the hill shone a
deep gold. It was the hour of the steaming kettle, of warmth
and the gathering of families; but doors opened and children
came running out down the hill, and soon they were gazing
at all these strangers, by now twenty or thirty of us, who had
come from they knew not where, tired and triumphant, and
had brought a new way of life to their very doors.

I have had like other men my ups and downs; Fate has given
me much and taken much away; but that day Fate gave me the
brush. From the hand of the Master I had it, the brush of the
finest fox that was known in all that country for many a year. I
have it still, what is left of it, in the very room in which I write,
and many an argument I have with Monsieur Alphonse, who
says that to keep this tail of a fox, now in such poor repair,
shows that I am no serious politician. Nor am I, but I argue

with him for the sake of my memories, and because I have
never known him really serious himself, and because I would
burn every political paper of both of us if in the smoke of that
burning I could see by any necromancy some vision of the
hunt that we rode that day across twenty miles of some of the
finest pasture of the old Ireland I knew. There it hangs on the
wall, and I turn from it once again to the scene that still shines
in my memory; the whips collecting the hounds together again,
men climbing up again on to tired horses, the children gazing
silently, the town above us now glowing with lights, and I turning round and asking its name as we rode slow down the hill.
"Clonnabrann," sang the children.

CHAPTER XIV

All the colour went out of the earth and into the sky. Fields
grew dull, trees very black, and grey mists slipped abroad
like ghosts going out to a gathering. We spoke little, riding
home; there was little that words could do. Someone spoke
of another great hunt that there had been, but it was long ago
and in another country. Then talk died down again. The sky in
the west was green, with bright layers of scarlet and gold. I was
staring into it for nearly a mile as we rode, and when I dropped
my gaze to the hedges I realised that down there night was
already among us. A horse struck a spark with his hoof, and the
illumination from that single spark showed that day was indeed
gone. Then red coats went black. White patches on hounds
bobbing down the road were visible, but all other objects only
added a darkness to night. And then a spark again flashed out
from a horse-shoe, a golden glow among dark shapes, shining
but for a moment, yet lighting vistas in my memory still. And
here's a theme for the follower of almost any art, a spark in the
night. Its huge appearance, its beauty, the mystery of shapes
gathered round it, and of the darkness beyond; its brevity;
and, all things being material for art, its eternity, lingering in

memories and having its obscure effects through them upon later years, and handing these effects down the generations, at which point perhaps the philosopher takes it over. The scientist too has a little to say about it, trying to destroy the mystery upon which the artist works, but no more able to do so than the artist is able to say the last word about it. We must just leave it glowing. But tired and happy men followed no such speculations. They saw the glow, it added its beauty to the deep content of their mood, and they rode on thinking, if not too tired to think, of poached eggs at their journey's end.

I was a neighbour of all these people, as well as the son of a member of the Hunt committee, yet hitherto I had been among them something such as is called up in my mind by the words one reads now and then in the foreign news, a minister without portfolio; who is probably in reality a hearty and well-contented person, though always pictured by me as a man lacking something. But to-day with that brush in my pocket, and for so long as it lasted; longer than that, as long as that day's memory lasted; I had my portfolio. Henceforth I was one of them; and that year, young as I was, I was made a member of the Hunt.

Another memory that I have of that long ride is the glow of port by lantern-light. One man had suddenly urged his horse into some sort of a brisk trot and gone on ahead of us: his house was on our road, only a few yards back from the very roadside, and when we came up, there he was outside his hall door with a lantern; and soon he was giving us port in claret glasses, and the port glowed near the lantern. Queer things one's memory carries far into another century.

And a few miles further on I parted from them all with affectionate farewells as they took the road to Gurraghoo and I the road home, the magistrate with whom I had talked at the meet, and the Master himself, both offering to ride with me to our gates. "You don't think you'll meet any of those four blackguards in the dark?" said one of them. "Better let us see you home."

But I wouldn't take them out of their way on their tired

horses. "They couldn't know where I am," I said, "after a hunt like this." Which they agreed was true enough, and we said goodnight.

The last few miles I walked beside my horse. But I had not gone far from where I said goodbye to the rest, nor yet dismounted, when my horse shied suddenly, and I saw a figure step from the dark of the hedge. First the stranger spoke to my horse, seeming to soothe it instantly, and I recognised the voice of the man with whom I had talked in Gurraghoo; and then he spoke to me.

"Are you all right, Master Char-les?" he asked.

"I am that," I said.

"What kept you so late?" he said. "I've been here three hours."

"We had a great hunt," I told him.

"Glory be to God," he remarked.

Then I told him how we had gone to Clonnabrann from the covert beyond Clonrue. It was too dark to see his face, but I knew that he was looking up at me wondering.

"And you saw the end of it, Master Char-les?" said he.

"I did," I answered.

And he gave thanks to God again, and said: "All the gentry will know you now, Master Char-les; and you'll not be feeling so lonely without your father."

And I trotted on.

When I got to our lodge on the Clonrue road, with my tired horse dragging behind me as we walked, a sleepy lodge-keeper who, but for me, would have been by now in bed, opened the gates and let us through and then locked them up for the night. I too was sleepy and our talk was brief. I remember the little fires glowing dimly in the demesne, burning heaps of branches that the snow had broken and that now had been tidied up and were being burned, but looking more like fires that gnomes had lit for warming small brown hands secretly while man was out of the way. Then I had a long talk with Ryan, but what either of us said I do not remember. I remember the glow of the hall when I came to the house, a brightness hurting the eyes. And I was not very hungry, as I would have expected to be. And that is about all I remember of that evening.

I woke quite early next morning. I woke with the pleasant sense of treasure in the room that a buccaneer might have felt, when overnight he had come by a good share of the treasure of Spain, or some merchant or pirate who by any means has newly come by a little sack of pearls, only needing to be strung. So, only needing to be tidied up by a taxidermist, lay raw and fresh on my pillow the brush whose mouldering remains hanging here beside me to-day cause Monsieur Alphonse to say that no Englishmen are serious; and I point out to him that I am not an Englishman, but a representative of the Irish Free State; and Monsieur Alphonse apologises in that whimsical way he has, which is really no apology at all, but is completely disarming.

I soon went round to the stables, and there I saw Ryan, in with the horse, running a hand down one of the fore-legs from knee to fetlock.

"Good morning, Ryan," I called out.

"He'll hunt no more for a long time," said Ryan. "He has a big leg on him."

I hardly believed it, and in my disappointment I retorted to Ryan: "I thought you said he had wings."

"And so he might have," said Ryan; "but he could have lost all the feathers out of them between here and Clonnabrann."

And in the end I had to accept Ryan's judgment; both the fore-legs were hot, and he would not be fit for a long time.

I had set out to write down memories of an Ireland fast passing away, so that something might remain of it, if only on shelves where books sleep and are seldom disturbed, and dust gathers softly as the days and the years go by; of hunts that led a field of over two hundred, with a hundred men in red coats, where now there are twenty or thirty out at the most, and five red coats to be seen; and of the life of an Irish gentleman on his estate. Briefly I meant in my idle moments, which are very many here, to do the little that a wandering pen may do to check the flight to oblivion of pleasures and occupations that Ireland knew once so abundantly. What oblivion can never claim, what outlasts histories, is consequently irrelevant to my purpose. Yet, only yesterday there occurred an episode, trifling enough to the casual onlooker, which turned my memories far aside from the work I had planned for them, to contemplate once again the very first of those unchanging and time-defying things. I had been writing down my memories in the morning, and they set me thinking so much of Ireland again that either this or an impulse that I can never explain urged me, almost compelled me, to go down to the station to see the Overland Express come in at 12.25. On this train, that contains mostly travellers from other countries coming to drink the waters at the well-known springs in this State, I thought that I might see an Irish face once more. I went on to the platform without paying the usual schlwig, almost the equivalent of our penny, which is one of my diplomatic privileges, and saw the train come in. A commissaire was going along the first-class carriages with forms that had to be filled in, merely the full names of the traveller and of his parents, the correct address of the house in which he was born, his exact age, the number of his teeth (this purely for identification), his religion and occupation, the number of his motor-car and the name of his usual laundress. The whole thing took no more than a minute. I noticed that all the German first-class passengers enjoyed doing this, and that all the English ones submitted to it. The third-class passengers have to register at a bureau. Then I saw the commissaire go up to a lady whom I could not clearly see in the dark of the railway-carriage, but I saw from a certain air that he wore that there was some kind of charm about her that brightened the commissaire's eye and even seemed to illumine a little his rather absurd uniform. He began to ask his questions, he began on behalf of the country he served to attempt to reduce the lady to a formula, as it was his duty to do. Fifty passengers had been so reduced already; none had complained and many of them had enjoyed it. But Irish people do not like forms and formulæ. And this was an Irish lady. She was thinking of her luggage, and he of the mathematical formula by which it was his duty to sum up all human souls on that train in possession of a first-class ticket. At first I did not hear what they said. He was on the platform and she inside the carriage. When she came into the doorway I saw an elderly lady, but one with an air and a grace well able to account for that bright look that had come in the eye of the commissaire; a look that she had not missed. He had already asked her, I suppose, eight or nine questions, and as she stood there he politely asked her her age. Then she turned on him. He was looking up at her still with that rather foolish expression that was his tribute to those feminine graces about her.

"Seventy," she rapped out. "And ripe for the grave."

So falls the hail on the apple-blossom.

The bright, foolish look fell from his face, but his politeness did not desert him.

"Ah, no, madame," he said.

"Should I come here to drink your foul waters if I weren't?" she said.

And they have a foul taste, though very medicinal.

And in the end he never got his form filled in, but filled it in himself from imagination; and did it so well that when he brought it later to me, who could have filled it in to the tiniest detail, I left it just as it was.

But the moment she spoke I knew her. I went forward then, and at first she didn't remember me; so I told her my name, and she gave me the old smile, that all those years never altered; and it was that smile that has interfered with my memories, turning them from a chronicle of things that are passing away, to what will not pass away while any life remains to watch stars or dawn on this planet.

I too was shocked to hear her say she was seventy, for I had remembered her seventeen. She was about a year older than I. I have lived to see that being seventeen is no protection against becoming seventy, but to know this needs the experience of a life-time, for no imagination copes with it. Try it yourself, reader. Look at any young girl, lithe, athletic, full of strength and dreams, and try as you look at her to picture her seventy. The picture before you blurs the imagination's picture. You

cannot see the two. And another thing you cannot do: you
cannot hold your forefingers before you horizontally, nearly
touching, and then revolve one of them one way and one the
other. We are always more concerned with one thing at a time
than our intellect chooses to recognise.

And so it was that once she was seventeen.

I did not tell you that she was in the hunt to Clonnabrann. I
had not meant to write of her at all, but Fate thrust her among
my memories yesterday morning, and they will not leave her
now. I see her still so clearly, I who saw her yesterday; I see her
standing on the grass by the side of the avenue at Cloghnacurrer, as I rode up on our carriage-horse; medium height, a
very slender figure, a face not thin but rather as though it had
been chiselled first to an exquisite profile, long ago in Greece
by a sculptor, and afterwards copied in Heaven from the cold
marble and given there the colour and warmth of humanity;
a darkish dress, no hat, the wind in her hair, and above everything her grey eyes. That slender figure that more than fifty
years cannot efface from my memory, is surely undimmed by
a day; and the figure that I saw yesterday in the train, perhaps a
little burlier than the dapper form of the commissaire, cannot
oust from its place a single one of those visions that I have
brought from the past, and that I cherish more than a child
cherishes bright shells and pebbles that it has taken home from
the seaside, and for whose sake I principally live. And the eyes
are the same as ever. Well then, a letter came about noon the
day after the hunt, brought by the postman from Gurraghoo,
and sent there on a horse, a letter from Mrs. Lanley, and that
was Laura's mother; and Laura Lanley was the lady who
years later refused, I am afraid rather unreasonably, to tell the
commissaire the number of her teeth, the name of her laundress or the address of the house in which she was born. And
the letter invited me to come over to tea at Cloghnacurrer that
day, and asked if I would mind bringing over to show them, the
brush of the Clonrue fox. So might the Queen of Sheba have
asked Solomon if he would mind showing her his treasure of
gold and ivory, and though that wise mind would have known

that it was said to please him, still it would have done so. So I took the relic and rode over, five or six miles on the carriage-horse, past Gurraghoo to Cloghnacurrer; and that is where I saw her, not for the first time, but it is the time when she seemed to walk into my memories for ever. I saw her standing by the avenue as I rode up to the house, and I dismounted and showed her the brush, and she looked at it with just the same expression with which she saw it again yesterday, when she came to have a cup of tea with me; and Monsieur Alphonse, who had escorted her to my rooms, saw her thus, standing in silence. And Monsieur Alphonse said: "I see, then, that it is a holy relic."

"No, no!" I exclaimed.

But, before I had time to stop him, he crossed himself. I tried to explain, but all he said was: "Pardon me, my friend, if I have said you are not serious, because of this. I see, now, that it is your religion."

"No, no," I said, and finding that I was making no headway with him I turned to Laura, knowing that she could do it, and said to her: "Please explain to Monsieur the Attaché."

And Laura said: "Yes. It is our religion."

I was in despair then. "What will you think of us?" I cried to Monsieur Alphonse.

"My friend," he said, "I respect all men's religions. I have no exalted post. To the contrary. But I should not be even where I am if I had not shown that respect always."

And he turned to the old brush and crossed himself again.

"That's right," was all that Laura said to him.

I am once more fifty-two years ahead of my story, but the events of yesterday have disturbed the quiet routine by which I was jotting down memories every day as a man writes a diary. Well then, I showed that brush to Laura Lanley fifty-two years ago, and she gazed at it in the same stillness that made Monsieur the Attaché act so strangely only yesterday. And how easily she might have had that brush for herself; so easily that I think that only by some look of hers at the Master, that I had not seen, or perhaps merely by turning away from him, the vacancy can have been left open to me. I could not give it to her, for such things cannot be given by ordinary men, but must come direct from the hand of a Master of Fox Hounds. She gazed at it and we walked to the house talking of that great day, that was then so near to us, and the memories of which were shared among so many. How many remember it now?

CHAPTER XV

We must have had tea early; for I remember going out with Laura afterwards, and the sunset still lingered. I have the impression of a warm evening while we walked on gravel paths through the shrubs of the garden. I think that walking slowly in those latitudes, after sunset in January, would kill me now; so the warmth that seemed to come from the glow in the western sky cannot really have been sufficient to warm us without those hopes and emotions that come no more. Their splendours, it must have been, that kept us warm. What we talked of I do not remember. But I remember there came a time, as we walked in that evening, when I wished to tell her of strange lands, and of things and people seen that she did not know; but I had never travelled, and knew the land round about us less than she did, and there seemed no such places of which I could tell her anything and my boyish whim seemed frustrated. And suddenly I thought of Marlin and the way over the bog to the pools that glimmered in sunlight, and thence, as he had so often told me, the bog, narrowed and all hemmed in and yet wandering free to the ocean; and a little way over the water, the land to which the dreams of so few had gone. Of this I could tell her. And so I began to speak of Tir-nan-Og, the land of the young. As she heard me her eyes darkened, and I saw that no land to which I could have travelled, had I been able to follow wherever youth's spirit led, would ever have excited that interest that was awakened in her by the mention of Tir-nan-Og, which from its place outside geo-

graphy exerts through the twilight that curious lure to which
Marlin had wholly surrendered. It is strange indeed that talking of Tir-nan-Og seemed to strengthen its frontiers; and, sentence by sentence, as though they were the steps of a traveller
walking westwards through twilight, Tir-nan-Og came nearer.
Over the shrubs and through the branches of evergreens, now
blackening with the approach of night that seemed to come
first to them, we both glanced westwards to where the day was
sinking: on what shores, we wondered.

At first I had asked her if she believed that the bog went
all the way to the sea, as Marlin said; and she fully corrobo-
rated him. So much for geography. And then I spoke a little
of Irish legends, like a traveller of strange lands fearing his
wonders will not be believed; and she told me other legends
of this land of ours. Mere incredulity unarmed, without its
weapons of ridicule, would have swept Tir-nan-Og out of my
thoughts for ever, and better perhaps if it had, even regarding
only my interests in this world; but the tales she told from old
writings upon the outskirts of history, and I from the talk of
Marlin, so bore each other out that a new land seemed gradually lifting into sight of our wonder, with streams and gardens
clear enough at any rate for our hopes; and how much in life
is no more certain than that? It was easy just then to believe
in such a land, if I did believe in it, for I was walking in the
twilight in Ireland, side by side with youth in its triumph and
in its power. What miracles might not be achieved by such a
radiance? As for immortality in unfading gardens of the West,
that was little more to imagine than the belief which we both
held firmly, that this radiant youth of ours would be with us
always, and that the longings our hearts had then would never
pass away. Time was then a grey spectre that other people had
seen, like the phantom told in a ghost story before a pleasant
fire, but not a power whose lightest finger had touched us, or
of whom we had any fear.

And then I told her of Marlin, and Marlin became for us the
pioneer of this strange new world we had found for ourselves,
a kind of gate-keeper at the border of fairyland. He was so

clearly a citizen of Tir-nan-Og, and yet he lived here on the
solid land that is mapped; and the thought of him linked the
two lands, as that sunlit stretch of water out by the bog's horizon seemed to link them whenever I saw it. I told her, too,
something of Marlin's mother, and of the witchcraft of her,
and of how she had foretold me of Clonnabrann; so that
always after that, whenever we spoke together, there seemed
to be something of magic tingeing our talk, a background of
wonder behind Laura and me that others had not got, or so it
appeared to me, as though we stood together before curtains
of rare fabric veiling a witch's chamber, or draping windows
that looked from some sheer tower far over enchanted lands.
Then as the light went out of the sky and colour grew more
triumphant, and mystery as though on tiptoe stole into the
sleeping air, we spoke again of the West and the Land of the
Young. And if Tir-nan-Og have its foundations more firmly
based upon the dreams of a few people, growing, I fear, fewer,
than upon whatever land there may be in the Atlantic a little
out from our coasts, then how much of its twilight may not be
lit by the love of Laura and me, which soon rose up and glowed
as we talked of Tir-nan-Og? It shone upon all my youth and lit
many years for me: may not some rays of it have ripened the
apple-blossom on those immortal branches?

These thoughts that I set down to-day I have shown to
Father Svlonenski, who lives at the back of the cathedral here,
not far from my house, to ask if they touch the safety of my
soul; and he says that there is no danger, but that at the time of
which I write my soul was indeed in peril.

CHAPTER XVI

After that walk in the garden I went home with a good sensible
horse to take care of me. Had I walked there to-day—Ah, no,
it is as I have said; the cold would probably kill me; but were I
young to-day, and were Laura young in that garden, I should,

I suppose, have driven away in a motor, and I should not have been fit to drive it. Or would it have scattered my dreams, in the way that machines do, and left me changing gears without harming the clutches, and forgetful of Tir-nan-Og? But I think my old horse understood, and he brought me home with my head full of soaring thoughts, and of visions of happiness in this earth, visions whose borders lapped like a rising tide on the shores of the Land of the Young.

The moon was about full and my hunter lame, so that it was time to go to the red bog; and next morning Ryan drove me again to Clonrue. And as we went we talked history, the history of men like me and men like Ryan; not about Kings of France and their favourites, Corn Laws or conquests, but about the fox and the line he took, and of those who followed. Now and then a law comes, and in the course of decades affects the countryside, increasing the narrow-banks round smaller hold-ings, or filling the hedges with wire, and the close observer may note its effect on gardens and thatches, and, in the case of some great law, even the habits of the people for a little while may be touched by it; but the following of the fox is our history, and all the lesser grades of sport; a tapestry of figures with horses, greyhounds and guns on the eternal background of agriculture.

And I noticed that Ryan had forgiven me for laming the horse, and I saw from this that I must have gone well in the hunt; not that Ryan ever expressed any annoyance with me, or retracted it, nor did I hear a word of what was said of that hunt to Ryan, nor know who said it. Now that so many in Ireland can read, and newspapers are in nearly every cottage, news prob-ably travels a little slower and far less accurately; but in those days men spoke vividly of what they had seen themselves, to those who were keenly interested in it, and a good tale not only outlasted a daily paper, but went right down the generations.

I think, though I do not know, that some enquiries were being made that day in Clonrue about the identity of the man who had waited three hours by the side of the road to see that I was all right after the great hunt. Whether this were so or not

I could not say, for I closely followed my father's advice in his letter, and kept out of politics; but some enquiry must have been afoot, for there was not a man to be seen in the street; the doors of the houses were shut, and any men in sight were working hard in the fields. It is inconvenient never to refer to the man in the long black coat by his name, which by now I knew; but for reasons which I will mention later it would be injudicious, and even tactless, to do so. We passed by Clonrue, its white walls gleaming in silence, and came to the bohereen running down among willows, till it seemed to catch sight of the bog and suddenly stop in terror. Certainly there was a strange, an enchanted, look about that land on which the Marlins lived that might well have awed such an orderly thing as a road, or its little relative a bohereen. It is not that I think that Mrs. Marlin could have enchanted it; rather I think that living there all her life on that wild willowy land beneath the frown of the bog, that in this flat country seemed to rise up almost like a mountain, the queer haunt had given her whatever powers she had. Certainly one would expect some difference in the ways and abilities of the citizens of some town, living amongst their kind, and entirely surrounded by the works of man, from the ways of one who for companionship had chiefly the voices of curlews ringing through miles of emptiness, and whose news of the seasons must have been brought by the varying notes of birds; at whom the moon must have peered through the willows, more of a neighbour than he can ever be to the cities, and to whom the white mist rising up from the marshes at night must have seemed a friendly spirit. Were it otherwise, surroundings would be without their influence upon us, which means that Mother Earth would have no say in the bringing up of her children.

I believe that my father had had some intention once of putting an iron fence across that land, from the bohereen down to the bog, which with the help of the stream would have enclosed a rushy space that two bullocks might have grazed, but the men that came to dig the holes for the fence had seen such fury smouldering in the eyes of Mrs. Marlin that in the end nothing had come of it and the land was left as it was. That land and the stream that ran through it were things so primeval and sacred to her that to alter them at all must have seemed to her the bewildering sacrilege that altering the tides by an hour or so, if we could do it, or rearranging a constellation, would seem to most of us.

Marlin I found, as I so often found him, gazing out over the bog to the distance, where wide pieces of water near the horizon seemed always gathering sunlight.

"Ah, Master Char-les," he said when he saw me, "I was waiting for you. It's the full of the moon, and the snipe will be all on the red bog."

"Will the geese come, Marlin?" I asked.

"God knows that," he replied. "It's over three weeks since they were shot at. Begob they might."

Then he took one look at the wind, which he did by turning his face to it till he could hear the sound of it equally in each of his ears, and we set off at once across a part of the bog, walking straight into the wind, towards the low line of hills that bounded the heather in the direction of Gurraghoo.

"How did you get on in the hunt?" he asked.

"Well enough," I said.

And snipe got up at the sound of our voices.

"Don't fire at them," said Marlin. "There's no man living could hit them walking up wind."

It was his old way of worshipping the golden idol of Tact before the goddess Truth, if they got in each other's way. And I took his good advice, and we spoke again of the hunt, and I told him how his mother had foretold to me the end of that famous run.

"Ah, she would know that," was all that he said.

"How can she tell?" I asked.

"Begob, she knows," said Marlin.

And I could pry no further.

To our right lay the bare horizon, and sometimes as we walked I saw Marlin glancing thither, and knew that his thoughts were away by the paths of morass and mosses with the bog's long wandering to the shore, and the land that lay a little way over the water. But in this world, to which his thoughts came instantly back, his only care was to give me a good day's sport. Once more I tried to dissuade him from his heresy, but my words fell lame and unpersuasive, since Tir-nan-Og had been the topic of conversation between Laura and me: more than that it had been; almost Tir-nan-Og had been the land to which our spirits had roved and in whose orchards they met; sometimes, to this day, if I dream I am young, it is there that my dreams go, and to this day Laura is there with them. And, if by day I think sometimes of holy things Heaven will not grudge me these straying and frivolous dreams, which come seldom now, and which I fear, Hereafter, may never come any more.

When we came to the dry land under the low hills we turned and set out to walk across the bog, with the open horizon now on our left, and the path to Tir-nan-Og, as I had come to think of it. I took the speck of a white cottage on the other line of hills as my guide and walked t'wards it all the morning. The wind, which was now behind us, came rather from over my left shoulder, so Marlin walked on my right, and most of the snipe he put up flew across me. I did not shoot well; but among all the excuses there are for missing a snipe I had this time a fairly valid reason. I was stiff after that great hunt, as I always am after the first hunt of the year, unless I have been riding about a good deal; and in shooting snipe there is one thing you have to do before you aim at the twisting bird, and that is to get your own balance. Every step on the bog is chosen; were it left to chance, the chance would be about even on each step finding a safe landing, or taking one down into the quiet slime that Marlin used to say was bottomless. The snipe seldom gets up exactly as both feet are firmly planted, so that sometimes one has to shoot from off one leg, even aiming while stepping forward, and firing before planting one's leading foot on the tussock; and, if one attends to this last matter first, the snipe is well away over flashing pools and dark heather before one has time to turn to him. The perfect balance that can leave the step to itself and concentrate upon aiming needs supple limbs, and in spite of youth all of my muscles that are the most important for balance were stiff and even aching. Even my arms, though this mattered less, and certainly my left one, were a little slower than usual; so that every snipe had a handicap in his favour of a fifth or a tenth of a second, which was all that most of them needed. On my side I had the consolations of Marlin, always forthcoming, always sufficiently varied; imaginative, and yet never crossing the line at which any inaccuracy would have been obvious. By one o'clock we were still out on the bog with the dry land far before us; I had shot a few snipe, and we chose a suitable one of the bog's million islands, on the heather of which to lunch. Once more I offered Marlin sandwiches, but the offer was received with the polite indifference with which a well-bred dog would refuse a handful of grass; not that dogs never eat grass, but they eat it rarely and prefer a bone; even so Marlin preferred whiskey. And sitting there with the bog all round me, and with that soft wind blowing, the thought suddenly came to me that in a few days I should be back at Eton, following up the intricacies of some Greek verb.

"I go back to Eton on Thursday," I said to Marlin.

"That's a fine school," said Marlin.

"It is," I said.

"Don't all the gentry send their sons there?" he said.

"Some of them," I replied.

"Sure, there's no school like it," he said.

"There is not," said I.

"But, sure, there's no use going back to it," he said.

"I'm afraid I've got to," I answered.

"But if you were too ill to go?" said Marlin.

"I'd have to be very ill," said I.

"Begob," said Marlin, "there's diseases that men know nothing about, that Dr. Rory over at Clonrue knows the same as an old woman would know the name of her cat."

"I'm afraid they're rather quick at finding out those sort of diseases," I said reflectively.

"Begob," said he, "not when they have Dr. Rory to deal with.

And the geese will be coming in of nights to the bog from now on, like chickens into a fowl-run."

Such temptations do not come to most boys, their parents see to that; and what aggravated the temptation was that Dr. Rory had been in the hunt to Clonnabrann, and I had the feeling he would do anything that I asked.

"No," I said, "I can't stay away from Eton just to shoot a goose." And I looked out over the bog, set in its pale emerald crescents of low hills which did not wholly encircle it, and away and away over brilliant islands of moss in lakes the size of hearth-rugs, and still away and away, till clouds were lifting from the shores of the lakes; and, as I looked, the loneliness of that strange land found a voice, and two notes floated down, as full of magic as any of all the sounds of the sky, and I saw for a moment against a mountain of cloud that musical rover the curlew. "And besides," I added, "I couldn't be sure of finding Dr. Rory in time."

"He's in Clonrue this minute," said Marlin.

Honestly, had Marlin not said that, I should have let the difficulty of finding Dr. Rory defeat the temptation. But Marlin's words drifted me further. Had a good education attracted me more than the cry of the curlew, I should perhaps have some better occupation now; and yet I am very comfortable here in large well-furnished rooms; and wishing that anything in the past had been otherwise is idler than wishing for the moon, to which man may one day attain, but to the past never.

So I got up there and then and set off with Marlin over the bog, back to his mother's house, only tarrying to make my bag of snipe up to half a dozen in order to send them to Mrs. Lanley.

We climbed by the steep soft precipice with which the bog ended and frowned down on that land in which only the Marlins lived, and we came to their white walls gleaming below the dark of the thatch. Marlin brought me in, and when his mother saw me I perhaps brought back to her mind a mood in which she was when last I had been there, for she stood up from her chair and raised her right hand high, and began to speak of the great cities of Ireland that were further down the stream that ran by the cottage. "The world will know them," she said, "when Ireland's free. Our people will look down from their balconies on the navies of distant lands. The great ships of Africa will come into our harbours, and the treasures of Zanzibar. With silks of the furthest East and jewels from the Indies they will come to deck Ireland like a queen, and pearls will drop from their treasuries as they come, and run down the steps of our harbours into the water. All seas will know our ships, and the fame of our land will be in far men's mouths."

And she looked into the fire, or the smoke going up from it, for something she wished to see, and was silent a long while. Then she turned to me from the smoke. "Oh, Master Char-les, Master Char-les," she cried, "forget all I've said."

CHAPTER XVII

I walked over the land between the bog and the bohereen, where the willows leaned their cleft and aged trunks, looking as though they were enchanted by witches, or as though they were the very growth, and in the very place, that passed on the power of witchcraft to human beings from the ancient secrets of Earth. I walked up the bohereen and on to Clonrue, for I had told Ryan to come for me late, and it was not yet four. I found him at the centre of Clonrue, the public-house, in the stables where he had put up the horse and trap.

"I've come to see the doctor, Ryan," I said.

"Are ye not well, sir?" said Ryan.

"I have to go back to Eton on Thursday," I said.

"Begob," said Ryan, "you'd not be well enough for that."

"Do you know is he in?" I asked him.

And, as whatever information Clonrue possessed had passed through that room in which I found Ryan, he was able to tell me all I needed to know.

"He came in half an hour ago," said Ryan, "and will be there for another hour."

So I went over to see Dr. Rory, and found him in, as Ryan had said.

"That was a great hunt," he said as I was shown in by the parlourmaid.

"It was," I said.

"Are you well?" said he.

"That's what I wanted to ask you about," I said.

"What's the matter?" he asked.

"I have to go back to Eton on Thursday," I said.

"That's a serious matter," said he, "and with hounds hunting the way they have been lately, a good hunt nearly every day, though none of them up to the Clonrue hunt."

"Could anything be done about it?" I asked.

"You've come to the right man," said he.

I hardly knew what to say next.

And he said: "Have you anything of a cold? There's a lot of that about, and very dangerous things when neglected."

"I have not," I said.

"Well, did you get a fall in the hunt? There's lots of men think that doesn't matter, but there's no part of you that can hit the ground that may not suffer some damage or other."

"No, I didn't get a fall," I said.

Dr. Rory looked grave at that, and waited as though to see if I really meant it. Then he reached for a stethoscope.

"I'd better pound you," he said.

And this he did, and very uncomfortable such things were in those days; short ear-trumpets whose narrower ends were dug into one's ribs; and Dr. Rory's face grew graver and graver.

"Nothing wrong there," he said.

"I'm afraid I shall have to go back," I replied.

"Wait," he said, rather impatiently, like a thinker interrupted by some frivolity.

"I wouldn't take a certificate that wasn't true," I said, my conscience waking from sleep, though much too late.

"Nor you wouldn't get one from me that wasn't true," he answered.

"I'm afraid I'm quite fit really," I said.

"Wait," he said again, and added: "No man can be sure of that." And after a few moments' reflection he asked: "Have you been vaccinated lately?"

"No," I said.

"Then you'd better be," said Dr. Rory.

"Why?" I asked.

"Because McCluskey," he said, "is a tenant of your father's, and you might be going to see him. But it's my duty to advise you not to go, because if you did, you couldn't go back to Eton."

"Why not?" I asked.

"Because he has small-pox," he said. "It would be enough if you went in at his door. Only if you neglect my advice not to go, you'd better be vaccinated a day or two before you went in, so as to give whatever devilry there is in the lymph a bit of a start of the devilry that there is in the small-pox."

"Could you vaccinate me now?" I asked.

"I could that," he said.

So I was duly vaccinated.

"It'd be a good thing to wear gloves," said Dr. Rory, "they keep off all kinds of infection, especially the contagious kind, like small-pox."

"I will," I said; and he saw me off.

"Well, it's time you were vaccinated in any case," he said on his doorstep. "You'll be seventeen in a short while."

Next day I drove back to Lisronagh, to try for some snipe again, before they went from the red bog, and to see if the geese were yet coming in, as Marlin had said. As I walked from the bohereen I saw Mrs. Marlin a little way from her cottage gazing over those strange lands upon which she lived, with what looked like an anxious air, almost as though she watched against something that threatened them, an impression I only had for a moment, knowing of nothing that could ever affect those sparse deserted fields. When she saw me she turned her gaze at once from the future, or whatever it was that she watched with that anxious look, saying: "I'll call Tommy for you." And she turned and called her son with a high shriek that

must have carried as far as the voice of the curlew; and presently Marlin appeared, coming across the bog, and dropped
over the steep edge of the raw turf and walked towards me.

"There's a lot of the bog we didn't cover last time," I said.

"Begob," said Marlin, "you wouldn't cover it in a week."

So we set off, and, getting the wind right, we walked t'wards
the same green hills that had been before us on the previous
day.

I got more snipe this time, and all the while with every shot,
whether I missed or hit, I was learning, though imperceptibly,
how to shoot snipe.

But it was not so much to shoot snipe that I had come to-day
as to meet again that mighty traveller the grey lag; and, as we
sat having lunch on a tussock of heather, I on sandwiches as
usual and Marlin on whiskey, I asked him of the prospects of
seeing the geese that night.

"Begob, they might come," he said.

"What does your mother think?" I asked.

"Ah, begob, *she* doesn't know," said Marlin.

"I thought she did," I said.

"Sure, she does on days when she knows," said Marlin. "But
to-day she knows nothing."

What kind of power was it, I wondered, but did not ask,
that Mrs. Marlin had? And if she knew nothing that day, what
was troubling her as I saw her standing beside the stream that
morning? For something was. Looking backward I know no
more than I knew then, but I think that some shadow cast
from the future must have darkened on her and those fields.

As evening began to come down on the bog, scruples that
I had felt about not returning to Eton faded with the bright
sunlight, for an enchantment came with the gloaming over all
those miles of heather, an enchantment that no picture of any
bog can show you, nor any words of mine; and at the time
I knew of no parallel to that dim calm, haunted with fading
colours of earth and sky, but sometimes now I think that I find
a parallel to it when I hear the Ninth Symphony of Beethoven;
for somewhere near the beginning of the fourth movement

there is a quiet glory and a calm not of this world, that always reminds me, though so far in time and in place, of evening blessing those miles of heather and moss and water. And the curlews began to drop in with their wandering voices, bringing news down gleaming reaches of the sky, of the happening of events that concern curlews, news of which I could interpret nothing; their clear cries thrilled through the evening, giving me again and again some message that I almost understood, till I began to think and I lost it. In huge grandeur the sun set, and an awe went over the waste and reached me from the horizon, and a chill seemed to grip the air, and I felt there were bodings of things of which I should never know anything. Did Mrs. Marlin know? If she knew nothing of that hush that comes sometimes at sunset, that unseen finger lifted to still the world, if she drew no hint from the meaning with which it seemed overflowing, and understood no word of the shriek of the curlews, she was then an ordinary woman; but, if she knew any of these things, she had a book open before her from which she might have learned at least as much as anything that I suspected. Watching those sunsets sometimes and hearing the curlews I have often wondered only at my ignorance, and no whit at her knowledge, so much did that light and those voices seem to be telling, if only some sense just beyond our five were not sleeping.

In that great stillness through the glow of the evening we walked to the Marlins' cottage, whose walls seemed gathering in bright remnants of fading light, while the smoke from the chimney soared straight into quiet air. I saw her staring straight at the crimson layers over the sunset, in a sky pale blue or green, and we entered the cottage without her turning her head. When she came in later I felt she was going to prophesy, and in the end she said never a word, so that I drank my tea in silence, and soon set out with Marlin back to the bog, to the place at which we were going to wait for the geese.

"I think the doctor will give me a certificate," I said as we went.

"Sure, of course he will," said Marlin.

To Marlin the giving of such a certificate to a man who needed one was no different from giving him a tonic; but it is not for me to point out Marlin's simplicity: my own conscience is not entirely clear about the business, even after all these years. At any rate I did not explain to him that such a point of view was wrong: I was more truant than prig.

The air, cool on my face after the heat of the great fire in the small room, blew out of the gathering darkness, full of those promises that such lands seem always to offer to those that leave walls and roofs at about this hour, for hills and skies and horizons. I went straight for the old place where I had shot the goose before, but Marlin said at once: "Not there, Master Char-les. They've been shot at from there."

"Mightn't others come?" I asked.

"They'd go to their own place," said Marlin. "And the ones you fired at will have shifted."

So we went further into the bog. And Marlin found a place for me, and there I waited, with no thought but for the coming of the geese, while Earth darkened and the sky became like the jewel of a magician in which some apprentice to magic gazes deeply, but comprehends nothing. And while I waited the hush of the evening seemed to deepen, until quite suddenly into that luminous stillness there stepped the rim of the moon, stepped flashing like the footstep of a princess of faery coming into our world from her own, shod in glittering silver. And, as it rose, it slowly became golden, a vast orb holding me breathless, no pallid wanderer of the wide sky now, but huge on the edge of Earth like an idol of gold on its altar. I gazed at that magical radiance, forgetting the geese. And just as the lower edge of the great disc left the horizon I turned to Marlin to say something of what I felt, but said no more than: "It is a fine moonrise, Marlin."

But I had no need to say more: Marlin's eyes were fixed on that silent glory, staring straight into the face of the moon. For some moments he did not speak, hushed as all things else seemed to be by this wonderful visitor. And then he shook his head and said: "It's not for us, Master Char-les."

"Why, Marlin?" I asked.

"Maybe for you for a little while," he said thoughtfully.
"Yes, maybe for you, Master Char-les. For a year or two, then
no more. But we're all ageing here. It's only for youth, and
for those that are young for ever. It's to brighten the apple-
blossoms in the Land of the Young, and to shine on the faces
of kings and queens of the Irish, who have cast old age away,
with the lumber of time, on the rocks and roads of the world.
It's to glow in their eyes and to gleam in their hair, Master
Char-les."

And young though I was, and full of the wonder of the
moon, I felt that there was in the miles of gold on the water,
and in the enormous gaze of the moon itself, something, as
Marlin said, that was not for us.

"It comes up huge," he continued, "on the hills of Tir-nan-
Og, rising up in the West as it sets here, and larger than the
shield of the oldest giant, and brighter than we have seen it
and full of music. And they hear its music in the Land of the
Young."

And somehow I felt there was music in the moon, all those
years ago when I was not yet seventeen. And I said to Marlin:
"Does it make music?"

And Marlin stared towards it in the hushed evening; then
shook his head again, and said: "Not for us."

I got no geese that night. They came before the moon was
much higher, and passed near, and I heard their voices; but,
though the sky seemed brimming with light, things only a little
way off were swallowed up in the darkness. I heard them come
down on the bog, where night lay black and heavy; I heard
their wings beating the air as they stopped their flight, and for
a while the sound of their voices, then silence. I thought that
I could stalk them in the dark, and told Marlin so in a whisper.
He told me I could not do it, but I had to learn for myself. And
a difficult time I had getting through the bog in the night, till
the geese began to cackle, and very soon after that they were
gone.

The moon helped us out of the bog, and in half an hour we

were back at the cottage, where Marlin's mother was standing outside, a dark shape against the glowing wall, gazing silently at the moon. When Marlin came up to her he turned and followed her gaze, and they both together stared at the moon in silence, while I stood near them, not speaking. And at last Marlin spoke. "It's glorious upon the apple-blossom," he said, "in the orchards of Tir-nan-Og."

"It's for Ireland it shines," said his mother. "No other lands have such light from it. Not even Tir-nan-Og. And when Ireland's free we will build cities with golden spires that will flash back a light at which the moon will wonder."

"Not all the gold of the cities," said Marlin, "nor the gold that is still in the earth, can equal the glow of the blossoms of Tir-nan-Og when the orchards answer the moonlight. It's for the Land of the Young that it's shining."

"It's for Ireland," shouted his mother.

I had never seen them quarrel before, and did not know what to say. And now Marlin was gazing far over the bog and no longer listening to her.

"It's for Ireland," she repeated. "Look at the golden water. Look at the hills under the moon. And listen to that!"

For a white owl went by hooting.

"Aye, he knows," she said. "He knows."

And the owl gave one more cry, far off, and went out of hearing.

And she turned sharply to Marlin: "Do you still say," she asked, "that any land but ours has such light from the moon?"

But he was gazing, gazing away, and never heard her.

"Good night, Marlin," I said.

But he did not speak.

"Good night, Mrs. Marlin," I said then.

But she was still shouting at Marlin: "It's for Ireland. Ireland, I say."

And so I left them.

CHAPTER XVIII

I drove home in the huge quiet moonlight, wondering as we went at things that I wonder at still. I find it hard to tell what they are, for I am not a poet nor painter nor musician, but only an idle man jotting down memories, in which there is poetry, because they are memories of youth, but not through skill of mine; and the things that I would preserve upon this paper if I could are things that painters, musicians and poets handle, especially I think musicians, because words always seem to elude these things. But, briefly, I wondered if all that dome of sky, just washed, as it seemed to have been, with liquid gold, and the moon and its mountains, and the dark hills of Earth, and all the awe and the mystery that seemed floating between the two, were the real and vital things, as every emotion seemed to be telling me, or whether truth walked only in paths that the reason could follow. Well, I never worked it out and I cannot now. I'll write down facts instead; there is never any difficulty with them. When we got to the lodge I saw two men standing outside with rifles slung over their shoulders; I saw what it was before they spoke: I had been given police protection. And it has always struck me that one of the readiest ways of estimating a country's regard for law is to notice what arms the officers of the law are carrying: in England it is little batons, in France swords, in many countries revolvers, and in Russia the police used to have artillery.

"We've come to protect you, sir," said one of them.

"So I see, sergeant," I said. "But what if they come by the other lodge?"

"We've two more men there, sir," he said.

"And what if they get over the wall?" I asked him.

"We have a man in the house," he said. "And we patrol the desmesne every few hours."

"Good night," I said. And we drove on to the house.

This was evidently Major Wainwright's doing, and I did not like the idea of police protection at all. I felt that it would be ineffective; but, what was much worse than that, it made me a marked man, quite possibly tempting people to have a shot at me who would not have thought of it otherwise.

The presence of the police was a topic that Ryan avoided and I was left with my own thoughts. And what I thought was that, trouble now having been thrust towards me, I might come to need the protection that my father had had, and that had saved his life; and that I must find the way of the secret door for myself, for my father would never put it in a letter to be read by perhaps the very men that had sent the four to High Gaut.

I heard again from the butler about the police. Two were to sleep in the lodge by which I had come, two more would somehow find room to lie down in a smaller lodge, by a gate that we seldom used, and one had a bed in the house. I dined as soon as possible, then went to the library, and for the rest of the evening I occupied myself with the frame of the mirror, examining each square inch with the methodical care by which I felt sure that any secret, or any formula even, of mathematics or science, must in the end be discovered. Previously I had looked at likely places, edges of ornaments that gave a ready hold to the fingers, nobs that the thumb might press, loose bits of aged carving, and even cracks in which a knife might perhaps be used as a key; I had sought for perhaps three-quarters of an hour, till the irksomeness of the work had defeated my curiosity. But now a stronger motive than curiosity urged me, and I went over every piece of the frame with the same care with which the man who gilded it must have gone so many years ago. I only omitted such parts of it as my father could not have reached swiftly and easily, for he had gone as quickly and quietly as a man walking through mist. It was as though he had walked through the wall. And those words were really the key to the secret, for it was by walking that it was done, not by drawing of bolts or the handling of hidden locks; but it was many hours before that phrase chanced to enter my

mind, and a long time after that before it was any guidance to
me. But at last I tried walking straight to the mirror, as I had
heard my father walk into silence. I did it for no other purpose
than to see what part of the mirror, walking thus, was brought
most readily to my hand, for all that night I was looking for
something to handle. And I kept at it, for I thought that I
would indeed want that secret, and soon. And dawn came, as
I could see through chinks in the shutters, and I was still at it.
I drew the curtains and put out the lamps, and when the dawn
grew stronger I saw a picture before me that seemed slightly
different from the one I had studied all night. I thought I had
tried everything; now different tiny features about the carving
showed themselves, and I tried them all again. And then in the
brighter light, as I walked again and again towards the mirror,
to see what would come easily and naturally to my hand as
I walked, I began to notice a few inches of the design of the
carpet that was different from the rest. It was pointed like the
point of one's shoe, and I began to step on it. I think the secret
was well enough hidden: I had been eight and a half hours at
it, doing nothing else all the time, when the mirror dropped
before me in absolute silence, but for the tiny splash of two
drops of oil. It worked neatly, but very simply; all you had to
do was to walk straight towards it as though you were going
through, and you did go through. The left foot, two paces
away from the secret door, had to rest exactly on the mark in
the carpet, after that the length of one's next two paces tended
to be regulated by the distance remaining between the marked
step and the mirror; and, if you made those two paces right,
the third alighted on a piece of iron, shaped like the sole of a
boot and painted white, about a foot below the level of the
room on the far side of the mirror. Stepping on this white mark
closed the door. I saw then how my father must have walked
silently away in the very few seconds before the men came into
the library.

I stepped through on to the white and obvious mark,
the mirror lifted behind me, and I was in a dark passage of
stone. I could feel large grey stones in the walls, that is to

say I could feel they were limestone, but I had no matches. Wherever the passage led I now had a hiding-place, and no doubt an easy way out at the end, if I always kept matches on me; for there would be no object in having the exit secret; but without matches it was a slow walk in the dark, for I knew that there must somewhere be steps, the library being on the first floor and my father having got out-of-doors from it. I had to slide each foot along the stone floor, and at last I came to the steps, some spiral ones that took me to ground level and ended against a wall. But on the wall there was a handle easily found at about the same height as the handle on any door and, when I had pulled hard enough at it, it slid to the right, and a narrow part of the wall swung a little outwards, leaving just enough aperture for me to go through. Outside the first thing I did was to close the stone door, then looking about me I found myself standing under an ivy-covered wall that I knew well enough, and noticed now that the main trunk of the ivy had been twisted long ago away from the crack at the top of the door, and that tendrils that would have crossed the door so as to hinder its opening had been neatly cut, as though by a pocket-knife, not all in a straight line. The leaves leaned across the crack, though the tendrils did not, and standing a yard away there was no sign of a door. Cracks that I could see when I looked close seemed once to have been smeared over with mortar, which must have flaked away when my father left, and I resolved to put a touch of mortar where needed before the ivy was clipped again by the gardener. It was bleak and early morning now, and there seemed no way whatever of opening the door of stone from the outside. I felt all the colder for having had a night without sleep, and was wondering how to get in, when I caught sight of a column of smoke above one of the chimneys. So I went round to the back. Even then I found it difficult to make sufficient noise to attract the attention of Mary in the kitchen without alarming the policeman, who was there for the purpose of anticipating such efforts as mine to get in, and to act against them quickly. And a great deal of noise I had to make before Mary came; but in the end

I got in without waking the policeman. To Mary I said: "I've been taking a look round the house to see that there are none of those men about;" keeping altogether away from the means by which I got out of the house; and, however much Mary wondered, she could have come no nearer to that. I went to bed then and slept till late. And after breakfast I went to have a talk with the constable.

"I don't want protection," I said to him. "There's no need for it."

"There is indeed, sir," he said to me. "We are after those four men that came for Mr. Peridore. We know who they are. And they've all left their houses."

"Don't they live over the hills a long way from here?" I said.

"They do, sir," he answered. "Four or five miles beyond Gurraghoo."

"Then why would they come here?" I asked.

"They know we're after them," he replied. "And there's no one to identify them but yourself if they're caught. Wouldn't it be the simplest thing they could do to shoot you, sir? If you'll pardon my saying so."

"It might save them trouble," I said.

"Begob it would," said he. "It would be the right thing for them to do. I only mean from a legal point of view, sir. But you'd have to consider the evidence that you'd be against them in court. Sure, any man would do it. However, we'll not let them."

And I could not after that shake off the feeling that the constable was probably right. Once a man had considered proceedings in a court of law he must see that I was the principal obstacle to the defence; and they were likely to consider such proceedings with the police after them. I hung about the library a good deal during the morning, and practised steps that were exactly the right length to bring my second step from the mark in the carpet just to the edge of the wainscot. The three steps evidently worked like the three keys that are sometimes used to unlock a safe; for pressing upon any one, or on any two of the points, had no effect whatever. It seemed to me that during the day the five constables might be able to watch the place, but after dark I did not see how they could do it. And thinking about it made me only more uneasy. I tried to cheer myself by the thought that, if he had wanted to kill me, the man whom I afterwards met in Gurraghoo would not have told me anything that might be useful in my own defence, as that one should allow a foot when aiming at a man walking across at a hundred yards. But the thought soon followed that he did not at that time know that he was in any danger, and secondly that these men usually shoot at the back of the neck from a yard away, and are not so easily found walking about at a hundred yards. Nor was he the leader. But there soon came other thoughts to divert me, and the first of these was that I could take over my bag of snipe to Mrs. Lanley myself. It was also the day on which I must call on McCluskey, if I was to have that certificate that would excuse me from returning to Eton. Obviously Cloghnacurrer should come first. I told the constable, Geogehan, about this, and he said that he would see me to the lodge, and that the two men there would have to go with me in the trap.

So after lunch I set off with Ryan in the trap, Geogehan, with his rifle, walking half way to the lodge, and at the lodge the sergeant and the other man got up behind.

I brought Mrs. Lanley my snipe. I had sent her six only the day before, but I explained that they were small and might not be enough, and I had eight of them this time. I had no idea that Mrs. Lanley would not be amply satisfied that this was my sole motive for coming. I had not long alone with Laura, but we had a short walk to her rock garden, which at that time of year of course contained mostly rocks, and which I thought lovely. And we made some wild plan to walk some day over the bog to that point on the low horizon to which I used so often to see Marlin gazing, and then on till we came to the sea, where we were to look over the water at sunset to see if there were any glow in the sky from what might be apple-blossom beyond the horizon. It was not far for the dreams of youth to go, nor further than they might easily have taken us; though in the end we never went to look for the reflection of apple-blossom in the sky above the Atlantic.

After our short talk of Tir-nan-Og we parted, and I drove to McCluskey's house, who lived near High Gaut. His wife, who I believe had had small-pox years ago, was nursing him, and she shouted to me to keep away, but I went up and put my gloved hand to the half-door and opened it, and put my foot over the threshold and called out some word of greeting to McCluskey and came away. Then I drove home and wrote to the doctor, enclosing a note from the sergeant saying that he had seen me go in, which seemed to me to implicate the majesty of the law itself.

It was getting late now, and I kept a good deal to the library, the door of which I left open so that I could hear the sound of any feet on the stairs. I wrote to my father to tell him that I had found the secret of the other library door, in case he should be troubled at not being able to tell me, or should be arranging some difficult plan to get the news through secretly. The way I put it was: *I have been reading some of the travel books in the library, in case I should ever have to travel myself. I have opened three and closed a fourth already*. It was rather clumsy, but the very clumsiness of it would show him that I was trying to tell him something, and he would know what; but those who opened the letter on its way could never find out from it anything.

I had dinner and went back again to the library, still leaving the door on to the landing open. I sat late, reading before the fire, kept lingering there by an uneasiness since my talk with Geogehan, which made me reluctant to leave the only room in which I felt sure I was safe. The time came when I decided that I should go to bed, and still I put it off a little longer. A hush fell on the house, as though time itself were sleepy; and in the hush I heard a policeman's whistle. It was quite close, just outside; and I knew that Geogehan had seen the men he was waiting for, and that the sergeant and the three other men from the lodges would be here in a few minutes. In the still house at that hour, as I heard Geogehan's whistle, I was glad for the first time that I had been given police protection.

I waited, and sooner than I expected I heard on the stairs the heavy feet of one man and three more marching behind him. Geogehan had remained outside, every now and then blowing his whistle, I could still hear his feet on the gravel. "Geogehan's outside," I shouted, through the open door to the stairs, for it was Geogehan, not I, that had summoned the sergeant and his three men. "Outside in front," I added. And then the four men walked in who had come for my father.

I sat there saying nothing. And then the leader spoke. "It's the way it is, sir," he said, "that we want your help."

And then my friend, whose name I cannot give you, the man who told me how to shoot geese, said: "They hunted us out of our homes, Master Char-les; and we only just got away in time; and we came here. We've been about the haggard for the last two days and sleeping in the hay, but we never came into the house."

"Sure, we didn't wish to trouble your honour," said another.

"What did you do about food?" I asked.

"Sure, isn't Mary Ryan the blessed angel from Heaven?" said the man who had spoken last.

So that explained the food. Mary Ryan was our housemaid.

"And Mrs. Burke?" I said. She was our cook.

"Aye, the blessed old soul," he replied. "God will be good to her."

"Can you hide us, sir?" said the leader.

"I can," I said.

"The police saw us, sir," said my friend. "The place is full of them."

"Will you swear never to hurt my father?" I asked.

"We will indeed, sir," said the leader.

I looked at each one.

"Aye, sure we will," they said.

I turned round and walked away from them.

"For God's sake don't do that, sir," said the leader.

He saw where I was going. Last time they came they had sworn me by the piece of the true Cross. This time I was going to swear them. And the rest of them stood there silent; and not a sound in the night but Geogehan blowing his whistle again outside. I got to the golden casket and took out the cross. The leader, silent and uncertain, put his hand to his pocket. I don't know whether or not he meant to threaten me, but I threatened him first, for I spun round and lifted the cross. One by one they knelt and swore, but the leader would not. "God knows we're bad men," he said, "but there's worse behind us, and we have to obey our orders. We might never be told any more to hurt your father, or again we might. For God's sake, sir, don't swear us, the way we mightn't be able to obey orders."

"Do you want the curse of God on you?" I said, lifting the cross over his head.

And the cross won. I don't know if it would nowadays. But this was over fifty years ago; and the cross won. He went down on his knees and swore by the relic never to hurt my father. And he kept his oath. He disappeared soon after, and years later he was found by some turf-cutters buried at the side of the bog. He kept to his oath.

As soon as I had sworn the four men, I put the cross away, and told them about the passage, and the handle on the stone door at the other end. They could choose their own time about slipping out, whenever they heard the sound of the policemen all in the house.

"The blessing of God on you, Master Char-les," said the one that I knew best. And the others began to repeat similar thanks and blessings when I heard the sound of doors banging. It was the R.I.C.

"Wait there," I said, and walked to the mirror.

I lifted my hand to the frame as I went, so as not to let them into the secret of how the door opened, even though they knew of the door. But I must have started making my paces an inch too long, for the door did not open. And now I heard that booming noise such as might come from a drum of stone, which I knew for men's boots on paved passages. I think that the second of my two paces in front of the mirror went wrong, for I trod full on the mark in the carpet and my final step looked just right. Whatever it was I turned back and made some remark to the four men and then strode to the mirror again. The hollow sounds downstairs were coming our way. This time, just as my hand reached the frame, the three footsteps having fallen exactly rightly, the mirror slid down.

"Quick," I said. "Don't step on the white bit of iron. The last man step on it: it closes the door. There, shaped like a shoe."

They saw and began to go. I had to show them that secret. The only one that mattered was the three steps in the library.

"We'd stop and fight them, sir," said the leader, "but for their rifles. Rifles aren't fair."

It was always a grievance in Ireland that the R.I.C. carried rifles.

"Good-bye, sir," he said.

And then I heard steps on the stairs.

"Quick," I said again, and ran to the door.

I got outside the library just before the police came in. The sergeant was leading. He was actually on a mat that there was outside the door. There was only one way to stop him; I shook hands with him.

He was surprised, and looked at me strangely.

"I thought I heard steps up there," I said, pointing up the stairs.

"We heard a noise in there, sir," said he pointing into the library.

"In there?" I said. "There's no one there."

And when I saw I could delay him no longer, and he was about to go in, I said: "But you'd better search it."

I led the way in, going slowly the short way I had to go. And the room was empty.

"Now that all five of you are here," I said to the sergeant. I forget how I finished the sentence, but that much I said loudly at the end of the room near the mirror; and, if the four men in the stone passage did not know what to do then they were ill-fitted for Irish politics.

Of course I should have handed them all over to the police. Well, reader, you wouldn't have had this story. The Government had done more for me than for most men; they had given

me five armed men to protect me: they could hardly have been
expected to do more. And the five weren't enough. If I had
given up those four men, others would have got me within the
week, as others got my father.

CHAPTER XIX

That night I slept as tired men sleep, for I had been up all the
night before, and as men with good consciences are supposed
to sleep; for I knew that none of those four would hurt my
father now, but I did not look far enough. The days went by;
and one day, about ten days after they came, the five constables
were withdrawn. Somebody had asked a question in Parliament
as to whether this district was quiet; a minister had answered
that it was, and the questioner had contradicted him; and to
prove his point the minister had withdrawn police protection
from the one or two of us that had it in that county. My actual
case had the distinction of being mentioned in Parliament,
when it was explained that protection had been given to me
on account of my story of four men entering the house at
night and asking for my father; but that I had been unable to
name or even describe any one of the four men when questioned later, and no such men had been seen by anyone else
in that district. And the incident closed with these words that I
still remember: "'We must suppose that the gentleman calling
himself the Duke of Dover went to Paris for other reasons'
(loud laughter)."

The certificate that kept me in idleness apparently lasted for
twelve days, but about this time, with only a day or two more
to spare, I met the doctor riding by our gate as I was crossing
the road to shoot snipe. "What day have I to go back?" I asked
him.

"I've another case for you," he answered cheerily.

And he told me of a man that had mumps, about a mile
beyond the McCluskeys.

"It's a fine long infection," he added.

And when I heard that it would take me right over the next full moon, the lure of the red bog, which I had feared I should walk no more that year, became too strong for a conscience already enfeebled by my visit to the house of McCluskey, and any protests it still was able to utter were swept away by the doctor's cheerful directions. And so my ill-earned holidays were lengthened; and I may mention here that, for all the skill of Dr. Rory, I paid the extreme penalty of Eton when I got back.

Till the moon was full I shot snipe on the black bogs, and when snipe grew scarce I used to sit for pigeons as they came in to roost in our woods. And so I grew to know the evening almost as a neighbour, as you can never do in houses, where walls keep out the glow of its gentle light, and the lights of man overcome it. And what I gained by knowing the evening thus is something I cannot capture with words.

One day a man walked three miles to tell me that golden plover flighted over a field he knew. It was no field of ours, and I did not know him by sight. Why did he come? Well, to begin with, time to him seemed boundless. I do not mean time in general, what may be called eternity, but his own particular share of time, his leisure. And I think that those who feel they have plenty of time often find their illusion justified. If this be so, it is curious that it does not always apply to things of less value, such as money. Well then, out of his great wealth of time it was nothing to him to spare the two hours it took to walk three miles and talk to me and go back again. And then he was a sportsman, as they all were, and he enjoyed giving me a shot at the golden plover, as he would have enjoyed letting his long dogs after a hare.

And so I went one day to the high wide fields, on whose air the golden plover circled and raced every evening. Murphy came with me, a little distrustful of information not brought by himself, and took his retriever, and Ryan drove us over. It was broad day when we arrived, though the sun had set. I left Murphy with Ryan, and took some rugs from the trap, and

lay down on them in an old furrow that had been green grass
for years: it was not nearly deep enough to hide me, but the
hollow lessened my conspicuousness in the field. A dimness
came upon earth, a glow in the sky, and the great calm of
evening came down on us. A goat came up to inspect me, and
after some while went away again. Sheep came by cropping the
grass and passed to a far part of the field. Still no birds came.
Then, black as bats in that light, the green plover appeared,
and went away across the lucid pale-blue of the sky. And at last
I heard those notes that a golden flute might play, in the hands
of an elf or anything small and magical, and the white shapes
of the golden plover flashed by on their pointed wings, going
out of sight at a hedge, rising and pouring over it like a wave
over rows of rocks. Soon they were back over another hedge,
dipping down from the top of it and flooding over the field,
curving round the same pillar of air by which they had gone
last time, as though it were some visible flag-post for their aërial
races. I rose and ran to the place with my rugs, and lay down
again in a hollow. The next time that they or others came into
sight they danced on the air in another part of the field, but
I realised that if I started chasing them over the field I might
spend all the evening at it and get nothing; so I stayed where I
was. And the next time they came past me I heard the whirr of
their wings before I saw them, and then I saw the brown mass
going by and I fired, and they turned from the shot and flashed
white as they turned. They turned and went wildly away; and,
choosing one of the scattered shapes, I fired again and missed.
I had two birds down to my first shot. I don't know if there
are any sportsmen that avoid firing into the brown of golden
plover, choosing their bird with each shot, as I used to try to
choose them and have even succeeded in doing; but pouring
by as they do low over the fields when flighting, it is almost
impossible to choose one's shot, so I used large and few pellets,
which, when fired close, were likely either to miss or kill. They
had come with the last of the light, which still so illumined the
grass that I had no thought of night coming; and so I stayed
where I was a little while longer before going to pick up the

birds. They were quite close and the grass was short, and I had not yet learned that a golden plover, lying on the face of a field with nothing to hide it, can be invisible. Yet that is certainly so, even in day-light. The golden spots on the birds must possess the same brightness as the light on sere grass, and their spots of dark umber are so like the darkness among the grass-blades, that even by day one may pass one lying face downwards and not see it two or three yards away. More came by a little higher and I got one with my right barrel, but so carefully had I to watch and distinguish the falling bird among the rest, that all poured downwards from my shot till they were within a few feet of the field, that by the time I had marked the one dead bird among the fifty swooping ones I got no good aim with my left barrel, and shot no more of them. Looking up soon after that I saw a star, and realised that it was time to look for the two birds I had shot. The notes of many more were clear in the air, and the whirr of their wings, but I could no longer see them. The ground was darker than the air, and I only found one of the birds, till I whistled for Murphy. He came with his dog, when eyes could do no more, and a soft black nose took on the work from man. So we eventually got the two golden plover.

In a few more days I went to those fields again, while a young moon shone in the evening. Longer and longer it hung in the evening sky, lighting my quest for pigeons or golden plover, until it came round to the opposite side from the sun and was nearly full again, and it was time to look for snipe once more on the red bog. That was the February moon. On a morning that looked too bright for February, and that brought the snow-drops flashing out in large clusters, I drove to Lisronagh again; and Marlin came to meet me at the end of the bohereen. "I knew you'd come, Master Char-les," he said, "with the moon at the full. It's a great day to be going after snipe."

"And I want you to drive some teal for me too, Marlin," I said, "from the pools out in the bog."

"And so I will," said Marlin.

And with high hopes I set off with Marlin down to the bog.

The sky was bright and clear and the wind full of a splendour, a strength that one felt in one's blood as one breathed it in. When I asked Marlin after his mother he said: "She is in the house, cursing."

And then I heard for the first time of the Peat Development (Ireland) Syndicate, and how a man had come only that morning and looked at the low lands lying under the bog and had taken some measurements. And when Mrs. Marlin had come running out to ask him what he was doing, he had spoken of huts and machinery and so much Progress, that it had seemed to her that all the blight that there was in civilisation, threatened those willowy lands. She must have felt as a townsman would feel if he learned that brambles and bracken were about to cover his pavements. As we passed the cottage she came out. And the first words that she called to me were: "What is it at all that they are going to do, Master Char-les?"

"I know nothing about it," said I. For Marlin had not yet told me even all he knew.

"They are going to put down machinery," she wailed, "and to take the turf from the bog, and to cut my willows down. What is it all about at all?"

"Are they going to work the machinery by using the stream?" I asked.

"Ah, that great river of Ireland," she cried. "They shall never touch it. It's not the will of the hills, nor the bog, nor the north wind. They shall not harm Ireland's river. The storm and the hills and the night will never allow it. There's no blessing on such a notion from sun or stars or heather. And sure your father would never allow it, Master Char-les?"

"Not on our side of the stream," I answered. For I felt sure that he would not have allowed any company to come and spoil the bog.

"There's a power," she said, "that is hid in the heart of the bog, that is against all their plans."

What she meant I did not know, and as I knew little at all of the scheme of these people from what I had heard as yet, I went on with Marlin to the bog. And, being full of the zest of sport on that bright morning, I asked no more of the mechanical scheme, in which I scarcely believed, and came to the steep bog's edge; and there we were with the heather all before us, and the wind, as the smoke from the Marlins' chimney showed, exactly right for a walk straight on to the low horizon. Thither we started, a look on Marlin's face bright perhaps with that gleaming morning, but, as I thought, brightened from being turned in that direction in which, beyond the horizon, he believed lay Tir-nan-Og. Perhaps my own face was as bright with the hopes of sport and with all that glittering air.

We had not gone fifty yards, when suddenly, out of the sky, we heard a sound like a kid bleating in the emptiness over our heads. Or it was like a harp-string that has been touched and left to vibrate in B flat. More like a kid than a harp-string perhaps, because it was like nothing human or aught from the hand of man. The sky thrilled with it; the bog seemed changed by it; and so it was, for that sound heralded another season. It was the whisper of Spring. The snipe were drumming.

There was another ten days to go of the shooting season, but I turned round at once.

"The snipe are drumming," I said to Marlin, "I'll stop."

"Well, begob," said Marlin a little reluctantly, "when you hear that sound it's spring sure enough."

"It is," I said; "and they're nesting."

"Begob," said he, "maybe they'll be grateful to you next year, and give you easy shots."

Another and another drummed as we spoke, and spring seemed coming across the sky with a rush. I have seen in Japanese temples the carvings of little gods with drums and harps and flutes, running and flitting through clouds, and have wondered if this same strange and wandering music that I heard heralding spring had woken in priest or poet on the other side of the earth that vision of demon musicians in air above Fusi-Yama.

And still they beat the air with their spread tail-feathers that made this haunting sound. Looking up I saw one soaring and dropping, and soaring and dropping again, beating this music out of the air as it dropped, as though the air were a harp-string; and with all the sky ringing with spring I said good-bye to the Marlins; and set off for Eton next day.

CHAPTER XX

I said good-bye to Murphy, Ryan, Young Finn and a few others, and had a final talk with Brophy. Brophy always spoke as though my father would never return, or even write again, a view that I never held, but I gave him instructions on all points that he asked me about, pending the return of my father, and then left him to run the place. I said no farewells to Laura on account of my infection, such as it was. I had less scruple about bringing the infection to Eton, as I was doing for I was returning some days before the full period had expired; and it was while explaining to my tutor that I was no longer infectious, that I became involved in questions that led me to the old oaken block on which expiation is made for error at Eton.

Days passed, during which I acquired such education as I have, and learned something of the world in which I have travelled since; but Homer gave to one's fancy a world in which it travelled there and then, for the Odyssey is a mighty fairyland, along whose shores seafarers rollicked, a long while since, and hugely enjoyed themselves while they were able to keep on the right side of the gods, but were overtaken by deadly adventures whenever they were unable to delude authority any longer and the gods caught them out; but at all times they were quite untainted by the dullness and complexity of Greek verbs, so that I almost wondered how these jovial and lawless people came to be permitted in schoolrooms. And while my fancy had that old world of floating islands and monsters to roam in, my feet had the fields along the left bank of the Thames, wherever the beagles led them; a flat land with heavy soil I should say, and deep wide ditches, and white mists always rising up at evening; that is as my memory sees it; but the mud and the mist and the ditches may have entangled my memory unduly, as obstacles once surpassed have a way of doing. Certainly grand old willow-trees used to stand there: I can see them still with their huge shapes dim in the evening, but quite unhidden by time. And then I have memories of tea, which somehow outshine memories of banquets that I have attended since. And banquets remind me of some passages from the works of Edgar Allan Poe, which seem to have been missed by those that sometimes abuse Eton. As I feel sure that these passages would give them pleasure, I quote one here, leaving those for whom I quote them the excitement of proving them true. It is from a story called *William Wilson*, and tells of life at Eton:

"After a week of soulless dissipation, I invited a small party of the most dissolute students to a secret carousal in my chambers. We met at a late hour of the night, for our debaucheries were to be faithfully protracted until morning. The wine flowed freely, and there were not wanting other and perhaps more dangerous seductions, so that the grey dawn had already faintly appeared in the east, while our delirious extravagance was at its height. Madly flushed with cards and intoxication, I was in the act of insisting upon a toast of more than wonted profanity when my attention was suddenly diverted by the violent, although partial, unclosing of the door of the apartment, and by the eager voice of a servant from without. He said that some person, apparently in great haste, demanded to speak with me in the hall."

There is more, but the earnest student should consult the original.

Often in those days I was asked of my strange holidays, to whose startling events an even additional interest seemed to be lent by my visit to the block. At first I answered all the questions they asked me, but soon I saw that the English boys could not understand. Why not write at once to Scotland Yard, they said: why not leave the whole matter in the hands of the police: why not let the law take its course? Only the Irish boys understood.

I gave up answering questions, gave up talking at all of Ireland to those who were so little able to understand. Later I think they understood better. For one day, walking down town to buy various things for tea, and thinking of Ireland, I saw Brophy just as I crossed Barnes bridge. For a moment he seemed a vision, so remote did my home appear to me. And then I saw the wind in his unmistakable beard, and the look on his face. And the appearance of Brophy there, and that look on his face, told me that my father was dead. He had been murdered in Paris.

For an awful moment I feared that I might have been guilty of this by letting the four men free. Then I remembered how they had sworn, and knew that their oath would bind them as the administrators of the law would never have done. Nevertheless I told my fears to Brophy; and, looking round from old habit to see that none overheard him, he said: "It was not those men." I do not think he would have told me, but that he saw how distressed I looked, for far more is known in Ireland than anyone speaks of. He told me that the people believed that one of those four men had been told to go to Paris himself, either alone or leading the other three, and that he had refused and had been shot; and that the rest of them were still in the country, as all the people seemed to know, though the police could not find them. The funeral was to be that day in Paris, or had already been. News had come slowly, because my father had been living quietly there, probably not under his own name, and his address was not known until the French police discovered it two or three days after the murder. I fear that the address he gave me for letters may perhaps have been the means whereby he was traced; he might have been followed when he went to get the letters; but one can never know. It was all the more of a shock to me because I had supposed that once my father had got abroad he was safe, but, with plenty of money at their disposal, it was no harder for the men that were after him to follow him to Paris than London.

Everyone at Eton seemed to understand better after this, even though the English boys said little, and the Irish boys hardly anything at all, the latter having come by the habit, even thus early, of avoiding talk in public about religion or politics, and so much in Ireland comes under these two headings. I was offered leave to go home, to look after things there, for a few days; but I would not take it, for there was nothing there that I could attend to better than Brophy, and I was a little ashamed of the leave that I had taken already, to see the end of the shooting.

But when the short Easter half was over I returned to Ireland, and stood once more on the platform of that railway station that the joy of arrivals and the sorrow of departures have stamped more vividly on my mind than many worthier objects, and the soft south-west wind met me, and the low hills seemed to beckon to me, and two or three outside-cars were waiting for my choice. A good deal of iron, a quantity of white-wash, and ferns hanging out from cracks in a wall wherever the whitewash had crumbled, how can it seem so beautiful to me? The station-master welcomed my arrival as though trains ran for that purpose, and a couple of porters, coming towards me full of leisure and greeting, gave the impression of having rested on that platform since I had left for Eton, waiting quietly for my return. I picked the best-looking horse, and my luggage was piled up in the middle of the outside-car, and some on the right-hand side, where the driver sat, while I sat on the left, and soon we were off down the road between two stone walls that had been gathered there from the fields to give the grass a good chance to grow, and to guide the road on its way and to prevent it from ever being lost in the bog. Sometimes a black-thorn leaned over a wall, all a mass of white blossom, like a lady of some enchanted people dwelling beyond the hills, who had strayed to take this look at human folk going by; clearly a blackthorn as you look at it, but what may it not have been a moment before?

Heather and ruined towers are the principal objects that meet the eye of the traveller by that road. And in summer travellers sometimes come that way. Then is the time to see it, with the heather all in bloom and sunlight on the old towers.

Yet even in sunlight they wear a mournful air, so vividly do they bear testimony that someone had tried to civilise that waste of bog and heather, and that the waste had won.

We drove to Gurraghoo. And a little beyond the village a boy of eight or nine slipped over a wall of loose stones and bits of peat and sticks and odd things growing, and stood in the road before us.

"I have a message for you, Master Char-les," he shouted.

"Who is it from?" I asked.

"They said you'd know," he answered.

"But what were their names?"

"I don't know."

"What were they like?"

"I don't know."

"What's the message?"

" 'It wasn't us,' " he said.

"Was there anything more?" said I.

"They just said: 'It wasn't us,' " the boy answered, and was gone over the wall. A few willows standing in a field that wild Nature seemed to have given up to cultivation lately and grudgingly, was all that there was to hide him once he went from the wall, but I saw him no more. I had given him no answer, nor even told him I understood him, or let the driver see that I did; but I understood.

CHAPTER XXI

A green mist came out upon thorn trees, a grey mist upon poplars, and clumps of willows seemed welling up in pale flame.

Two days passed, while through woods and fields, and over the hills and the marshes, went the procession of spring, to the music of wood-pigeons cooing. It came like something new out of strange lands, that had never come before. The thorn trees went brilliant green, and the leaves of the chestnut came like moths from the chrysalis, fresh and intensely bright and with wings not yet unfolded.

The mist of the buds on the poplar trees grew whiter, and the green of the thorn was now brilliant and deep. Elms were fountains of yellow, beeches pale Indian red, and the trunks of the trees had now a spectre-like look, standing pale amidst so much colour. A glow lingered long after sunset about the oaks and the beeches, a ruddy light in which, yet, there was nothing green. Among them here and there the larch stood in his splendour, perhaps the most brilliant emerald in all the crown of spring. And the cherry was like a cloud, if clouds are there, in heaven. A faintly greenish tinge began to appear on the white mist drifting from poplars. The buds of the rhododendrons began to burst; primroses were at their full, and the daffodils dying.

And then one night upon all this floral infancy there came the rain. A rainbow shone before sunset, enclosing a cloud-mountain that glowed with a dull red: below it earth shone with that splendour that comes sometimes just before sleet. Chestnut, beech, chestnut, from where I watched at a window, were standing alternately, shining green, red, and green; and further away an elm was flashing the yellow mass of its seed-pods, though as yet it had no leaf. Then fell the sleet like a thin curtain of gauze, and trailed away pale-blue over the grass, leaving an azure sky where the clouds had towered, which rode away on the north wind, still glowing, to the other side of the earth.

And all that night rain fell, and the wind went round, and in the morning there were yellow flashes against the dark of the beeches, as though a painter had intended to paint the Spring and had recklessly painted a brilliant branch in cadmium and left it forgotten, staring amongst grey trunks in the gloom of the grove. On the bright brown of the oak-buds a dull gold came to appear, and now the laburnum's buds showed minute tips that were yellow. Cowslips came peering out, as early stars appear; but the dandelions flashed forth like distant suns at their zenith. And all these splendours of Spring were shining for me with a brightness that was magnified by youth, and by the thought that I should soon see Laura. I somehow thought that in an unheeding world Laura and I understood the glory of leaf and flower, and the rejoicing symphony of blackbirds and thrushes; so that birds sang and leaves shone largely for us. There was justification for this belief at the time, for the mention of any of these things at Eton, or elsewhere, usually met with derision, as though there were something evil about the song of a bird, or contemptible in a flower; but Laura even knew the name of every bird that sang, from hearing its notes alone when the bird was hidden. And, looking back on these things, I find another justification for the belief that birds sang and young leaves flashed chiefly for us. For music is poured out for ears that can hear and sympathise, and beauty is shown to those for whom it has meaning; and, whether birds and leaves knew for themselves, or whether they were guided, Laura and I were a fitting audience then for blackbird and thrush, and our wonder was not unworthy of what the leaves had to show.

I had been back two or three days when I got a letter from Mrs. Lanley, asking me to go over to tea in two days' time to see a new game that had been invented: the rules of it were— but I need not tell them to the reader, for the game was lawn tennis. On the morning of the day on which I was to go to Cloghnacurrer the Spring was shining for me with magnified glory, when a shadow fell, such as often comes in April from clouds full of hail, passing across the sunlight suddenly: Dr. Rory rode over. For a while we spoke of my father. "Who got him?" I asked. For though I had read the man's name in the Press, it meant nothing to me.

"No one from these parts," said the doctor.

And that bore out what Brophy had told me, and the boy outside Gurraghoo; for the doctor was sure to know.

And after the doctor's condolences he came to what he had ridden over to tell me, and this was the shadow that fell on me through the bright leaves of the Spring: "Marlin is dying," he said.

"Marlin!" I said. For I had thought his energy inexhaustible.

THE CURSE OF THE WISE WOMAN

Not only was he ready to walk the bog with me whenever I came and for as long as I liked, but he did it scorning such sustenance as I needed. "Why! He could go all day on only half a glass of whiskey," I added.

"That was the trouble," said Dr. Rory.

"But Marlin was never drunk in his life," I said.

"No," answered Dr. Rory, "he never took enough to bother his head."

"Then what is the matter?" I asked.

"He took more than his kidneys could manage."

I had never thought of that; I had read of men who died of consumption, and had got the idea from my reading that it was a rather romantic death, and I envied those who could take their whack of whiskey without ever showing a sign of it; but I had never thought of the kidneys.

"I must go and see him," I said. And then I thought of my visit to Cloghnacurrer. "He's not dying at once?" I added.

"Not at all," said the doctor.

"A few weeks?" I asked.

"A week, anyway," he replied.

"As bad as that?" said I.

"It's bad when your kidneys won't work," said Dr. Rory.

Poor Marlin, the news was as sudden to me as one of the storms of Spring; and I decided to go over and see him the very next day.

"It will be all right to go to-morrow?" I asked.

"Oh, yes," said Dr. Rory.

"You are quite certain?" I asked.

"Absolutely," he said. "He's still walking about in their bit of a garden."

Once more I asked him, and he answered me that Marlin would live at least for another week. And not till then did I decide to see Laura first.

So I drove over to Cloghnacurrer and they showed me the new game, which had already been going two or three years in England. I remember the line drawn across the court, with the idea, I think, of starting the game gently; and, as the narrow

space was considered hard to hit, the server was given two
shots at it. The line was drawn, as of course it still is, where the
top of the net just obscured it even from a tall man serving, and
must have been intended to make an overhead service impossible; but, if so, the inventor had forgotten that the racquet can
be held so much higher than the eye that the ball can reach
where the aim cannot. But it did not much matter what the
rules were, so long as there were rules: it is from these that
a game develops. Nor did the rules matter much to me, for I
soon went off with Laura to see her rock-garden, and to talk
of our land, as two explorers might talk of Africa, but with a
sense of ownership such as none can feel for any solid land; for
our imaginations not only had travelled there, but had their
share, with all who had ever dreamed of that immortal apple-
blossom, in building Tir-nan-Og. But there was a sadness in
our talk, for I told her of Marlin's illness, and I was feeling as a
traveller of far lands might feel when some old heathen hunter
that once has guided him goes home to his gods.

Then the rock-garden; and all the flowers bowing to the
sun, where it came through a gap in some chestnuts from
the South. It had passed to the West by now, but the flowers
were bowing to the point at which it appeared in its greatest
splendour, bent stalks and nodded heads, a bow as graceful
as though they had learnt it by moonlight, watching some
dainty dance before the Queen of the fairies. Saxifrages, both
white and pink, the humble veronica, anemones and oxlips,
all bowing the same way; then there were primroses and
primulas, cowslips and polyanthi and the tall grape-hyacinths
and one or two yellow poppies. The primroses had the same
appearance of having strayed there from the woods that squir-
rels have when they enter a walled garden, though one of the
primroses had already flashed to a bright colour, as though in
good living it had forgotten the dells of the hazel. All this was
at the edge of a grove of Portuguese laurel, whose old trunks
twisted like dragons in the dimness under the leaves, a space
between Laura's garden and the rest of the grounds, through
which foxes went by night and nobody went by day. And

beside the rock-garden stood one short tree, of great age, but lopped to within three feet of the ground, a Portuguese laurel strayed from the dark grove, which, as evening wore on, grew more and more like a gnome. The rock-garden itself was a ridge of grey granite which had thrust up through the soil and through other rocks, like a giant that in a restless moment had once heaved a shoulder up, and then had slept again for a million years. And any winds that came from the West, through the gorgeous green of the chestnut, were sweet with the scent of the flowers of common laurel, out of sight, but enchanting the garden. In such a spot we might surely have been content with Earth. Yet it was not so; for we spoke of the orchards just over the rim of the sea, in the land where youth was immortal, as though there were not time enough for the love of Laura and me. Little I thought then of Marlin, I fear, though without him my fancy could never have wandered thither; unless that sadness that seemed so near to our joy came only from the bad news I had had of him and not from the shadow of Earth, which always falls heavily near to any brightness that shines from hope or dream that transcends its mighty bulk.

CHAPTER XXII

There was a conference only two days ago in my sitting-room, between Monsieur Alphonse and me, and two gentlemen that Monsieur Alphonse said were members of the government of this State, though I doubt if really they were anything more than the members' secretaries; and in any case we decided nothing, and I only mention it for the sake of a curious comparison, which is that the memory of the details of that conference is less vivid in my mind to-day than the things that I heard and saw on a morning fifty-two years ago when I drove over to see Marlin, hoping that, after all, Dr. Rory may have been wrong. I went to Clonrue first, to see the doctor, impatient for some better news than what he had given me only the day before, and I even got it, for he had seen Marlin again, later that day. "He's walking about a good deal," he said.

"Then he'll live longer than you thought?" I asked.

"Ah, I think he will," said the doctor.

And from that I tried to get him to say that perhaps he was wrong after all, and that Marlin would yet recover. What he said I cannot remember. But what does it matter? I was only asking him to echo my hopes. Dr. Rory's words could not turn Fate back to walk the way that I wished. Yet neither he nor I ever guessed the end of Marlin.

"What way are you going?" he said to me then.

"There's only one way," I answered.

"Ah, but you can't get down the bohereen," he told me.

"Can't get down the bohereen?" said I.

"No," said Dr. Rory, "they are making a road along it."

"A road?" I exclaimed.

"Yes," said the doctor.

"What ever for?" I asked.

"The Peat Development (Ireland) Syndicate," he replied.

Then it was true. What had almost seemed like ravings, when Mrs. Marlin told me, was mere accurate information. They were going to spoil the bog.

"But did my father ever give them leave?" I asked, clinging to a last hope, for it was not like him to allow syndicates and such things from towns to make a mess of the countryside.

"They bought an option for fifty pounds," said the doctor. "And now they've taken it up. You'll get a rent from them."

"I don't want their rent," I said. For it seemed like selling Ireland piecemeal, if they were going to cut the bog away. One did not feel like that about the turf-cutters, who all through the spring and summer had their long harvest of peat, that brought the benignant influence of the bog to a hundred hearths, and that filled the air all round the little villages with the odour that hangs in no other air that I know. Indeed the very land on which the Marlins' house was standing had been once about twenty feet higher, and had been brought to that level by ages of harvests of peat, or turf as we call it. And the land that was left was still Ireland. But now it was to be cumbered with wheels and rails and machinery, and all the unnatural things that the factory was even then giving the world, as the cities began to open that terrible box of Pandora.

"Why did my father do it?" I asked.

"He only sold them the option," said the doctor. "He never thought they'd come here with their nonsense. And fifty pounds is fifty pounds."

"What are they going to do?" I enquired.

"Compress the turf by machinery and sell it as coal," he answered.

"What nonsense," I exclaimed.

"Of course it is," he replied. "But there's a lot of money to be made out of a company. And when it's got an address beside a bog, and is actually working there, it will look much more real to investors than when it's only in a prospectus. Not that it doesn't catch some of them even then."

"I wish my father hadn't done it," I said. But that was no use.

"They'll be broke in a few years," said the doctor.

In a few years: that seemed terribly long to a boy.

"They'll ruin the bog," I said. "Can no one stop them?"

"I'm afraid not," he answered.

It seemed so wrong that all that wonderful land, so beautiful and so free, should be brought under the thraldom of business by a city so far away, that my thoughts in their desperation turned strangely to Mrs. Marlin.

"Could Mrs. Marlin do anything?" I asked.

"I'm afraid not," he said.

"Couldn't she lay a curse on them?" I continued.

"She might curse their souls a bit," said the doctor reflectively, "but they'd think more of business."

In despair I left him then, and went on to see Marlin.

"We'll go by the other road," I said to Ryan. "They're spoiling the bohereen."

And Ryan muttered something, as though he were cursing the Peat Development Company, but with an amateur's ill-

trained curses; not like Mrs. Marlin. So down the road we
went, the other road from Clonrue. And, if it is not too late,
why does not some museum preserve a few yards of an old
road, as it used to be before even bicycles came to cover it
with their thin tracks? It's clear enough in my memory, with
its wandering wheel-tracks, its pale-grey stone bright in the
sunlight, and the cracks that ran through it everywhere from
its unstable foundation, as soon as it neared the bog; but when
I and my memory are gone and all my generation, who will
remember those roads? I suppose it will not matter. They will
lie sleeping, deep under tarmac, those old white roads, like the
stratum of a lost era for which nobody cares. But who cares
aught for the past? That pin-point of light called The Present,
dancing through endless night, is all that any man cares for.

So we drove down the other road, and along the side of
the bog; and the little cracks were running among the wheel-
tracks as though the bog had often whispered a warning,
telling that he was amongst the ancient powers, of which the
earthquake was one, and that he suffered roads as all these
powers suffer the things of man, which is grudgingly and for
a while. And half a mile or so from the Marlins' cottage, at the
nearest point to which this road came to them, I got out of
the trap. My walk lay over the level land from which the bog
had receded, or rather from which it had been pushed back
by man: on my left, all the way as I went, the cliff of the bog's
edge stood like a wave of a threatening tide, dark and long and
immanent. Square pools of sombre deep water lay here and
there under the cliff, with a green slime floating in most of
them, and the green slime teeming with tadpoles. I sat down
by the brink of one of these pools and looked at it, for the
sheer joy of being home again. I looked and saw little beetles
navigating the dark water like bright pellets of lead, and rather
seeming to be running than swimming. Then an insect with
four legs skipped hurriedly over the surface, going from island
to island of scarlet grass, and a skylark came by singing. Above
me in the mosses beyond the top of the bog's sheer edge the
curlews were nesting, their spring call ringing over the pools

and the heather. Beside me a patch of peat was touched with
green as though it had gone mouldy, and up from it went a
little forest of buds, each on its slender stalk, for spring had
come to the moss as well as the curlews. In amongst the soft
moss grew what looked like large leaves, but so fungoid was
their appearance that it was hard to say whether they belonged
to the moss, or were even vegetable at all: rather they seemed
to haunt the boundary of the vegetable kingdom as ghosts
haunt the boundary of man's. Strangely ill-assorted were those
gross leaves and the fairy-like slenderness of the stalks. I could
have sat there long, watching the activity of the two kinds of
insect that scurried over that water, or looking at the history
of the ages in the coloured layers of the peat, which is always
written wherever an edge of Earth is exposed, if only one can
read it; and all the while the skylark sang on. I could have sat
there idly all day in deep content, only that an anxiety thrilled
through my content, and drove me on, urging me to hasten
to hear the worst about Marlin. And so I walked on, under
the bog's edge, with peaty soil underfoot, on which sometimes
rushes grew, now all in flower, and sometimes heather, young
and very green and sometimes, almost timidly, the grass; for
the grass came mostly along the tracks of the turf-carts, and
where the earth was most trodden, and by little bridges across
tiny streams, as though only in the immediate presence of
man could it dare to usurp that land where the bog so recently
reigned. And all the way as I went over that quiet land there
went beside me a chronicle of the ancient shudders of Earth,
old angers that had stirred and troubled the bog; for the long
layers, tawny and sable, ochre, umber and orange, that were
the ruins of long-decayed heather and bygone moss, went in
waves all the way, sometimes heaving up into hills, the mark
of some age-old uprising, sometimes cracked by clefts that
sundered them twenty feet down, as though they still threatened the levels so lately stolen by man. And even that land that
man had won for himself faintly shook as I trod it, making the
threat of the bog all the more ominous. I passed innumerable
little ditches, dug to run off the water that came down from

the bog, so that the things of man might grow there and not the things of the wild. And over all of them were little bridges for the turf-carts to cross with their donkeys, for a man on foot could step over the ditches anywhere; trunks of small trees heaped over with peat and sods; but the trunks were all rotting away, so that only a prophet could tell whether man would hold that land, or whether the damp and the south-west wind and the bog would one day claim their own again.

Presently I came on turf-cutters at their work, digging out of the brown face of the soft cliff their foot-long sections of peat, four or five inches thick and wide, with an implement that seemed a blend between a spade and a spear. I don't suppose that has altered since I was living in Ireland, nor for some centuries before that. And another thing that can scarcely ever have altered is the little turf-cart in which the pieces of fresh wet peat are drawn away by donkeys, for it has the air of having been there for ever, and I do not see what it can ever have altered from, for it is so simply primitive that it must have been nearly the first. The superstructure was like that of the wheel-barrow and little larger, but it was the wheels that had been left behind by receding ages from man's very earliest effort at drawing loads. These were merely two trunks of trees, hollowed a little where the axles should be and leaving a pair of crude wheels at the ends. An iron bar ran through the core of each trunk, connecting it to the cart, and on these the trunks revolved. Two donkeys dragged the little load away to be stacked and to dry in the spring weather, with a little heather on top to keep off the rain. In those stacks the long, brick-like pieces of chocolate-coloured turf would dry to pale ochre and be carried to the cottages to take their part in the struggle against the next winter. Two men with long black hair were working the face of the bank as I came by, cutting in level lines, as though they were taking bricks layer by layer off a wall; so that when they had come to the blacker layers underneath, and had gone as low as they could and met the water, the edge of the bog would have receded along the width of their working a distance of four inches. We greeted each other as I passed, and I went on over grass and bare peat and rushes, and over the little bridges, till I saw far off the willows that grew near the Marlins' house, shining like sunlight coming through greenish smoke. I saw the willows that I knew so well, now glorying in the spring, but I saw with a pang light flashing on roofs that were strange to me: mean buildings had come already, with the swiftness of an encampment, to that land that had always seemed to me as enchanted as any land can be. And what would come of that enchantment now? So elusive a thing, among that cluster of huts, could never survive the noise, the ugliness, the ridicule and the greed. I felt sick at heart at the sight of them; and in my despair I knew nothing that could protect the ancient wildness that was such a rest and a solace to any cares that one brought to it from the world; and, feeling helpless myself, I placed no confidence in any help that could come from Mrs. Marlin.

CHAPTER XXIII

When I saw the willows shining I hurried on, for anxiety drove me on over the little bridges to hear the news of Marlin. The curlews uttered their curious cry on my left, beyond the wavy strata, while above me a skylark sang on and on and on; and, amongst all the cries of the birds and the gleam of the willows, my melancholy deepened, standing out all the blacker against the splendour of spring.

And then I saw Mrs. Marlin, far off, in her garden. She was not hurrying, she was not wailing; and I knew how grief would have racked that dark woman, giving a wild movement to her strides and a certain terror to every line of her. Or if I did not know to what fury grief would have urged her spirit, I saw at least, and even at that distance, that no great passion was driving her; although later, when I came nearer, I saw often a quick uneasy turn of her head towards the new huts and the dam that was building across the stream, as though a malevolence smouldered in her, or she rested from recently cursing; but at least Marlin was not dying; and, suddenly relieved of that fear, I walked towards her with all my anxieties gone.

"How is Marlin?" I asked, when I got within call of her.

"He's all right, sir," she said.

I came a few paces nearer.

"I am delighted to hear that," I said to her. "The doctor gave a very bad account of him."

And she laughed at that, with rather a sly look.

"Ah, what does he know?" she said.

"Where is he?" I asked.

"Ah, he's gone," she replied.

"But Marlin, I mean," said I.

"Aye. Sure, he's gone," she answered.

"Gone?" I said. "Where?"

"Over the bog," she said.

"But what way?" I asked.

"A rainbow showed him," she said.

"A rainbow?" I muttered.

And she went to the door and opened it for me, and we went in. And she offered me a chair before her great fireplace and sat down on a chair herself and gazed into the red embers of the turf, which never break into flame. And then she said: "He was very ill. Ill as the doctor said. But, sure, what does he know of anything, only of the affairs of that world?" And she pointed away from the bog.

"He was lying there in his bed yesterday evening, ill as the doctor said, and I was trying to get him to take some medicine, when he turned to me and says: 'Mother, I must go. For if I stop any longer I'll be dying. And I'll not die in this earth.' And I says to him: 'Ireland's a good enough land for any man to die in.' And he says: 'Not when it's Hell you'd have to go to; and it's where I'd go from here.' And at that he rises up from his bed and puts on his boots, and gives one look round at the cottage. Then he gives me a kiss and sets off, and there was a rainbow shining. And no sooner had he climbed up by the bank of turf and set his foot on the bog, but the rainbow

begins to go further and further off. And he follows it all the
way to the everlasting morning."

I don't exactly know what she meant by that, but she
pointed through a window as she spoke, in the direction in
which the sun usually brightened far patches of water, away
by the bog's horizon, all the morning; the direction in which
so often I had seen Marlin's eyes stray.

"But how far did he go?" I asked.

"To Tir-nan-Og," she said.

"But how did he know the way?" said I.

"The rainbow showed him," she answered.

What had happened to Marlin? I wondered. Where had he
gone?

"How far did you see him?" I asked.

"Away and away," she said. "And the rainbow before him."

"But he couldn't walk out of your sight," I said. "A sick man
couldn't have done it."

But still she pointed away to the far horizon, where the
water shone and no hills bounded the bog.

"The night came on," she said, "after the rainbow left him."

Her words frightened me. You can't walk the bog out there
in the night; or it is very nearly impossible.

"You should have called him back," I said.

"Call back a rainbow!" she exclaimed, with a gust of laughter.

"No, Marlin," I explained.

"Nor him, either," she said. "They were both of them going
away to the glory of Tir-nan-Og, the rainbow from the dark
world and the coming of night, and my son from damnation.
Little they know the rainbow from his few visits to these fields,
little they know it that have not seen it glorying in its home,
entwined with the apple-blossom of the Land of the Young;
and little they know of a man till they have seen him in the
splendour of his youth among the everlastingly youthful in the
orchards of Tir-nan-Og."

For a moment I feared she would try to go after him, and
drown herself, thinking she could not go very far in safety, at
her age, over the bog. "You're not going, too?" I asked.

"I'll never see him there," she said. "God knows I'll never see him there, having stayed on Earth too long, till my feet are slow with its weeds and my soul with its cares. Though I'll say nothing harsh against Earth, for the sake of Ireland. And I have one thing more to do upon Earth yet. For I have to speak with the powers of bog and storm and night, and to learn their will with the men that are harming the heather."

"Show me the way he went," I said, and got up from the chair; for I felt sure that a man as sick as he was could never have walked far over the bog. And she rose and came with me out of the door and we walked to the bog's edge, I impatient to find Marlin and trying to hurry her, she without any anxieties and only concerned with her reflections, which she uttered as we went.

"It's by the blessing of God," she said, "that mothers never see their sons grow old; bent and wrinkled and haggard. It's the blessing of God. And they should not see them die. A few days more and Tommy would have died, there in his bed beside me; and no art of mine could have hindered it; for I have no power against the splendour of death. But he rose and walked away out of the world, where age cannot overtake him, and where death is only known from idle stories told in the orchards by those that are young for ever, for the sake of the touch of sadness that gives a savour to their immortal joy. Weakness and wrinkles and dying, they are the way of this world, and the shadow of damnation creeping nearer. But he has walked away from the world and away from the shadow."

All the while I was trying to hurry her, picturing Marlin lying a mile away out in the bog, for I feared he could scarce have got further; and how would a sick man fare, out there all night?

"Was there any frost?" I asked her; for we still had a touch of frost sometimes at night, and she was nearer to these things than I in our large house.

But she only answered: "Aye, the world's cold," and gazed away before her with happy eyes as though she went to her son's wedding.

"Hurry," I said, for she would not quicken her pace. "Or we'll find him dead."

"Ah, no," she said. "He would not wait for death. And why would he, with damnation prepared for him by those that are jealous of the land of the morning?"

I don't know whom she meant; and, God knows, these are no words of mine, but only hers still haunting my memory, where I fear they should not be, and would not be if I could banish them.

And so we came to the steep edge of the bog and she climbed agilely up, and I after her; and for a while we walked in silence over the rushes. The moss lay grey all round us, crisp as a dry sponge, while we stepped on the heather and rushes, the heather all covered with dead grey buds, the rushes a pale sandy colour. I had never walked the bog in the spring before, and was surprised at the greyness of it. But some bright mosses remained, scarlet and brilliant green; and along the edge of the bog under the hills lay a slender ribbon of gorse, and the fields flashed bright above it, so that the bog lay like a dull stone set in gold, with a row of emeralds round the golden ring. A snipe got up brown, and turned, and flashed white in turning. A curlew rose and sped away down the sky with swift beats of his long wings and loud outcry, giving the news, "Man, Man," to all whose peace was endangered by our approach, and a sky-lark shot up and sang, and stayed above us, singing. The pools that in the winter lay between the islands of heather, and that Marlin used to tell me were bottomless, were most of them grey slime now, topped with a crust that looked as if it might almost bear one. We knew the way to go; the way that I had so often seen Marlin's eyes gazing, the way that Mrs. Marlin said straight out was the way to Tir-nan-Og: I could see the water flashing over there, though the grey moss was dry about us. The fear that I had had that Mrs. Marlin would come to harm in the bog I had now entirely forgotten, for she stepped from tussock to tussock surely and firmly, with a stride that seemed to know the bog too well to falter even with age. We came, with the skylark still singing, to pools that were partly water and partly luxuriant moss: strange grasses leaned along them and burst into flower. More and more pools we met, and less grey moss, and presently the wide lakes lay before us, to which Marlin had looked so often. I stood on a hummock of heather and stared ahead, then looked at Mrs. Marlin. There was nothing but water and rushes and moss before us. We were as far as a sick man could have walked, apart from the danger and difficulty of all that lay ahead. If Marlin had come this way there was no hope for him.

"You are sure he went this way?" I asked, and knew that the question was hopeless even as I asked it.

Her face all lighted up, looking glad and young, and with shining eyes she gazed over the desolate water, and said: "Aye, he went this way, this way; away from the world and the shadow cast by damnation, black as tar on the cities. Aye, he went this way."

And then I knew that Marlin shared with the Pharaohs that strange eternity of the body that only Egypt and the Irish bog can give. Centuries hence, when we are all mouldered away, some turf-cutter will find Marlin there and will look on a face and a figure untouched by all those years, even as though the body had obeyed the dream after all.

CHAPTER XXIV

Then I brought Mrs. Marlin back from the bog, thinking she had gone far enough, and knowing that the part of it to which we had come was dangerous walking even for a young man. For these were the waters that Marlin called "the sumach," or some such word that I do not know how to spell, a mass of stored rains that grew heavier every year, till it flooded in under the roots of whatever growth gave a foothold, and floated the light surface of mosses and peat, till everything trembled round one as one walked: one called it the shaky bog, the most dangerous of all the kinds of bog that one walks. These waters were the source of the stream that ran past the Marlins' house; but, as more rain came with the storms than left with the stream, the whole weight of the bog was increasing.

"We must get all the men we can find, and search the bog for him," I said, when I got her back to the safe grey moss and the heather. And at that she laughed with peals of her strange wild laughter.

"Aye, search the world for him," she said. "But he will not be there. And it's not the world that wants him, but Hell. And Hell will not have him either. It's the orchards of Tir-nan-Og that have him now, with the morning dripping from their branches in everlasting light, golden and slow, like honey. Aye, and the evening too, and both together; for Time that troubles us here comes not to those gleaming shores. Age, desolation and dying; that's the way of these fields; and not one wrinkle, nor sigh, nor one white hair, ever came to Tir-nan-Og."

"We must look for him," I said. For it was a duty to do all that one could, even if the search seemed hopeless; and I did not wish her words to turn me away from it, as I feared that they soon would.

"Aye, search for ever," she said, "and you'll never see him. But I shall see him often."

"Where?" I said.

"Where would it be," she answered, "but about his mother's house and over the heather that he knew as a child, and on mosses by pools where he played? Where else would he go when he comes from Tir-nan-Og, and the jack-o'-lanterns come riding the storm through the darkness, and go dancing over the bog?"

"How will he come?" I asked.

"On the west wind," she answered.

"We must search for him," I said, sticking to my point, which it seemed harder and harder to do.

"Aye, search," she said, and went off again into peals of her wild laughter, which rang far over the bog and frightened the curlews.

"How could he get to Tir-nan-Og?" I asked. For if there was

any chance of finding him, it would have to be done quickly, and she would not see that it was serious at all. I spoke to her all the more impatiently for the fear that I soon should believe her, and do nothing at all. And one ought to do something.

"He'd go by the way of the bog till he came to the sea," she said. "Didn't he know the way well?"

"And then?" I asked.

"There'll be a boat there, lifting and dropping with the lap of the tide," she said; "and eight queens to row it; queens that have turned from Heaven, and yet slipped away from damnation. Hell has not their souls, nor the earth their dust."

"How could he know they'd be there?" I asked her.

"How could he know?" she said. "I told him."

But that made things no clearer. Then she gazed away over the bog and went on talking: "'Hell would have me, mother,' he said, 'if I stay here.' And when I saw he was bent on leaving the world, I said I'd help him; for he knew the way over the bog to the shore, but he'd never been on the sea. And I went one stormy night to the bog, when the wind was in the West and all the people of Tir-nan-Og were riding upon the storm, and by the edge of the water where they were flashing and admiring their heathen beauty, I called out to them: 'Ancient People, there's a man that would share your everlasting glory; and Hell wants him, because he has turned his face to the West. How shall he go to find you?'

"And with tiny voices they answered me through the storm, voices shriller than the cry of the snipe and small as the song of the robin, they whose voices rang once from hill to hill over Ireland; and they said: 'To the sea, to the sea.'

"'And then?' I said, 'Oh ancient and glorious people?'

"'What would you have of us?' they asked.

"And I lured them nearer, by a power I have, and said to them: 'By that power, I need your help over the sea.'

"And they said to me: 'When will he come?'

"And I answered: 'One of these days,' which is the only time we know with the future, and all we ever will know, till it is dated and mapped as is should be.

"And they repeated one to another, with their small voices, 'One of these days,' till the message passed out of hearing. And I made my compact with them out there on the bog, swearing by turf and heather, as they swore by blossom and twilight. For a danger threatened the bog and I swore to guard it, and they swore to carry Tommy over the water and bring him to Tir-nan-Og. Eight fair girls, they said, that were queens of old in Ireland, would bring him over the water, waiting for him where the bog ran down to the shore, upon the day that I said. And Tommy would know them, apart from their beauty and apart from their crowns of gold, by the light that would be gleaming along the sides of the boat; for the boat would be made from the bark of birches growing in Tir-nan-Og, and the twilight that shone on them in the Land of the Young would be shining upon them still. And whether it was night in the world, or whether noon or morning, the twilight of Tir-nan-Og would be shining upon that birch-bark."

I tried to picture a boat glowing gently in twilight while it was noon all round, with the sun bright on the water; or, more wonderful still, the birch-bark iridescent in the soft light of the gloaming, while all around was night. But thinking of this only drifted me from my purpose, which was to find a number of men and search the heather for Marlin. I was in two minds; one was the mind that listened to Mrs. Marlin telling of Tir-nan-Og, of which I had already learned so much from her son; the other, a more disciplined mind, told me that the bog must be searched for Marlin whether there seemed any hope of finding him there or not. The more useless this appeared the more I clung to it, lest Mrs. Marlin should lure me to forget it altogether, and a duty remain undone.

"We must search for him," I repeated.

"Aye, search," she said indulgently, as though the search were some trivial rite that custom idly bound me to. And I think she knew from the tone of my voice that I somehow had not my heart in it. "Would they fail me?" she went on. "Never."

And I saw from her far gaze westwards, and the light in her eyes, that she was thinking of those eight queens.

We came to the bog's edge, where deep fissures ran down out of sight, as though the vast weight of the bog were too much for the banks that bounded it; and from that high edge I looked over the land lying round Marlin's cottage that had always seemed so magical to me, the land over which the old willows brooded in winter and were like an enchantment in spring, and I could have wept at what I saw. And what I saw is well enough known: I need hardly describe it: a large number of small houses meanly built, and all exactly the same, denying any difference between the tastes of one man and another, nor caring anything for any man's taste, nor expressing any feeling or preference of builder or owner. It was as though men without any passions had built them all for the dead.

They were barely finished, but men were already living in some of them, and work had already started on building the dam and putting in the wheel that was to be turned by the water and which would set the machinery clanking in the ugly house they were building. The world is full of such things, little need to describe them; the only concern that this story has with them is to tell that they came down dark upon that spot to which first my memories went whenever I was far from Ireland, racing there quicker than homing pigeons, or bees going back to the hive. And not only had they spoiled the magic that lay over all that land, deep as mists in the autumn, but they were there for the purpose of cutting the bog away; not as the turf-cutters take it, with imperceptible harvests, slowly, as years go by, a few yards in each generation, but working it out as miners work out a stratum of coal.

It was to these men that I now appealed, calling out to them from the high edge of the bog and telling them that a man was lost out there in the heather. They came at once, and I soon had about thirty of them, some of them English and some the men of Clonrue. "Begob," said one of the latter to me, "if you set Englishmen walking the bog it's soon a hundred men that we'll have to look for, and not only one." But oddly enough it was the Englishmen that took charge as soon as we started off, though they got very wet over it.

"We'll find your son for you, mam," said one of them. "Don't you worry."

But she looked fiercely at him and only answered: "Do you know the way to World's End?"

"I expect we could find it, mam," was all he said to her.

Her eyes were blazing, and then she burst into laughter. "And you'll only be half-way to him then," she said.

Then we all spread out to about half a mile and walked in the direction of the deep part of the bog, from which Mrs. Marlin and I had just returned, and heard her laughter still ringing in mockery of the thirty men that were trying to find her son.

We went back over the grey moss, about twenty-five yards apart, the bog-cotton flowering round us, a bright patch at the tips of the rushes, the skylark high above us singing triumphantly on.

"It's got on her mind a bit," said one of the men, as Mrs. Marlin's laughter rang out behind us.

"I'm afraid it has," I said. For I could not explain Mrs. Marlin to an Englishman.

"We'll find him all right, sir," he said.

But he only saw that the heather was not high enough to hide anyone lying there from a searcher passing within twelve yards: he did not know the deeps of an Irish bog.

"Don't step on the bright mosses," I said.

We went on till Mrs. Marlin's laughter faded from hearing, and the only wild cries we heard were the cries of the curlews.

When I came again to that waste of water and moss, where trembling waves ran through the bog from every footstep, the line of men drew in from either side to the edges of that morass, each man seeming drawn towards it without anyone saying a word; and we all looked over the water and brilliant mosses in silence. I realised then that in bringing these thirty men over the bog I had done a conventional duty in which there was no meaning whatever.

We turned round and each man took a different line to the one by which he had come, so as to cover more ground on the way back, but nobody searched any more. I knew that they were not searching, but said no word to them, for my thoughts were in Tir-nan-Og.

CHAPTER XXV

When we came back to the land of fields and paths with no more hope of ever finding Marlin, his was not a loss over which I merely mourned for a few days: I feel it still. I feel to this day the zest that went out of my life when I knew that I should no more walk the bog with him, and even thought of laying my gun away and never walking the moss and the heather again, as to-day I could lay down my pen and end this story, were it not for one thing. And that one thing is that the bog itself was threatened; all the wild ways he had shown me, mosses and rushes and heather, the home of the curlew and snipe, and the grazing-grounds of the geese, all those enchanted fields and the magical willows lying under the edge of the bog, all were to be spoiled, hidden, sold and disenchanted by that terrible force named Progress. And Mrs. Marlin had made her compact to protect it, with certain powers that were of the bog itself. No one else promised to save it. Would Mrs. Marlin do so? That was the interest that burned in me now that Marlin was gone. And the less I spoke of it to anyone the more it loomed in my thoughts. The very heart of Ireland appeared to be threatened, for the bog seemed that to me then, as it seems to me still; and it was the only bog I knew. How clear those anxious days are yet in my memory. I might look out of the large window of the room in which I am sitting, and pass my idle hours in jotting down what I see, the motors in the sunlight flashing up the wide street, sometimes a cart with horses, plumed and decked with bright harness, from some farm out in the plains, the different kinds of people, idlers wasting away the passing hour, hurrying men seeking something from some hour yet to come, perhaps equally vainly, statues of famous men of whom

I know nothing, great porticoes and façades of the high houses, sometimes even a butterfly lost from the fields, illumining for an instant these sheer cliffs of man, a cat amidst all the clatter and hurry of men attending placidly to her own affairs; the bright clothes of the fashion that passes, and now and then some women, in from the lands beyond, bright with the dress and the ribbons of the fashion that never passes, the age-old fineries of the peasant's dress; and evening coming on with its outburst of lights; but I could not write an account of the passing moment here as I could of the anxieties that troubled me then, multiplied as all troubles are multiplied always by youth: I foresaw the bog vulgarised by noise and machinery, then cut away altogether, and lastly a litter left of all those bits of iron and old hats, papers, cinders and medicine-bottles, that together make up rubbish-heaps, where once the bog had wandered wild for the curlews, as once for the Irish elk. And the bog was to me what the desert is to the Arab.

When last I saw Mrs. Marlin on that day, her laughter had ceased and she was standing silent on the high edge of the bog, looking down on the level lands, once the home only of willows, and now as I have described it, and worse. She was looking at the row of new huts, and at the men going back to their work on the dam and laying down narrow rails, and there was a look on her face such as an eagle might wear on a high cliff watching lambs. I turned to go to her and ask her about the compact she said she had made, and to ask if anything could save the bog, but suddenly I despaired and went away.

I walked back again all under the edge of the bog, where the strata were troubled, as they lay in their sleep, by the violence of old upheavals, and the wavy lines here and there were arched upwards until they cracked. And where the cracks ran deepest, fallen masses of turf lay half-submerged in the square pools of dark water looking like blocks of masonry tumbled down by an earthquake, only that their squared edges and whole bulk were soft. I should never see Marlin again, and the bog I loved was threatened, but the skylark sang on.

I came to the road and found Ryan, and told him the news about Marlin.

"Begob, a man must go some time," he said.

"Ryan," I said, "did you ever hear tell of Tir-nan-Og?"

"I did not," he answered.

But I talked of the orchards over the sea in the West, and the twilight caught up in their blossoms for ever and ever, and the queens of old there everlastingly young; till he admitted that he had heard of it.

"Could Marlin have got to Tir-nan-Og?" I asked.

"Begob," he answered, "if a man starts in time, they say among the wise women that Hell can't get him."

And I spoke again of the splendours of Tir-nan-Og, telling, as Marlin had told me, how the glow of the apple-blossom was brighter than any colour seen in the western sky, floating over the sunset, and that the bloom on the face of the immortal maidens was fairer even than that.

"Hist," said Ryan, "let us not speak of that land" (he would never name it), "for if a man's heart turn towards it and he comes to die in bed he dies in mortal sin."

"Hell would have him then," I said.

"Why wouldn't it?" Ryan answered.

Beyond the bog a green dun watched over the waste, built once by men at the edge of the fields that they grazed, and protected on one side by the bog all the way to the horizon, for the bog was there then as now. What kind of men were they, I wondered. What was their heaven? Did they know Tir-nan-Og? And where was Marlin's spirit? Vain speculations that led my fancy to the mists that surround our knowledge, and through which there is no seeing.

We drove first to Dr. Rory's house, and I found him in.

"Marlin's gone," I said.

"B'Jabers," said the doctor; "but he should have lasted a bit longer."

"He walked away over the bog," I told him.

"Walked away over the bog!" he exclaimed.

"He was looking for Tir-nan-Og," said I.

"Ah," he said thoughtfully, "he might do that."

"What would happen to him?" I asked.

And Dr. Rory said nothing.

"Is there such a place as Tir-nan-Og?" I continued.

And a look came into the doctor's face as when a man suddenly remembers things that are long gone by.

"You see, I've been studying medical books for fifteen years," he said.

"Yes?" I interposed, or something to keep him talking.

"And there's nothing about it there," he said.

"Nor about Heaven either," said I.

It was Father MacGillicud that I should have gone to, but I daren't, for it is mortal sin to think of Tir-nan-Og as I was thinking of it.

"Before you studied medicine at all," I asked, "did you know of Tir-nan-Og?"

For a moment I thought that he was going to say "No."

"When one is young," he said, "one has a lot of foolish fancies."

If I had agreed, or disagreed, that would have been all. But I was silent.

And after a moment or two he went on. "It's like this," he said. "I used to read old histories years ago. And there was surely talk about that country once. About Tir-nan-Og, I mean. And there's no doubt the priests made a great fight against it, a terrible great fight. And in the end they won. Well, it's the same in either world, if you'll take advice from an older man; and it's this; always to keep away from the beaten side. There's no good ever comes from going near them; the folks that are beaten, I mean. They've nothing left for themselves, and they're not going to help you. Heaven or earth it's just the same. And there's another thing; besides getting no good out of the beaten side, the other side get to hear of it if you go near them, and they're against you at once."

"That's what Marlin said," I told him. "He said that he knew that Heaven had turned against him."

"And why wouldn't it?" said the doctor. "Sure it's right that it should. Wasn't it Marlin that began it? And there's another thing, speaking of fights in general: if it's not much of a fight, and one side's beaten at once, the winner may forget all about it. But if it's a close thing, as this was, and against a country of that beauty (for could there be anything lovelier than young girls in the pride of their beauty walking through endless orchards in blossom that never grows old?) why, then the winner's always afraid he may have to fight again; and it's little mercy you'd get from either side when they found that you had leanings towards the other. And I don't presume to blame them: it's the same everywhere."

"I'll take your advice and keep away from it," I said.

"Do," said the doctor.

And it was a good deal for me to promise, for in some odd way or other I thought that some nook of those orchards was the arbour of Laura and me; and there's no saying what fancies may come sometimes to youth. It meant also that I should never see Marlin again.

"I don't say," the doctor continued, "that if you're over in England, or if you ever travel abroad, you mightn't be thinking of Tir-nan-Og for a bit. It's hardly known outside Ireland, and the true faith had no trouble with it: they never had to fight it there, so there's no bitterness, if you know what I mean. But it's very different here. It's not much more than a thousand years since they beat it. And what's a thousand years to Heaven?"

If I did not entirely take Dr. Rory's advice, it kept me at least from coming too much under the influence of Marlin's heretical faith and his mother's witcheries, temptations that have little hold on me now, but I write of days when all temptations were strong whenever they came at all. And let me, so that I may tell an honest story, not brush aside influences now, because they were fanciful, false, or contrary to the known truths of religion or science; for none of these disqualifications has the weight of a feather in keeping any doctrine or influence away from youth. It was a perilous influence, and was near me, and I think it was Dr. Rory that saved my soul. I think it is saved: I find all temptations that come to me now so weak that I think it is surely safe. Yet had it not been for the advice of Dr. Rory to turn from Tir-nan-Og, who can say what would have become of it? It was not the doctor's job to save my soul, but through some queer aptitude of the Irish people they are always doing other men's jobs as well as their own.

"Have a drink," said the doctor.

And then I remembered that I had had no lunch, and it was well on in the afternoon.

"May I have some tea?" I said.

And it leaked out about the missing lunch, or his kindly hospitality drew it out, and he had some eggs boiled for me; and soon we were talking of what weighed most on my mind from the future. Out of the past the loss of Marlin was the trouble that most oppressed me, but the danger that threatened the bog loomed heavily in the future.

"What will they do to it?" I asked.

"It will take them a very long time to cut it away," he said.

"But they'll cut right into it," I complained. "And there'll never be snipe on it, with all that noise and machinery round the edge, and the geese will never come to it again."

"They might not be there very long," he said.

"Why not?" I asked.

"Maybe the curses of Mrs. Marlin might be too much for them after all," said he.

"But you said they wouldn't care about curses," said I.

"I said so," he answered. "But there's something about a curse that the men might not like, that are doing the work for them. Day after day and Mrs. Marlin still cursing them; they might get tired of it after a while. And she'd do that. And at nights too. Queer things, curses. Even the things we know are queer; bacilli and all that. But they're nothing to the things that we don't know."

"I suppose they're not," I said.

"B'Jabers, they're not," said the doctor.

"But is there any way of stopping them?" I asked.

"There's one way," he said.

"What is it?" I asked.

"But it wouldn't do," he said.

"What way were you thinking of?" I persisted.

"Some of the people about might ask them to go," he said.

"They'd never listen to them," said I.

"There's some they'd listen to," said the doctor. "But it wouldn't do."

I turned to my boiled egg then, for I was very hungry.

"We searched for Marlin," I said after a while. For the doctor had asked nothing about that.

"Yes, yes, of course," he replied. But he said no more.

CHAPTER XXVI

Those would have been happy days, but for the loss of Marlin, and but for the rails, the huts, the dam and all the machinery that I had seen preparing against the helpless bog. Spring came to its full glory: the leaves of the chestnut lifted and spread out, and the great blossoms towered up from among them; the birch shone green and the lovely lilac appeared, and the oaks were a mass of gold. In all this splendour I walked at first with a heavy heart, but a boy's spirit is nearer than mine is now to whatever influences sway the leaves and set the snipe drumming, and I think it was not very long before there was something singing in me with the joy of the birds and with the brilliance of flowers, though I had not thought it could be so, so soon after Marlin's loss. Yet all the while anxiety for the fate of the bog was weighing on me; anxiety for its silence, for the voices of all its wandering birds, for its wildness, for everything that passes away at the sound of the clank of machinery. Man is the enemy of many an animal, but so they are of each other, and still there is room for all; it is only when he makes an ally of steam and the Pluto-like iron machine that the terrible alliance sweeps all before it: mystery flies away, solitude with it, and quiet is gone with the rest; and all the tribes of the air that love these things, and know them as we shall never know them, are away to the wilder lands. The remoteness, the wildness, the beauty, of the bog were somehow all round my heart-strings: it was as though someone were planning to spoil the Evening Star. I talked to Brophy about this syndicate that had come to trouble Lisronagh, and to Murphy and even young Finn, for I often found that the less men were educated the more they appeared to know of what was going on. But none of them could tell me what was going to happen to the bog, for that depended on the intentions of men in a remote city, and they were men who had double doors to their offices, and double windows, so as to prevent any noise coming in while they were making their plans.

Fox-hunting was over, and it was of course the close season for game-birds; the only things unprotected now, besides those birds that keepers call vermin, being the rabbits. Even to these I would not take my gun, so much was it associated with memories of Marlin, and I left it where I had put it away on the day that he and I heard the snipe drumming. I took instead a small rifle, which, though it has some features resembling those of a shot-gun, entails such different methods in using it from those of the man with the gun, that they are the implements of as widely separate sports as are a bat and a hockey-stick; and with this I whiled the long evenings away. The rifle I used was called a rook-rifle, named after a rather dull sport, which I very seldom practised; for the young rook is barely able to leave its branch, let alone its tree, so that the only skill required to get him is one accurate shot, a very different thing from the necessity of having the first shot accurate. It was a .250; that is to say its calibre was exactly a quarter of an inch; and it was an ejector, but I had got the blacksmith of Clonrue, who did many odd jobs of other men's trades, to put the ejector out of work; for the flick of a finger-nail will throw the small cartridge out, and I had noticed again and again that a rabbit will often sit still after one shot, with ears up, wondering what the sound can have been; then comes the click of the ejector, after which I have never known the rabbit to stay. It is the sound of the bullet that he hears, close to his head. But what was it? Where is the danger? The ejector tells him that.

But this is only a trifle, for one has only to get one's rabbit first shot, and the ejector is then a convenience. A far more necessary precaution, and one without which one cannot hit any animal without the probability of wounding him, was the removal of the shiny line on the back-sight. No part of a back-sight should be shiny, but if the very centre of it shines, just where the bright foresight rests, it is impossible to tell in the sunlight, away from the gun-maker's shop, whether you are taking a fine sight or a coarse sight; whether, that is to say, you are seeing the tip of the foresight through the glare, or the whole of it, or even perhaps none at all. Yet nearly all makers of rifles put then, and still put to-day, that little silver line just where it does most harm. That it is on account of some ancient ritual of the gun-maker's I know, because none of them have ever told me the reason for it; it is more sacred to them than reason; and because one gun-maker told me once that it was in order to show if the sights were upright, an answer obviously made to conceal the ancient ritual. Or perhaps they only put it to brighten the rifle, so stimulating its price. I blotted the bright line out with some paint that I got from a carpenter, and then I could see the very tip of the foresight shining in the back-sight's black valley and could take as fine a sight as I needed, seeing more and more of it up to seventy-five yards, at which range I took the whole of the little bead; and further than that I aimed a bit over the rabbit. Another detail, for such as care to know it, is that I used hollow-pointed bullets, which by expanding do the work of a much larger bullet and are more merciful, if one can use such a word of any of the means whereby man procures meat for himself, than a solid bullet; and the ricochet does not travel so far. There was a green bank sloping up to a long wood, and along the edge of the wood ran a line of hawthorn, already powdered with whitening buds on those branches that saw most of the sun. There when the fields were quiet and the grasses cool, and the rabbits stole out of the wood, I used to go with my rifle. The old hedge waved in and out, even as it had been planted; but with some of the bushes prospering in the sunlight and others shadowed by trees, with some leaning one way and some another, and with trees from the wood behind here and there thrusting right through, I could get fresh cover every hundred yards. It was along this slope as much as anywhere that I learned to shoot with a rifle, and grew to know something about stalking, although I used to ignore one of the most important things about it; the direction of the wind; and for years I used to notice, without connecting it with the wind, that there were days on which all wild things seemed haunted by such a feeling of danger that, if I only showed the top of my head, every rabbit for over a hundred and fifty yards would run at once for the wood, while on other days they would hesitate, even at fifty yards, when the whole of my head and shoulders had come into view, so long as I kept still. To use the word stalking of this tiny sport seems almost ridiculous, and yet I know no other word for the approach of a man with a rifle to any animal whose meat he desires; one must put one's wits against the little animal's wits, humbler but much sharper, and one must learn to shoot straight, not to make noise, and to do as well as one can without the cloak of invisibility. I learned in those days too how to cock a rifle without making a click, for the hammerless weapon was not yet invented: one did this by keeping one's forefinger pressing the trigger while one lifted the hammer with one's thumb. A click just before aiming would have been, if not a warning, at least a hint, to the long listening ears. Sometimes crawling flat, and sometimes on hands and knees, I used often to get within fifteen yards of a rabbit before firing a shot, or in a lazier mood I would take the shot at seventy-five yards. The knuckles of my left hand, the three furthest away from the thumb, got rough and hard, because, carrying the rifle in that hand, it was the back of it that one walked on when on all fours. I never knew till those days, what the deer-stalker knows in Scotland, that birds can speak to the other animals. So hard is it for man to speak with man when separated by no more than a frontier, that it surprised me the first time that I saw twenty rabbits sent hurrying to safety by no more than a single remark from a passing rook, who had seen me stalking them, though I was out of sight of the rabbits. And I learned that a rook does not merely say Caw, having, at least, one note of warning that probably means Man, and another that certainly means "Man with a gun." I learned too that a small bird among trees would go on and on repeating a warning note until hundreds of hidden ears must have been thrilled with the menace; and, however quietly I went after that through the wood, I would see fewer rabbits, and those that I saw would be at once away. And so by pitting myself against the rabbits I came to know a little about them, and about their other enemies; and I know no other way in which I could have learned as much. Nobody standing behind a chess-player and watching him play can learn half as much of chess as the man that is playing against him, for rivalry is the essence of the game, as it is of the woods. And in learning something of rabbits and those that prey on them I learned nothing of men, but a good deal about nations; for it seems to me that the law of the woods is the law of life, a law from which every man escapes under the shelter of the laws of his country, that protect his life and property, more or less; but where is the nation that can leave any property unprotected, or trust its life unguarded? Seeing so much more of our own affairs than of the affairs of nations, we get the idea that slaughter and rapine are only the methods of such as the fox and the tiger, but undefended land in Europe or in any other continent survives no better than meat that cannot escape in the wood; and wherever a little weak country thrives it is not in spite of this law, but because of the interests of some powerful neighbour, as the mice in a lion's den are safe from the panther. And lest any that follow a simple tale be irked by a touch of philosophy, I close this chapter.

CHAPTER XXVII

I had absolute freedom, all those holidays, to do whatever I wanted. An uncle, my father's younger brother, had now become my guardian. He was a man of charming manner, and let me do what I liked; in return for which I naturally gave my consent to whatever he recommended in the affairs of the estate that my father had left me. He often consulted me, always giving me two courses to choose from. Of some rents that were to be invested he would say: "If you would like the money invested at 3½ per cent in what are called trust funds, I will do it for you; but if you would sooner have it invested at twelve per cent in a company that I can put it into, which is equally good, you only have to tell me." And I told him.

He never spoke of finance without smiling.

Well, one evening I was enjoying this care-free life as usual; and yet it was not care-free, and perhaps a boy's life seldom is: day-dreams of Laura took up two-thirds of my time, and anxiety for the fate of Lisronagh took up half of it. And that is not correct mathematically? Mathematics never came into it, nor any other branch of human reason, which was quite incompetent to control my day-dreams, or to allay my anxieties. But one evening I was out with my rifle, on the long slope under the trees, and had come to the end with half a dozen young rabbits, and was coming back on the other side, where one got more light late in the evening, for it was the western side of the wood. I had stalked some rabbits to within fifty yards, and was kneeling behind a bramble that had run out from the wood. The sun was setting, but brightly, so that I had ample light on my foresight, and there was a row of rabbits feeding a few yards out from the trees. I had chosen my rabbit, rejecting the easier shots that stood out large and clear, for they are usually the old does. I was perfectly covered by the bramble and was just aiming through the top of it, when suddenly all the rabbits ran. I remained hidden and silent, and waited to see what it was that had frightened the rabbits, and saw nothing. And then I looked behind me; and there was the man standing of whom I have told you before, the man in the long black coat.

"Begob, Master Char-les," said he, "sure I've spoiled your shot."

"Never mind," I said.

"Sure I wouldn't do that," he answered, "for the wealth that there is in the world. But it's the way it is that I wanted to see you."

"What about?" I asked; for there seemed a certain divergence between the interests of him and me.

"Weren't you asking a lot of men," he replied, "how long that English company was going to stay at Lisronagh?"

"I was," I said, knowing that my words had had ample time to travel over the bog and up into the hills beyond Gurraghoo, which they would do at about the pace of a man running, and not making the mistake of supposing that such news could not travel, merely because I did not know how.

"Well then," said he, "we could have them out of it in a week."

Never had I known a greater temptation. I loved the bog; I have not the right to say that I loved the dwellers therein, for I shot one in every fifty thousand of them, but it grieved me to think of them driven away, by all that comes with machinery, from the nesting-grounds that were theirs for ages and ages. I should have shouted "No," and left him. "But at least," said Satan in the deeps of my mind, "know what the temptation is before you do anything hastily."

"How would you do it?" I asked.

"Begob," said he, "if one of them met with an accident one night, and another the next night, and then another, and if nobody quite knew what happened them; and then one more, four in all. Sure, four would be enough. Begob they'd all go."

For one moment I dared to think of Tir-nan-Og, if I lost Heaven.

Then I said "No."

"It's a pity," said he; "and sure no one would know. And you'd not know yourself, Master Char-les. You might come to me and say, 'How did those men die?' and you might ask any man in the world, and there'd be no one to tell you, no man living in the world."

"No," I said. "No."

"They'll tear the very soul out of the bog," he said. "And the guts of it."

I just found myself able to say "No" again.

"It's a pity," he said once more.

Then I walked a few steps on my way, slowly and watching for rabbits, and believed he was coming behind me. But when I looked round he was gone.

I went on with my humble sport; more rabbits came into view, and, though the sun soon set, I was able to get four or five more, for there were great numbers of them at this hour out on the dewy grass, and I had a wide V to my foresight, which obscured as little as possible of the light and the object at which I was aiming. Ten rabbits are more than one can carry in one hand without dropping one every few yards, and it was, as I had already discovered, a very wearisome thing to attempt; so about the time that the sun was gone from the grass, and even from the top of the wood, and only shone now on the breasts of pigeons going late to their homes, I sat down and paunched the rabbits; I then slit the sinew at the back of one of the hocks of each rabbit and slipped the other leg through, and cut a stick from a tree and hung all the rabbits along it by the crossed hind-legs. All I had to do then was to hold the stick at the point of balance, and the burden was more than halved, even without the paunching.

I have always considered that in those days I learned the secret of rifle-shooting; not some obvious thing such as people often tell you is the secret of doing some simple work, but something rarely practised and either little known or not credited; and that is to shoot with both eyes open. Many believe that it cannot be done, which if true would dispose of it; but, if it can be, a man with two eyes must see double as well as a man with one, and it is seeing that counts; I do not mean seeing the sights accurately aligned; any man with a steady hand and any eyesight at all can do that; but seeing the landscape, of which all animals that are ever hunted by anything seem to form a part, and seeing just where the animal emerges from the ground, and seeing which are his ribs and which the larger portion of him that should never be regarded as part of the target at all, because there a bullet only wounds, and a sportsman who is unable to kill should be well content with the next best thing, which is to miss. And miss I often did in those days, and often since; but I spent my boyhood with a rifle, and gradually came to know a little about it.

As I got home the Evening Star appeared. I dined early, then sat and thought in the lonely house. Had I said enough to dissuade my strange friend from the project at which he had more than hinted? And the more I thought of it the more awful my responsibility seemed to grow, for the origin of this dreadful plan had been my anxiety to save the bog, often and eagerly expressed, whereas all I had done against it was to utter a few emphatic negatives. Thinking, which makes things so much clearer, builds up the outline of fears, then fills the outline in, till a great dark edifice stands blackening the future. What could I do to make certain that what I feared would not happen? I never had known where this man lived, and knew no way to find him. He appeared when he wished to, but I never knew when that would be. And I knew that it would be useless to warn the men at Lisronagh. Suddenly I thought of Mrs. Marlin. What police could not prevent, or conscience restrain, would not be done against the word of a Wise Woman. I must see Mrs. Marlin before anything had time to be done and get her protection for the men of this syndicate, though they were her enemies and mine.

Next morning I breakfasted early, and then set off with Ryan along the road to Clonrue. I would not even stop to talk with the doctor, whose advice I had come to rely on, but drove on to the spot at which the cracked white road came nearest to the cottage of Mrs. Marlin, and thence I hurried over the springy soil, jumping the little ditches, and thinking little of the beauty of spring or the ugliness of mean buildings; till I came to that cottage standing amongst the willows, that had now so sad an air that I suddenly pictured the tent of the leader of a lost cause, with his enemies camped around him. And there was Mrs. Marlin flaming in her garden, as far as spirit can flame or eyes burn. Gusts of anger I had seen in others, flashing out into curses, but here was an anger that seemed quietly burning on, as though it never abated; and this was the woman to whom I had come for protection for the very men that she hated. I was terribly uneasy, but could only go on.

"Good morning to you, Master Char-les," she said.

"Good morning, Mrs. Marlin," said I.

And then I blurted out the cause of my coming, naming the man that I had met in the twilight. "He is going to kill some of those men," I said. "And he must not do it. You must stop him."

And she burst out laughing.

"Is that all?" she cried. "They've the curse of the north wind against them, and storm and moss and heather, and the curse of the ancient powers of bog and hill. Is it any more that they want?"

"They do not," said I, "and you must not let that man harm them."

"Harm them, is it?" she said. "They need no harm from man."

And I stuck to my point. "Then you will forbid him to hurt them?" I asked her.

"Sure, I will," she said.

I thanked her.

"And let them watch for what's coming," she added.

"When?" asked I.

And she answered me: "In the time of those that wait."

There was a look in Mrs. Marlin's eyes that seemed so far from here that I never asked her who they were that waited, being sure that the powers she spoke of would be something

beyond my ken. Nor could I hope to know when their time
would be. So I left Mrs. Marlin, trusting well enough that no
danger from men would dare to cross her path to trouble the
workmen that had settled down round about her, and wondering what danger there could be from others, and who those
others were.

CHAPTER XXVIII

I was easy now in my mind about the syndicate's workmen;
for I knew that my guardian demon, as I might term my friend
from whom I parted at the edge of the wood in the twilight,
would not dare to kill anyone in the face of the curses of a
Wise Woman. But the old trouble returned with even greater
weight, the doom that was hanging over the bog and the quiet
lands lying under the long black cliffs of it where the lovely
willows grew. It was no real solace to me that the workmen
were now safe. What were they to me? One could not abet,
permit or instigate murder: whatever ages had civilised us in
that old house of High Gaut had presumably taught me that
much, even without the help of Eton; and mere reason told
one the same. But my heart, which did not reason, was with
the rushes and heather, and the stooping willows, grim and
weird in the winter, like old prophets foretelling storm, and
shining now as though a flame were exulting, yellowy-green
from their branches. No teaching could make me care for these
strangers as I loved this wild land, and all the grief of which
a boy is capable was darkening now round my heart, when I
thought of the bog about to be partly spoiled and partly to
be cut altogether away. I fell to wondering what pools would
be spared, and what particular patches of heather or moss
that I knew; and then I brooded that, whether spared or not,
noise and a crowd and litter would spoil them all. My thoughts
turned to Laura: she, they said, would be able to help me. And
then old tiresome Reason said: "How could she save the bog?"

Thus conflicting thoughts making negations of each other filled my head, their sum amounting, I suppose, to nothing.

It was the day after I came back from seeing Mrs. Marlin that I drove over again to Cloghnacurrer, in order to enquire when the cub-hunting would start, as I had an idea of buying another horse if I was likely to get hunting enough before the end of the summer holidays. This was early May, and cub-hunting started in August, so that my enquiry may seem to have been curiously early, and so it was, but I was shy about going there without any reason at all; and, the shyer I was the more stupid my subterfuges became. I did not speak of Marlin, indoors at the tea-table. Not till I was walking once more with Laura, in the soft light that seemed to float for ever at Cloghnacurrer amongst a million leaves, did I tell her how Marlin went to Tir-nan-Og. I could not have said that indoors. Someone would have said: "I heard he had fallen into the bog and was drowned." And I could no more have denied that than a pane of glass can resist a stone; and all Tir-nan-Og would have been shattered by the words. It is right that it should be shattered. Yes, yes; it is right. There is no warrant for it in our religion; it is never mentioned in the Lives of the Saints; not only that, but it is deliberately avoided. It cannot be doubted that there is mortal danger in it. Monsieur Alphonse, here, mocks the idea of any danger from Tir-nan-Og, and he is not the only one to do so when I have mentioned that land; but it is easy for men living in temperate climes to mock perils of ice in the Arctic, or lions in African nights; and any whose fancy has once roved westward from Ireland knows, as I knew, the mortal peril threatening the soul. Under those trees that day at Cloghnacurrer I spoke, perhaps for the last time, perilously of Tir-nan-Og. I spoke of it as though that land, and not Heaven, were the lawful land of our hopes, and as though Marlin were already among those orchards in which his heresy trusted, waiting to welcome Laura and me with a smile of youth on his lips, and a light of youth in his eyes, which would flash still young and smiling as long as the oldest stars. And Laura, dear soul, never checked me, as she should have done, and we talked on together of those blossoms gleaming in spring, and the golden and ruddy apples heavy with autumn, flashing on the same bough; and, shining in and out among blossom and apples, the gliding rainbow that had seen Marlin home.

And then I turned from the peril that threatened my soul to the sorrow that troubled me here, and told Laura all I had seen at the edge of the bog, and how a factory was to be built by the stream, and the bog cut into and spoiled. What could save it, I asked her? And we spoke of the Hunt Committee, who cared little enough for the bog, as it was the one place they could not ride; and then of politicians, who cared about it no better, as there are fewer votes on the bog than on any equal area. And last of all, I do not know why, but last of all I came to the thing in which I trusted most, the curse of Mrs. Marlin.

"What do you think of curses?" I asked.

"I don't like them," said Laura.

"Could Mrs. Marlin's curse stop them spoiling the bog, do you think?"

Laura thought for a while: I can see her grey eyes still, in that soft light under the trees, brought down the years by my memory. And then she said: "They'd be carrying a lot of weight if they tried to compete with it."

What would Mrs. Marlin do? We talked long about this, and came to no conclusion. But a hope coming dimly from an uncertain power that lurked in the strange woman remained a secret between us, and cheered me during all the anxious days of the summer, during which the Peat Development (Ireland) Syndicate pushed forward hugely its plans for bringing factory and huts to the haunts of willow and curlew.

CHAPTER XXIX

It was very soon after this that I went back to Eton, to the calm old buildings, the red may and the chestnuts, and then the willows that with a pang would remind me of those almost enchanted lands lying under the threat of Progress. I do not know what I learned that half; perhaps unconsciously words clung to my memory which I thought had escaped me entirely, but my heart all the while was shadowed by the machines that darkened Lisronagh. "Wilfully dreamy," said one of my reports; but they were dreams that brought me no pleasure. How would some townsman feel who loved his city, and knew that a band of farmers with their ploughs threatened his very pavements and would tear his high buildings down? As he would feel, fearing that turnips would thrive where his busses ran, so I felt and feared for Lisronagh. I had one hope in this trouble that shadowed me, and that hope was in Mrs. Marlin. I had rejected the help of my friend in the long black coat. Ought I not to have rejected, too, any help from Mrs. Marlin? But I was powerless to gain her help or reject it, where the affairs of the bog were concerned. She loved the bog with a fiercer fury than I did, and if she should defend it I could no more turn her aside from whatever she planned than I could turn the north wind back when it swept the bog in the winter. And yet what could she do? I had no one in whom to confide about it. The priest in Slough, to whom I used to confess, was English and knew nothing of witchcraft; and merely warned me against it, which it was his duty to do. There was more than one master who encouraged one to bring him one's troubles and difficulties, but how could I tell him that what was wringing my heart was that an Irish bog was going to be developed commercially, incidentally paying me rent, and that my only hope was in the curse of a witch? Then there were boys with whom I sometimes approached this subject, but they seemed to know nothing of witches. Why this was so I never knew, for most of their fathers were magistrates, who must all have taken the oath to suppress witchcraft, which every magistrate takes. Yet beyond these attempted approaches I never got, and never found the understanding I sought for, still less the sympathy.

And then one day there came a letter from Laura; and it told me of Mrs. Marlin. Laura knew how I should be thinking of the fate of the bog, and the hope that I had in Mrs. Marlin's curses, a hope slender enough, yet the only one that I had. No one else would save it; not even the Blessed Saints would help me there, knowing well enough that it was along the edges of just such bogs as that, and indeed only there, that the heresy still survived that set men turning westward when they prayed, and thinking of youth and twilight instead of the joys of Heaven, and praying to those of whom we may not think, if we are to hope for salvation. And I am sure that Laura knew I should have found no one to talk to of the thought that was most in my mind, and knew how welcome news of such things would be. Indeed I think Laura knew everything, except how to spell. I have all her letters to-day, and I notice it now when I look them over again, trying to lure from their leaves old moods of mine and old memories: she certainly could not spell. Her letter said: "She is walking along the edge of the bog. She goes along the top of the bank every evening. The men say she looks very black. I've seen one of them, and he said she looked 'terrible black.' But so she would in that dress of hers in the evening, up against the sky, in that light. Though it may have been her looks that he meant. You know she has pretty dark eyes. I don't mean pretty, but you know what I mean. And if they got flashing it might look a bit like a thunderstorm to them. The Englishmen laugh at her, but all the Clonrue men have left. I'm afraid that won't save the poor bog, as they got more men over from England by the next boat, and it did no more than stop half the work for a day. But I thought you'd like to know she's done something. More power to her, but I'd like to see her save the old bog yet. But I don't know how. Her curses seem only to work on the Clonrue men. Those English don't understand them."

And there was a lot more, ending up with "I am sure you are in sixth Form now"; just as when writing to a curate one might say: "I am sure that you are a bishop." I have not exhibited her spelling to eyes that might only mock peculiarities that to me were once almost sacred, and so I have altered it here, though for myself it always seemed better just as it was.

When I wrote to thank Laura for her letter I asked her to

keep an eye on Lisronagh, and to let me know what was happening to it. And she wrote again in a week, telling me about the wheel below the dam in the stream, and the factory and the huts; but I knew from the way that she wrote that things were worse than she said.

The sorrows of exile seldom last for life, and, when they do, a man still preserves in his heart the image of his home; but I could not keep from the picture my memory made of that part of Ireland that I loved best, the dark smear of machinery that knowledge put vividly into memory's picture. And one day when this was heavy, as always, upon my mind, there came another letter from Laura. "No one goes to Lisronagh any longer," she said. "They're afraid of Mrs. Marlin. The Englishmen are working there, but no one goes near them. They hardly go out from Clonrue on that side at all. I'm afraid it's all up with the bog."

And in spite of the last sad sentence, the letter brought me encouragement, for that told me no more than I knew; while the rest of the letter strengthened the only hope that I had, a dim feeling, too crazy for me ever to speak of it and so to embolden it with the understanding of friends, an uncertain hope that Mrs. Marlin would somehow keep to the compact she said she had made with those that she told me had helped her son to the West, a curious faith that her curses could even yet, so late in the nineteenth century, be able to struggle and win against the might of machinery. At least she still held to her purpose.

And so the summer half wore softly away, as though three months of sunshine had slipped down the Thames, whose gliding by those fields might have taught me that all things drift away; but nothing ever taught it to me, so that it bursts on me only now like a surprise.

CHAPTER XXX

I came again to High Gaut. Bright sunlight on the white-washed walls of the station; welcoming faces, and an outside car; then the long white road by bogs and towers; and so home. Brophy, Murphy, Ryan, young Finn, I saw them all again, and everyone in the house. And then on the very day that I arrived I set off with Ryan in the afternoon to drive to Lisronagh. I had not told Ryan where we were going till I got into the trap at the door, and when I said Lisronagh Ryan said to me: "Is it shooting you are, sir?"

It was still July, and of course I was not going shooting, as Ryan knew well enough. "No," I said, "but I want to see what those Englishmen are doing."

"Wouldn't they be able to tell you all about that in Clonrue?" said Ryan. And I saw then that for some reason Ryan did not want to go to Lisronagh.

"I want to see for myself," I said.

"Begob there's not much to see," said Ryan.

I wondered why he wished to avoid Lisronagh, but did not know how to find out.

"What's going on there?" I asked.

"Begob, I don't know," Ryan answered.

"I hear the people of Clonrue have all left it," I said.

"Begob, they have," answered Ryan.

"Weren't they giving up a good job?" I asked.

"There's jobs," said Ryan, "that a man might not do if he were starving."

"What kind of jobs?" I asked. And Ryan thought for a while.

"Any job with a curse over it," he said.

"I heard Mrs. Marlin was cursing it," I said straight out; perhaps too straight for Ryan's tastes.

"Maybe," he said.

"Shall we go and see?" said I.

"Maybe the old horse couldn't get so far and back," he replied.

"Didn't he often do it before?" I asked him.

"Aye," said Ryan, "but he was younger then."

"Not much," I said.

"And the oftener he did it," said Ryan, "the more it wore him out."

"Let's go and ask the doctor about it," I said.

"Begob, we will," said Ryan.

There were mysteries that the doctor did not know, but probably none within fifteen miles of Clonrue; and I had no doubt I should get from him what it was that was frightening Ryan.

But the doctor was not in, and was not expected back for another hour, so we drove on for Lisronagh, Ryan driving slower and slower. We were not gone from Clonrue when I noticed people watching us from the doorways, and children putting their heads up over low walls, to see who it was that took the road to Lisronagh. At the end of the village we met a group of men standing in the road talking. I knew one or two, and they all seemed to know me. They greeted me, and I them. And then one said: "Is it to Lisronagh you're going, sir?"

"It is," I replied.

And at that they muttered and looked at each other.

"It's a fine great bog," I said.

"Indeed it is," said one of them.

"And I'm wanting to see it again," I continued.

This produced scarcely any answer at all, and Ryan was gazing ahead of us down the road as though he heard nothing. A direct question would have brought me no information.

"Would you care for a drive down to the bog?" I said to one of them that I knew.

"Begob, sir," said he, "I'd like it. Only I have my old mother to look after. She's a long way past sixty now, and if I were away all that time, she'd wonder what had become of me. Begob, she'd be that anxious, she might die of it."

I asked another. "Sure I've my work to do in Clonrue," he said.

All this while an old woman that I hardly noticed at first was coming towards us down the street. Now she arrived beside us and lifted up her voice.

"Ah, Master Char-les," she said, "don't go to Lisronagh. I'm an old woman now, but I never had anything to do with wise sayings, or any of them things at all. But there's things going on of a nightfall at Lisronagh that it's best for the likes of us to keep away from, and best for you, Master Char-les."

"What things?" said I. And the men were all standing silent, as they heard the topic that they were avoiding thus blurted out.

"Mrs. Marlin," she said.

"Is she putting a curse on the place?" I asked.

"Begob, she is," said the old woman; "and worse. For she goes up into the bog and calls on those at night, that it is not for us to name."

"That won't hurt me," I said.

"Begob, they'll hear her," she answered. "Don't go near it. For one night they'll come."

"Well, thank you for warning me," I said.

"Begob, it's a good warning," she said, and looked at me; and then went slowly away.

There was a strained silence among the men, and Ryan seemed to have heard nothing at all.

"Then to Lisronagh," I said to Ryan.

He gave a slow flick with his whip and the horse moved off at a walk. One man chewed a straw, another searched his pocket for a bit of tobacco to put in his clay pipe, a third turned to find a more comfortable spot in the wall against which he was leaning; none of them spoke; and Ryan and I and the horse went on alone, and saw no one in the fields and no one in the road as we went, nor did anyone in Clonrue seem even to look towards Lisronagh.

What I saw and heard in Clonrue, and far more what I felt, filled me with sudden hope. For months I had said to myself:

What can Mrs. Marlin do? But here was something she had done. There was a fear in Clonrue, and the fear was her doing. Might it not in time extend to the other workmen? Foolish hopes like this in the end add weight to our troubles, and the very first sight I had of them at work as Ryan reluctantly drove down the old bohereen, now a wide road with hard surface, scattered my hope at once, and left me all the forlorner for having clung to it. It was not only the awful progress the work had made, but the whole attitude of the workers, that seemed to show me something solid and real, beside which Mrs. Marlin's curses were mere shadows.

"Will you be long, sir?" said Ryan as I stepped down from the trap. And I saw that he feared to wait there long in the evening, lest Mrs. Marlin should soon come out and utter her curses, and lest one of them should reach him from where she walked on the heather.

I went down to the factory they were building beside the stream, and went up to the foreman.

"I'm Mr. Peridore," I told him. "How is the work getting on?"

"Glad to see you, sir," he replied. "Getting on nicely."

It was indeed, and the wheel in the stream was already in position.

"You'll make a big change in the bog, I suppose," said I.

"You wouldn't know it in a year, sir," he said.

Some look of sadness I could not conceal in my face he must have noticed, and added: "Well, sir, it's no use as it is, is it?"

"No," I said.

I had not the heart to say more, and we should have been standing in silence, but that he suddenly said: "She'll be coming out soon now."

"Who?" I asked.

"The old woman," he told me.

"What does she do?" I asked him.

"Only a bit o' cursing, sir," he said.

"Does it worry the men at all?" said I.

"Not a bit, sir," he said. "She's only enjoying herself. They know she means no harm by it."

No harm by it!

"But the Clonrue men," I said, "I heard they'd left."

"Oh, them," he said. "They felt a bit funny about it, and we let 'em go. They weren't much good."

"They tell me no one comes here now from Clonrue," I said.

"No, sir," he said. "They've a funny way of looking at things, those people. But we don't want 'em."

And then the door of Mrs. Marlin's cottage opened and I saw her dark figure come out, and walk through all the shabbiness and untidiness that now littered those lands; and so she came to the high edge of the bog and climbed fiercely up and stood on the heather; and there she raised her arms slowly, with fingers clutching, and stared at the men and the factory, and one saw her against the sky as Laura had said. Then she turned her back to the factory and gazed away over the bog, and seemed to be speaking with people far away; but, if she was, she was only muttering to them, for one heard no sound of her voice. Then she turned round again and began to curse the factory, first in English, then in Irish, and then in what seemed to me some older language, all the while with arms stretched upward threatening the men.

"Bloody old kipper," said the foreman.

CHAPTER XXXI

I hurried back to the road of the lost bohereen, for I was anxious about Ryan, not knowing what he would do when the witch appeared; and I found him with the trap turned away from Lisronagh and the reins gathered up in his hand, looking back at the bog with quick glances over his shoulder. The old horse, that seemed so tired coming, trotted fast away from Lisronagh; and half-way to Clonrue, whenever I looked backward I could still see that dark figure prowling above the huts: Ryan too saw her often, although she was the last thing that he wished to see, but he could not help glancing. The Irish evening that I knew so well fell softly round us, making Ryan shiver; but I drew strange hopes from its colour and shadows and gloaming. Not till we reached Clonrue was Ryan himself again.

There we found Dr. Rory returned, and I went in to ask him for a cup of tea.

"What's going to happen at Lisronagh?" I asked him over the tea.

Dr. Rory was silent, as though trying to remember something. And then he said: "It's no use telling you that I know. I've been studying scientific things all these years, and it's no use pretending that I'm in touch with what's going on, as I was once. It's very seldom that the same man knows much of science, and about the things that were known before ever science came. I knew one man once that knew the two things, but it gave a queer twist to his brain, and in the end he had to be certified. If there's things out there on the bog that aren't in books you must ask someone that hasn't puzzled his wits by reading, for there's more things in books than any man could possibly believe or understand. It's like trying to drink Niagara. And I've come in the last few years to think that I understand nothing. So you mustn't ask me."

And yet I saw that there was something in Dr. Rory's mind that he would not tell me, because it was contrary to all his studies, and to deny them would be to deny his whole profession and the good work he had done in Clonrue for years.

"Can Mrs. Marlin save the bog?" I blurted out to him.

"Ah, what do I know?" said Dr. Rory. "What do I know?"

"You know a great deal," I said.

"I know nothing," he answered.

It is strange to reflect, looking back at it through the years, that the shadow that brooded over the far end of Clonrue, the feeling that prevented them going a yard along the road to Lisronagh, was the one hope that brightened those days for me. If Mrs. Marlin was all they feared, she could save the bog. That at least was the feeling I had in the twilight, driving away from Clonrue, but I do not think that it lasted long; and Reason, on the side of the doctor's learned books, said: "She can do nothing."

Those were anxious days, and I think that those who have somewhere amongst their heartstrings a deep love for any soil will understand how it was with me when I saw the willowy lands round the Marlins' cottage already lost to sight under huts and machinery, and all their enchantment gone, and the menace that threatened the bog looming nearer and nearer. They will understand me because we have all of us one thing in common with oak-trees, the need of some soil to love, and though we are able to travel far away from it, and to spend years in cities, yet it is not so with our hearts; they send down tendrils deep into that soil, and pine when they are transplanted.

I went again to Lisronagh, riding the hunter, so as not to bring Ryan back there against his will. Again in Clonrue I found that curious turning away of everyone from the direction of Lisronagh, and found there from a few words with some of the men, rather from what they indicated than from what they actually said, that not only were they afraid of Mrs. Marlin herself, but they had a fear of meeting the men that were at work on the factory, or of associating with them; not because there was any boycott, but because they feared there was something that might befall these men, and feared to be entangled in it themselves. What could Mrs. Marlin's curses do? I asked. What could curses in general do? And always I was met with the same answer: "Sure, I don't know." Or some variant of the same answer, with which these men guarded a secret. I dare say in London, if one asked a bank clerk how much money his bank possessed, one would meet there similar evasions.

As I rode on from Clonrue I found again the empty road and no one in the fields, no one between the village and Lisronagh, till I saw the men of the syndicate.

I found the foreman again and asked him more precisely what was going to be done to the bog. He gave my horse to one of the men to hold and walked with me along the face of the peat, where the bog rose sheer from the fields about Mrs. Marlin's, and showed me where the darker stratum ran, below the layers of brown and saffron and ochre, and told me how they were going to quarry this out, and then cut shafts through the bog in every direction, so as to work as many surfaces as possible; for they only wanted the blackest layer that lay below the rest and had been already compressed by the bog above for tens and scores of centuries. Then they were going to compress it more by machinery.

Against this scheme the heather for miles and miles, at the height of its beauty and multiplied by the pools, seemed to cry out, but—alas—only to fancy, unless that beauty had so inspired Mrs. Marlin that it had some share in her voice now ringing wild through the evening, for it was the hour at which she paced the edge of the bog and cursed the Peat Development (Ireland) Syndicate. For a while I was a little ashamed of the trouble the foreman was taking and the consideration that he was showing me; then I looked away over the lovely heather, and my heart went out to Mrs. Marlin's curses.

Passing the factory on the way back he would have told me how they were going to compress the peat, as he called what we call turf, but I only cared to hear how they would harm the bog, and asked him how far they were going to quarry into the bank. "Several feet," he said. "Yards, where we get a specially good layer."

"But how will you stop the bank falling in?" I asked.

"Shore it up with timber," he said. "Quite easy."

"The whole way along?" I asked him.

"Yes," he said, "there's plenty of trees."

So all those willows were going too, and probably those little groups of pines that marked the place of cottages far away, where they were gathered round those small and lonely dwellings to help them in the defence of man against wild and windy spaces of untamed heather.

"And then we're going to cut a lot of lanes through the bog, sir," he said; "and work both sides of them. We get that black layer at about seventeen feet."

It is that that would tear the soul out of the bog, as my strange friend had said, and the guts of it. And in my despair I asked him when they would start on that.

"We should get going with half a dozen of the big lane-ways before Christmas," he said. And, as though this were not enough, he added: "And we should push them across the bog in little over a year."

It was then that my Irish heart sorrowfully regretted what my English education had taught me, to interfere with my friend who would have killed these men. But that was done now, and, having no more to say to the foreman, I got on my horse again and rode sadly away.

To whom could I go? Not to the man that had promised to help me. It would have been better to have left him to go his way when he first made the suggestion. It would be murder to go to him now. Not the doctor, for he had insisted he did not know. There was only Laura.

So to Cloghnacurrer I rode over next day, and had tea with Mrs. Lanley, and told Laura the bog was done for. We were walking, as I told her, in the heavy scent of limes, and the sunlight was oozing down through the myriad leaves, and a chorus of bees was glorying in the blossoms, and my doleful news seemed all the sadder against the splendour of summer. But Laura would not agree that the case was hopeless with the land that I so much loved.

"There is Mrs. Marlin," she said.

"She can do nothing," I answered sadly.

"But she promised to," said Laura.

"To whom?" I asked.

"Those people," said Laura.

It was true. I had told her of Mrs. Marlin's compact with whatever she fancied drifted over the bog.

"She can do nothing," I repeated, clinging to my melancholy as though there were anything good in it.

"Let's ask her," said Laura.

And so we arranged to drive over and see Mrs. Marlin one day that week, and a new hope rose in me from Laura's belief in the powers of the Wise Woman.

The day came and Laura called for me in the afternoon, driving a dog-cart, as we used to call them, with a groom seated behind. That I was strangely exhilarated I remember still, even if I can no longer recall the actual feelings with which happiness came to one then. But the brilliant lights and the black shadows of youth cannot really be seen from the twilight. I was happy to be with Laura, happy too in the brilliance of that sunshine of early August, on one of the last of the fine days of what was so far a glorious summer, and I was stimulated by the hope of help from Mrs. Marlin, renewed by Laura's encouragement, though I had a feeling that it was the last of my hopes, like the last plan of an invaded people when defeat seems tainting the air.

"We'll see the doctor too," said Laura. "He seems to know something, from what you said."

"He won't say anything," I told her.

"Never mind," said Laura.

So we called on Dr. Rory, and found him in. And I think he nearly said to Laura what he would not say to me, when she asked him what there was that could save the bog. But all that he said in the end was: "If there's anything in all I've been learning for fifteen years, the old woman's mad; and if there are any powers roaming the bog that she has the knack of calling on, why then all I know is as no more than one pebble by the everlasting sea."

"Ah well, I'm afraid she's mad, Charlie," said Laura.

"And a small pebble at that," added the doctor. "And I wouldn't say she was mad."

We drove on, and the men that were standing about in Clonrue, though they took their caps off to Laura, said nothing, and watched us in a curious way when they saw the direction we took. And no more men or women did we see, till we came in sight of the men at work on the factory, moving amongst huge wheels and bars that had lately arrived, and that looked like the skeleton of some monstrous thing that had no concern at all with the animal kingdom. I think the sight troubled Laura, but she said nothing, and, leaving the trap with the groom, we went straight to Mrs. Marlin's cottage. For all the dreadful change that was around us, the dim long room, with a window at each end and the great fireplace, remained the same as it ever was, as though I might yet shoot geese on the bog again. And there was Mrs. Marlin sitting before her fire, which she probably burned all through summer to keep out the damp from the bog.

"I've brought Miss Lanley to see you," I said.

And she welcomed Laura and gave her a chair.

And at last I could speak straight out, with no concealments or subterfuges, for Mrs. Marlin loved the bog with a fiercer love than I did, and the trouble that had burdened my mind so long was a matter to speak of openly.

"They're spoiling the bog, Mrs. Marlin," I said.

And a fierce look entered her eyes, and it was a wild look too, and perhaps a little crafty.

"They wish to," she said.

"Will they do it?" I asked her.

"It's against the will of the bog and the north wind and the storm," she answered.

Still I had learned no word of the fate of that glory of heather, and Laura sat saying nothing.

"Will you keep your compact," I asked, "with those of whom you told me?"

Then she shot up from her chair with flashing eyes, standing tall and straight as the queens of whom Marlin dreamed. "Will I keep my compact?" she said. "I swore it by turf and heather, as they swore by blossom and twilight. Will I keep my compact with those that helped my son, rowing him over the sea with eight oars, and all of them queens? Did they keep their oath by blossom and twilight? And is Irish heather and Irish turf any less than the holy things of the Land of the Young? Will I keep my compact with them? Aye, while Ireland lasts. And what would I say on nights when they're drifting over the bog, and what would I say to Tommy, if I could not swear an oath to the queens of the West and abide by the oath that I swore?"

Still Laura said nothing.

"Yes, I know that you'll keep to your oath," I said.

"Do they swear oaths and break them in Tir-nan-Og?" said she.

Still Mrs. Marlin was standing tall before me.

"No," I answered.

"Then not in Ireland," she said.

Gradually she calmed, and sat down again, and I had not really learned anything.

"They are going to begin cutting right through the bog before Christmas," I said.

But she smiled and shook her head, and went on shaking it, still with the smile on her face.

"Mrs. Marlin," I said, "I love the bog as you do."

"It's the heart of Ireland," she answered.

"When will you save it?" I asked her.

And she was angry no longer, and said, as though she were trusting me with her plans: "I must wait for my allies, and only one's here."

And Laura helped me then.

"Have you great allies?" she asked.

"The giants of the earth," Mrs. Marlin answered. "The bog and the north wind and the storm."

"What will you do?" I asked.

"I wait for those that are not yet come," she said.

She meant of course the north wind and the storm, but I saw that I had questioned her too directly, and that she would say no more. And so I rose, with my vague hope, and we left her.

I remember, as we drove back, a stupendous sunset; vast armies with banners, and monsters, rode by under wonderful mountains. And rain fell all that night, and all the next day; and for most of the night after that it was still raining.

CHAPTER XXXII

We had a cricket-ground at High Gaut, and a local team that throve when my father was young, and that throve again during my youth, and teams used to come over and play us from Gurraghoo and still further; but I remember we had no more cricket that summer. It rained a great deal in August, and then in September it settled down to rain for nearly the whole month. I hoped that it would hinder the work of the syndicate, but the work went remorselessly on. When it was near the time for me to return to Eton and the factory was nearly finished, I decided what for long had been daily perplexing me, which was that away from home I could not hope, and that without hope the anxiety I felt for the bog would be a greater burden than I could bear. In those long, glimmering evenings, with the soft wind blessing the grass, with huge clouds rolling inland like gods on the south-west wind, in the gentle light just before stars, among moths, with the owls hooting, and a curlew far away calling clear from the sky, I could hope that some help would come from the power of Mrs. Marlin. At Eton I knew that I could not. So I wrote to my guardian and begged him to take me away. I received a charming letter in reply: "I have come to a time of life," it read, "when my own pleasures are nothing to me, and if anything I can do can increase the happiness of others, I am only too glad to do it. I am writing to the authorities at Eton and will see what can be done."

So I was free to stay and watch the fate that was coming upon the bog, and at times to hope that Mrs. Marlin might save it; a hope I could never have hoped away from Ireland, out of sight of that strange apprehension she had already brought on Clonrue, and the loneliness she had made between Clonrue and Lisronagh. And all the while it rained. It rained through September, which was our worst month for wet; and during October we had as many days wet as fine.

At High Gaut they had given up all hope for the bog. Murphy tried to comfort me by telling me that there were plenty of snipe nearer than Lisronagh; which was true, but no consolation, with my heart-strings all entwined, as they were, with the heather. Ryan, although he had fear enough of the curses of Mrs. Marlin, never thought there was any chance of them frightening those workmen away, for he looked on the Englishmen as people that could not understand the ancient lore of witchcraft, and so to be no more moved by it than they could be alarmed by threats in a foreign language. Brophy, with the place to run for me, rather welcomed the idea of rent from the desecration. And young Finn, and Mary, the house-maid, and many another, said: "It's the will of God."

And not only did Mrs. Marlin's curse deter no more men from working, once the Clonrue men had left, but more men came over from England during September; and throughout that month they were working on the dark lower layer of peat all along the face of the bank. So far in did they cut, that by the time October came they could get shelter as they worked from the almost perpetual rain.

Sometimes I went over to see, but found little encourage-ment for my fading hopes in Lisronagh. Only in Clonrue was I heartened. There, unmistakably, had some power gone forth. Men were idle in the street who might have worked for the syn-dicate. If I spoke to them of Lisronagh, their answers avoided my questions, and they turned away from the subject as soon as they could. Some were silent altogether, and I saw none even looking in the direction Lisronagh lay. There nobody could have thought my flickering hopes about Mrs. Marlin fantastic: the lonely road to Lisronagh spoke of her power, the backs of the young men turned to it, and their silence, and the expres-sion one sometimes caught on the faces of women, vanishing just as one looked at it. If the syndicate had relied on Clonrue for provisions, or any other assistance, the curse of Mrs. Marlin would have prevailed. And yet it was to others than the men of Clonrue that Mrs. Marlin looked, and to others than mortal men. For one day in November; about the time that the earliest geese would have come, though they came to the bog no more; and the leaf was gone from the trees and the winds of winter were rising; Mrs. Marlin went up to the top of the edge of the bog, as she did every evening. I saw her go, for I had heard that the machinery was all installed in the factory and had now started working. This, I felt, was the end; so I had driven with Ryan to Clonrue and walked on by myself, to see the last of Lisronagh. It was raining as usual, but I had a good waterproof. On my way from what was once the bohereen, across the level land that seemed once to me almost enchanted, I heard, above the clatter of machinery, the voice of the foreman calling to one of the men. "There she goes," he was saying.

And I looked and saw the dark woman climbing the bank, and getting her foothold from the ledges the honest turf-cutters left, who would not have harmed the bog in a hundred years.

"Does it always rain like this here, sir?" he said as he came towards me.

I was hard tempted to say: "Yes, all the year round." And it was not, I fear, resistance of the temptation that prevented me saying it, but only the knowledge that he had no say in whether they stayed or left, but only some man far away, sitting dry in some office.

I had come to say farewell to the bog. Seeing Mrs. Marlin there, I wondered if there were any one last chance.

"Has she been giving you any trouble?" I said.

"Not a bit, sir," he answered, crushing my hopes, as a man on a quiet walk crushes insects he never sees. "It's only her way."

"The men don't mind her?" I said, though I knew the hope was vain.

"Not a bit of it, sir," said he. "She's just a bit touched in her head, that's all. A thing that might happen to anyone. They know that, and they just get on with their work. And look at her now, sir. Do you know what she's doing?"

And I looked at her gaunt dark figure, where he pointed, high on the edge of the bog. She had stopped in her stride and was stooping.

"Digging bits of peat into the stream," he continued, "to stop the water from coming down to us. That's the kind of thing she does. Been doing it now for three days."

And, sure enough, she was making a little dam across the sluggish stream where it left the bog; and I despaired when I saw it, for it seemed the maddest thing she had done yet.

"I'll go and ask her to stop," I said.

"It don't matter to us, sir," said he.

But still I left him and went over to Mrs. Marlin, for I felt she was bringing the bog and its people into contempt by the childish thing she was doing.

"How are you, Mrs. Marlin?" I said.

She looked at me and then went on with her digging: "I'm well, thank you, sir," she said, and tumbled another lump into the water that was lying deep against the dam she had made. "And I hope your honour is well."

"What's the use of that, Mrs. Marlin?" I said, pointing to the mess she was making.

"And what's the use, sir," said she, "of the work they're making the water do down there?"

"Little enough," I admitted.

"Then let it stay here," said she.

"Here?" I repeated.

"Aye, and there's work for it," she said.

"But, Mrs. Marlin," said I, "it will all be gone down by to-morrow."

"To-morrow," she said, and with emphasis so strange that I wondered. It was as though to-morrow were far far away, or as though the world would be all quite different to-morrow. And she never denied what I said, but went on digging the turf down into the stream. The rain was pouring down her face as she worked, and her old black dress gave her no protection whatever.

"But you are getting very wet," I said to the old woman.

She turned to answer me, then suddenly looked away as though she had heard the sound of some other voice, and straightened herself up tall, and stood and listened. Then she smiled with a glad look. And seeing her thus, with that look, in the wild weather, strange fancies came over me. I thought of a queen carried off after some lost battle, a captive, afar, for years, hearing all of a sudden the horns of her own people. So she stood silent, filled with a strange joy.

"It is the north wind," she said.

And, sure enough, a damp tendril of hair waved from her head southwards. Those were the last words she ever spoke directly to myself, for, though I heard her say much more, she spoke after that neither to me nor to any man, but to spirits and presences of which she was aware, powers of whom I knew nothing.

"Come," she said, but not to me. "Come as of old." Then she walked through the heather northwards, with the rising wind in her face, holding out her arms towards it. "As of old," she said, "with all the strength of the North and the might and splendour of winter. Darling wind, I know you."

And certainly the wind was rising now, coming full from the North, and the locks of her hair were straying. I had come with her, though she had spoken to me no more. "And old storms," she said, "come too." And she stretched out her arms and drew them back towards herself with clutching claw-like fingers, as though beckoning to something wild and fierce as her mood. For my part no such beckoning would ever have brought me, but I could imagine wild and savage things being lured by it. What she wanted with more storms I could not think, for the rain was heavy enough and the wind rising. And the rising wind brought more clouds, and put a slant on the rain that seemed to make it more penetrating. I luckily had my waterproof, but it must have gone right to Mrs. Marlin's skin. The rain was colder too with that bitter north wind driving it, and the wintry day was already closing in. But Mrs. Marlin's arms were out as though she hugged the rain, and she was uttering strange endearments to it. I would sooner have kept myself warm, but you cannot see an old woman die of exposure, so I took my waterproof off and offered it to her. I had never known Mrs. Marlin impolite to me, or other than courteous; she merely did not hear me, or see me any more. For the first time I felt ill at ease in her company, for never in her cottage was she without the airs of the perfect hostess that sets all her guests at ease; but now that awkward feeling had overtaken me of being one of a gathering of those that were greater than I, and of being forgotten amongst them. And if it were only a fancy it yet held me strongly, and remained with me all that night, the last thing I had thought to have felt while with that courteous old lady. When she would not take the waterproof I threw it over her and for a while it hung from her shoulders; but she was striding away to the North and still stretching her arms out, and the waterproof did not stay long; and when it had fallen off four or five times I saw it was useless and wore it again myself. All the while she was crooning to that horrible rain, and speaking to that fierce wind as though she were its equal. We came nearer to those pools by which Marlin passed when he went to Tir-nan-Og, those moss-bound lakes to which he always gazed, for they lay rather northwest of the point from which we had started; and I saw as the sun set on that splendour of water how much their mass had increased. For they were the sumach, of which Marlin used to tell me, the great store of the bog's water that kept all the mosses alive and their roots happy, and sustained and nurtured all that loved the bog, and made the steps of man unsure when he came, and made him come then as a stranger. And these waters always increased, for only one small stream left the bog; but the rain of the last three months had been unparalleled. At sunset a gust rose up that was worse than all the others; you could hear it coming over the tops of the heather; and when it reached us you could lean against it; and the cold as the sun went down increased immediately.

"You must come home, Mrs. Marlin," I said, and took hold of one of her arms.

But she did not hear me or seem to feel my grip.

"You are come, you are come, great wanderer," she said. "Your old self. From the ancient ice of the mountains." And she waved wildly northwards the arm that I was not holding.

Then she looked up to the clouds, that were lower and darker and hurrying. "You too, good shapes," she said, "kings of the sky, proud riders. You too. And welcome."

"You must come home," I said, tightening my grip on her arm.

Perhaps she heard me; perhaps she even spoke to me; but she did not look at me as she spoke.

"Hist. They are come," she said.

For the rest of that night, while the storm was continually increasing, she made her plans with those, whoever they were, that seemed to be all about her. And her plans were curses.

"Gather against them," she shouted, waving her arms aloft, even with the weight of my arm upon one of them, a weight she seemed not to feel. "Gather against them, old wind, and powers of storm."

Then suddenly she kneeled on the soaked roots of the rushes, and spread out her hands downwards, shaking off my hold with the suddenness with which she turned thus to earth, and began to speak to the bog. "Oh, ancient one," she said, "oh, beautiful everlasting, rise now out of sleep."

The rain was now lashing the pools and dripping from everything solid, and night was fast rushing down with it. Once I saw a star, and knew from that that the night was really come, and not only the darkness of the violent rain. The star was hastily curtained away by a cloud, and I saw no more that night. Then nothing but rain and darkness and the triumphant wail of the wind, as though some victorious power mourned over its enemies.

Lovingly she spoke to the bog, bending down to it over the mosses, crooning to it and softly beseeching it, but what she said to it I do not know, for she was talking now that language that seemed older than Irish, which I had once heard her use before, and which certainly was no language that men speak now. Kneeling there I thought I could put my waterproof over her, and tried to do so, but the wind took it out of my hand and into the night and I never saw it again. And she spoke still to the bog, caring neither for rain nor me. "Alarathon ahialee tharnee ekbathaton," are some words I remember yet, though what they meant I never knew, or in what language they were.

As the storm roared on, the night grew colder and colder, as though worse and worse weather were coming with every gust from the North. By midnight the cold was frightful. I could not leave Mrs. Marlin, and I was unable to drag her away. My voice may have been easily drowned by all that was raging there, but it was strange that she did not feel my hand on her arm, nor pay any heed when I tried to lift her from where she knelt, with her hands spread out to the rushes, as though she were indeed among some august assembly where neither she nor they noticed anything human. And every bitter gust that beat my wet clothes against me and set more cold water running all down my skin, she welcomed joyfully and with outstretched hands. Was she immortal, I wildly thought for a moment, that she still lived on, when by midnight I was wondering if even I, young as I was, would be able to last till morning. At midnight I thought the storm had reached its height, merely because I could not believe that it could be worse. The wind was no longer roaring, but the gusts were banging like guns. Suddenly it seemed to be blowing in every direction at once, and the rain was much heavier. In reality the wind was going round to the West, and thence whatever storms on that night roamed the Atlantic came inland with all their rain. I heard her voice calling out wild welcomes to them, and knew she was still alive, though I could not distinguish words or even what language she spoke in. And then the great lights appeared, the lights I had often read of but never seen, the will-o'-the-wisps over the deeps of the bog; and, strange as they looked out there on that desperate night, it was stranger to hear her crooning to them, welcoming them one by one, so far as I was able to make out from the tones of words that I could not hear. I was now too cold to drag at her arm any more, and no longer wondered that she could not feel my grip, for I no longer felt it myself, either her arm or the ends of my own fingers. And the huge gusts boomed on, and she was nodding and nodding her head to the lights that came with the west wind, and, I think, speaking to them. She seemed to have ceased from her wild appeals to the storm, and her wild welcomes, and seemed as though satisfied with something that she had done, and to be proudly announcing her deed to those to whom she had owed it. But I could only see her profile and her triumphantly nodding head; it was only by these nods, now, that I could tell that the black heap crouched on the rushes beside me was still alive.

The night raged on, and, instead of being crushed by the cold of it, she seemed to draw an energy from its fury which kept her pulses beating.

It seemed the longest night I ever knew. I was looking the way she was looking, which was to the West, crouching and leaning forward against the storm and the slanting sheets of the rain. And at last I saw the western clouds lighten, and knew that the dawn had come raging up behind me. I turned slowly round with limbs that could only move slowly, and barely keeping my balance against the might of the wind, and saw furious splendours of flame and gold wide in the eastern sky. Mrs. Marlin was still crouched there and still seemed to be speaking, as though no more content to abate her curses than the wind to cease from its raging. But, later, she and the wind seemed to end their fury together, for she staggered up from her feet and a great calm fell; and, after the last of the clouds had scurried past the sky was all a glittering Cambridge-blue.

Then at last Mrs. Marlin came with me, but a strange silence was over her; and, though she was walking now, she had the air of resting, while when she was standing or kneeling still for hours she had the air of such an outburst of might as could well have been the stored energies of years. Only her eyes were glittering, as though with a proud memory. She could barely walk, and perhaps she could not speak, and it was with diffi-culty I got her at last to the edge of the bog, and lifted her down from ledge to ledge of the peat-bank.

Little remains to tell of the day that, of all the days I have lived, remains most clear in my memory. The calm of that day was enormous. Not a breeze moved, not a leaf swayed on the willows, and when Mrs. Marlin's fire was alight again, the smoke went up and up as straight as a pine, till it was lost in the sparkling blue of the windless sky that at last was done with rain. After leaving Mrs. Marlin at her house, the foreman brought me to one of the huts, and gave me a change of clothing. The huts had survived the storm, and so had the factory, but anything that had been left lying about, even light planks, had been blown away like straws. "Never knew such a night," said the foreman.

Dr. Rory, after the storm, was out looking for broken limbs, and was prowling round the country like a wolf after a battle. As soon as I saw him coming towards the huts I was able to tell him that no one there had been hurt, and asked him to go and look at Mrs. Marlin, for she had not spoken since dawn and I did not know what the exposure of that night might have done to her. Dr. Rory went, and I finished a cup of tea that I ill deserved, considering how I hated the whole scheme for which those men were working. But after that wonderful cup I decided to bear the destruction of those wild lands that I loved, with a better grace. Then I went back to Mrs. Marlin's house. There I found that she had not put on dry clothes as I had, but had gone to bed. A thing natural enough and yet it alarmed me at once, for hardy and resolute people like Mrs. Marlin seldom go to bed by day except to die. And a look at the doctor's face did not reassure me.

"Is she bad?" I asked in a low voice that she seemed not to hear, nor did she seem to see me.

"Wasn't she out all night on the bog?" asked the doctor.

"Yes," I said. "I could not get her to come back."

And the doctor said no more.

He was sitting by her bed, and her eyes were open, but seemed full of things far from us and without interest. She lying there and the doctor sitting beside her, and I standing as still and silent as either; I do not know how much time went by us while none of the three spoke. I seem to remember the sound of the crash of the strides of Time, but it was only her old noisy clock beating out seconds. And then, I remember, she spoke.

"The bog's coming," she said.

"Yes, yes," said the doctor soothingly.

"The bog's coming," Mrs. Marlin said again. "Yes, yes," said the doctor.

And suddenly her voice was young and clear again, as it might have been years ago, out courting with Marlin's father.

"The bog is coming," she said.

And a very strange thought indeed came to me then. What, I thought, if it were true! What if that waste of moss and rushes and water were really on the march? What if the old woman spoke sense, and the bog were really coming? For so strange was everything that the Marlins had said, that it was hard to know what might be true. And with this strange thought in my mind I went out of the cottage. "Tommy," I heard her say most clearly just as I left.

I was in time to see the bank they had undercut arching itself into ridges. I had seen the waves in the strata along the bank, made by old tremors; but those were only ripples. It arched itself into low hills now, and they suddenly came towards us. The whole bog was moving. With the weight of years of rain and those last three months it was coming on over the lower lands, and rising higher and higher as it came. For as far as I could see, left or right, it was rippling and waving. I stood and gazed at it, and then ran into the cottage.

"She's right," I shouted.

"She's dead," said the doctor.

"We've got two minutes to save our own lives," I said.

Then he understood me. And the roar that the thing made helped him. For it had begun to roar like a tide. We both ran out through the door, and I saw that my two minutes were very much over-estimated, for we had barely one. I had stayed too long looking at it the first time. Dr. Rory gave it one look, then ran to the workmen, who had come out of their huts and were standing gazing at it.

"It's true," the doctor shouted. "It can do that."

For he knew the ways of the bog as well as any man, and knew that a bog can move, though he'd never seen it. And he got the men moving, and stopped all he saw that were running back to their huts to get some possession or other before they left.

"What about Mrs. Marlin?" I called to him. But he was busy saving the men, who had been slow to believe that what they saw was real, and paid little attention to me. "The bog must bury its own witches," he said.

The roaring was louder than a tide; it was like a waterfall. The bog came grinding on, turning over and over, while Dr. Rory just got the men away in time. It covered the level land, it covered the houses, it rolled the wheel that they had put in the stream to work their machinery for nearly a mile, and still the bog roared on with the weight of all that mass of water behind it, and all the new road that had been a bohereen lay eight foot under the bog when at last it rested. And that was the end of the Peat Development (Ireland) Syndicate.

CHAPTER XXXIII

I have lived fifty years since the bog moved over Lisronagh, leaving only the top of a meaningless ornamentation that they had built on the front of their factory, as a memorial of the syndicate that had worked there once for a while. Birds perched on it: it stood there for years, and is probably whitening there yet. And in those years I have seen many strange things, as who has not in that period that has held man's greatest wonders and four and a quarter years of his greatest violence? As for the wireless, I am wondering at it yet, and do not think I shall ever cease to do so. I have a set here in this room, and on evenings when Monsieur Alphonse does not drop in, and I am alone, I listen to men speaking in Rome, Toulouse and Madrid, and get to know the announcers by their various intonations and sometimes even by their breathing. Yet, looking back on all the things I have known, many of which, I feel sure, would in other hands be good material for stories, I see only three things that, if I could sketch, I could sit and draw to-day in detail just as exact as any artist with his model before him. And the first of these three things is Laura standing in her rock-garden; and the second is the four men kneeling before me, covering me with their pistols, while I held up the crystal cross; and the third is the dark outline of Mrs. Marlin kneeling in the dark night and stretching out her hands to the bog and beseeching it, but proudly, as though she and it and the North wind and the storm were four equal powers. If I wrote any more of my life I should have to exert a tired memory, and consult old letters, or fragments of diaries that seldom went further than January; I should have to turn the bright-lit pages of youth for pages that grow slowly dimmer and darker.

I never married Laura. We were engaged for several years. But Laura, who is a Protestant, would not give up what after all is only a heresy. She was never asked to give it up for herself, but only for possible children. God help me, and all the blessed Saints help me, I believed that in spite of all Laura would go to Heaven. And, God help me, I believe it yet.

I only once spoke to Laura of such things myself. "Do you want to go to Heaven?" I asked her.

"I do," said Laura.

"Will you get there, Laura?" I said.

"I will," said Laura.

"What do you think it will be like?" I asked.

"Galloping down wind for ever," she said.

I could never make Laura serious.

I lived on for many years at High Gaut, and saw many other lands, in wanderings that form no part of this story. Times changed and moss increased upon steps and gateways, and ate its way into woodwork, and a weed began to cover the paths that workmen once kept tidy. At first I did not notice it; and then one day I saw a small white blossom flowering like a mist down the whole length of a path. It was my uncle that brought the weed. And I cannot write of him for a curious reason. The reason is, he belongs to another writer. He was "the good old man" of *Stageland*, by Jerome K. Jerome. "When the good old man is a trustee for anyone, he can battle against adversity much longer. While that trust money lasts . . . he fights on boldly. It is not until he has spent the last penny of it that he gives way."

Jerome K. Jerome wrote that, not I; and the man is his property for ever, and I cannot write of my guardian and trustee, though he actually existed. Perhaps there was a touch of Pecksniff in him too, but I have no right to tell of Pecksniff either, for he belongs to Dickens. So let him rest.

The weed had grown very thick by the early nineteen-twenties; and then one day, to my great astonishment, I was invited to be the Minister of the Irish Free State to the country in whose capital I am now sitting over these memories. I had taken no part in politics, and done nothing of any kind to merit the offer. And the reason for it, that I was told soon afterwards, was as strange as the offer itself: I had been recommended for the post by a very prominent member of the Council of the League of Nations. Who the President of the Council was I did not know, nor the name of a single member, so rural was my life at High Gaut, and so out of touch was I there with those who were hoping to order and straighten out the world's destinies. I accepted at once. And so I sit waiting here for the conference that is to take place one day with the Minister for Extraneous Matters, which Monsieur Alphonse often assures me will be whenever the occasion is ripe. We are to discuss certain action on the part of this State, whether diplomatic or otherwise, with a view to bringing pressure against the continuance of partition in Ireland. They are certainly dilatory, for it is years since the Government first promised the conference; but then they are a dilatory people, and the ministers are often much occupied with the State's internal affairs. And I don't see what could come of it even if we did have a conference, for it is an inland power with no navy, and it is hard to see how they could give expression to their wishes in the matter. But those are my instructions.

My salary, and these fine rooms that I have free, enable me

to devote whatever of my income escaped from my uncle to
what has always been my hobby or my extravagance, call it
what you will, which is giving employment to those families
about High Gaut which have looked for it so long to my family,
that when we stop I do not know where they will find it. So
the place is still kept up by Brophy, who has scarcely altered,
except that his long brown beard is now pure white, like the
beard of young Finn, who died years ago. And Murphy died
too, and Ryan, and Dr. Rory. I think it's time I was going.

On my way out here I stopped an hour at Geneva. As
the train drew in I looked out over the station full of people
with alien faces, their very attitudes strange to me. A gust of
loneliness seemed to sweep over the platform. Suddenly the
station-master took off his hat, and I saw a man approaching
in frock-coat, tall hat and stiff collar, attended by what were
obviously secretaries. There was a little stir on the platform.
And then he came straight towards me. It was the man who
first taught me how to aim at a goose, the man in the long
black coat. I recognised him at once, after all those years. I
recognised him by his eyes. I do not think I shall ever forget
the eyes of those four men that knelt before me, looking along
their pistols, when they came to shoot my father. One died as
I have told, one was killed in the War, another got remorse for
something that he had done, and died like that; they said that a
curse was over him. The last of them stood before me.

Then I knew who he was.

"You have a fine job," I said, as we shook hands.

"Sure, any job is a fine job," he said, "after twenty years in
prison."

"Twenty years!" I exclaimed.

"The best part of it," said he.

"What was it about?" I asked.

"I got to arguing with a man about politics," he said.

"It was a damned shame," said I, because I felt some such
remark was called for, and because I was so happy to see an
Irish face among all those foreign ones.

And then I thanked him from my heart for what he had

done for me, and for remembering me like that after all this time.

"And why wouldn't I?" he said.

"I'm afraid it must have been a great deal of trouble to you to get this job for me," said I.

"Ah, not a bit," said he. "Haven't we got the nations by the throat? And we'll stand no bloody nonsense from any of them, not from the King of Rome himself. And wouldn't I get any job for you?"

I explained that the Roman Empire was long since over.

"Ah well," said he, "isn't there others as bad?"

"There are," I said.

We had a great talk, and I came on here.

I never saw him again. He died not long ago, and I wondered how it went with him. And the more I wondered, the worse and worse it seemed. And then the thought came to me: How does Heaven judge? The newspaper with the column that told of his death lay open before me. I noticed that one or two of its lines were wet, then saw that it was with my own tears. How, I thought then, if Heaven should judge like that?

RECENT AND FORTHCOMING TITLES FROM VALANCOURT BOOKS

Michael Arlen	Hell! said the Duchess
R. C. Ashby	He Arrived at Dusk
Frank Baker	The Birds
H. E. Bates	Fair Stood the Wind for France
Walter Baxter	Look Down in Mercy
Charles Beaumont	The Hunger and Other Stories
David Benedictus	The Fourth of June
Paul Binding	Harmonica's Bridegroom
Charles Birkin	The Smell of Evil
John Blackburn	A Scent of New-Mown Hay
	Broken Boy
	Blue Octavo
	A Ring of Roses
	Children of the Night
	Nothing but the Night
	Bury Him Darkly
	Our Lady of Pain
Thomas Blackburn	A Clip of Steel
	The Feast of the Wolf
Michael Blumlein	The Brains of Rats
John Braine	Room at the Top
	The Vodi
	Life at the Top
Michael Campbell	Lord Dismiss Us
Basil Copper	The Great White Space
	Necropolis
	The House of the Wolf
Hunter Davies	Body Charge
Jennifer Dawson	The Ha-Ha
A. E. Ellis	The Rack
Barry England	Figures in a Landscape
Ronald Fraser	Flower Phantoms
Michael Frayn	The Tin Men
	The Russian Interpreter
	Towards the End of the Morning
	A Very Private Life
	Sweet Dreams
Gillian Freeman	The Liberty Man
	The Leather Boys
	The Leader

Rodney Garland	The Heart in Exile
Stephen Gilbert	The Landslide
	Monkeyface
	The Burnaby Experiments
	Ratman's Notebooks
Martyn Goff	The Plaster Fabric
	The Youngest Director
Stephen Gregory	The Cormorant
	The Woodwitch
	The Blood of Angels
Alex Hamilton	Beam of Malice
Thomas Hinde	The Day the Call Came
Claude Houghton	Neighbours
	I Am Jonathan Scrivener
	This Was Ivor Trent
Fred Hoyle	The Black Cloud
Alan Judd	The Devil's Own Work
James Kennaway	The Mind Benders
	The Cost of Living Like This
Cyril Kersh	The Aggravations of Minnie Ashe
Gerald Kersh	Fowlers End
	Nightshade and Damnations
	Clock Without Hands
	Neither Man Nor Dog
	On an Odd Note
Francis King	To the Dark Tower
	Never Again
	An Air That Kills
	The Dividing Stream
	The Dark Glasses
	The Man on the Rock
C.H.B. Kitchin	The Sensitive One
	Birthday Party
	Ten Pollitt Place
	The Book of Life
	A Short Walk in Williams Park
Hilda Lewis	The Witch and the Priest
John Lodwick	Brother Death
Kenneth Martin	Aubade
Robin Maugham	Behind the Mirror
Michael McDowell	The Amulet
John Metcalfe	The Feasting Dead
Michael Nelson	A Room in Chelsea Square

Beverley Nichols	Crazy Pavements
Oliver Onions	The Hand of Kornelius Voyt
Christopher Priest	The Affirmation
J.B. Priestley	Benighted
	The Doomsday Men
	The Other Place
	The Magicians
	Saturn Over the Water
	The Shapes of Sleep
	The Thirty-First of June
	Salt Is Leaving
Peter Prince	Play Things
Piers Paul Read	Monk Dawson
Forrest Reid	Brian Westby
	The Tom Barber Trilogy
	Denis Bracknel
Nevil Shute	Landfall
	An Old Captivity
Andrew Sinclair	The Raker
	Gog
	The Facts in the Case of E. A. Poe
David Storey	Radcliffe
	Pasmore
	Saville
Bernard Taylor	The Godsend
	Sweetheart, Sweetheart
Russell Thorndike	The Slype
	The Master of the Macabre
John Wain	Hurry on Down
	Strike the Father Dead
	The Smaller Sky
	A Winter in the Hills
Hugh Walpole	The Killer and the Slain
Keith Waterhouse	There is a Happy Land
	Billy Liar
	Jubb
	Billy Liar on the Moon
Robert Westall	Antique Dust
Colin Wilson	Ritual in the Dark
	Man Without a Shadow
	Necessary Doubt
	The Glass Cage
	The Philosopher's Stone
	The God of the Labyrinth

CPSIA information can be obtained at www.ICGtesting.com
Printed in the USA
LVOW12s0718301014

411049LV00005B/527/P